A black WINTER

A Seasons Novel

KATE SMOAK

DEDICATION

For my daughter.
To show her that you can make
your dreams come true.

– Kate Smoak

CONTENT WARNING

This book contains scenes of graphic sexual content, depictions of alcohol and drug use, and deals with mental health issues like anxiety and eating disorders. It also touches on abuse. We advise readers accordingly.

Please note: This is the second book in a series of four where the HEA develops over the series.

CHAPTER
ONE

Mid-August
The day after the launch party

BRANDT

Riley enters Elissa's room, and when she freezes in place, my stomach plummets. Something isn't right. She darts into the en suite bathroom, but quickly reappears. At the same time as Riley, Rhys and I notice my overnight bag and a box on Elissa's bed. I watch as Riley rushes over and throws open the box. My whole body goes numb as she pulls out a single piece of paper with trembling hands. Her face screws up and instantly drains of colour. Rhys and I look at each other and jump up, barging into the bedroom.

I snatch the paper out of Riley's hands just as she falls apart with a wail. Rhys rushes to scoop Riley into his arms and comfort her.

I feel like a glacier. My frozen body aches as I read Elissa's hastily scrawled words. I can't move or think properly. Hell, I'm not even sure I can smell anything. It's like my brain has broken along with my heart. *She's gone?* I search the letter again for any information. My heart breaks a little more when I notice that the note is mostly for Riley, with just one small line meant for me.

Brandt and Riley,

I know you two will be together when you read this. I'm sorry for disappearing like this, but I just need some time alone. I can't live under my father's thumb anymore. I know you deserve more than a letter as an explanation or a goodbye, but I know if I were to do this face-to-face, Riles, you would talk me out of it. Or at least convince me to go to Fiji with you or something. Please don't look for me right now. I need time to decompress and figure some shit out.

Riles: I love you and I'm sorry for everything. Stay in the apartment. I don't know when I'll be back, so feel free to take my room. I'll be in touch in a few days when my head is a little clearer. I love you. xoxo

Brandt: I'm sorry…I don't know how to… I'm just sorry.

All my best,

E. xoxo

That's all I get? A "sorry," and nothing else? All the emotions I could possibly feel in this moment swirl around inside my core. My fingers curl into tight, white-knuckled fists. Only the sounds of the note crinkling in my hand and Riley's sobs fill the apartment.

"She'll be back soon," Rhys says quietly. I'm not sure if he's trying to soothe Riley or convince me. "Elissa probably just needs a breather. There's been a lot put on her the last few weeks."

That last part seems to have been enough to soothe Riley. She snorts, wiping her tears and snot on the blankets of Elissa's bed. She's left nothing behind other than her sheets and a few scattered items of clothing. Riley shuffles into the bathroom, closes the door, and the room falls silent. It feels like the floor has shifted underneath my feet and I'm free-falling into darkness.

November, three months later

The last three months have been a blur. After Elissa left, Harold lost his shit and dumped the entire department on me. So, instead of taking care of my other responsibilities within Collins Global Collective, I've had Rhys taking over most of the operations until I can get out of this fucking department. Rhys has been accommodating, but I pay him well for that, and he is the CFO, after all. He should do his share when it's called for.

It's been three months of long, grueling nights at the office. Burying myself with work to keep myself from thinking about *her;* then burying myself in someone else to keep from hurting over her. Sometimes I don't even go home— my office couch has gotten a lot of action these past few weeks. And when I say action, not only do I mean sleeping, but *sleeping.* Selena, my assistant, has been volunteering to stay late and help me with the tasks that Elissa was suppos-ed to be in charge of. I've unofficially promoted her at this point, but I keep holding out, like a fool, praying Elissa walks back through the door. But even if she did, I don't know what I'd do. She shattered me by running away.

"Brandt," Selena purrs. I shift my glance to her. I'm sitting behind my desk, typing on my computer, and she's lounging on my office couch. She hitches her black pencil skirt up to mid-thigh and traces little circular patterns on her legs with her middle finger while she sucks in her bottom lip, biting on it firmly. Her eyes are on me, dark with temptation.

"Come over and take a break for a bit." She pats the small space on the couch beside her.

Her eyes light up when I push away from my mahogany desk and stalk toward her, cuffing my sleeves around my muscular forearms. Her tongue glides along her lower lip and bites down on the soft pillowy skin. When I reach the couch, she shuffles off and sits me down. She straddles me, her skirt bunching up around her waist, and pulls me in for a kiss, the collar of my shirt gripped in her tiny fists.

Selena's soft lips crush against mine and she instant-ly probes her tongue into my mouth. Her hand slides around the back of my neck and up into my hair, tug-ging on it hard as she rolls her crotch against mine so I can feel her wanting heat through my pants. I break our kiss so I can French kiss her neck and she moans like a porn star in my ear. My dick gradually gets harder, and when I close my eyes, I imagine only the flash of silky copper hair and sharp blue eyes. Selena jumps off me and saunters over to my desk, pulling out a silver packet from the bottom drawer.

Selena settles herself back on my lap, her lips meeting mine in a slow, sensual kiss. She pulls at my bottom lip, softly sinking her teeth into it. Her hand slides down my broad chest, popping open the buttons of my shirt, and she rubs up and down my washboard abs for a few moments before descending further. Selena thumbs open the button on my trousers with one hand while the other grips my neck for support. She drags down the zipper of my pants and shoves her hand into the opening of my boxers, freeing my cock. Her long, manicured fingernails rake gently along my shaft, making me twitch before she wraps her tiny hand around me, priming me for the condom.

With the foil packet between her teeth and forefinger and thumb, she slides off my lap to her knees, tears open the condom and rolls the rubber onto my hard cock, pushing it down with her mouth. Before coming back up, she sucks both balls into her mouth and swirls her tongue around them. She leaves a trail of kisses along the side of my dick and up my chest, tickling the golden blonde hairs there, tonguing wet kisses over my abs.

Selena straddles me once more, pushing her thong to the side and positioning herself over my tip. She loops an arm around my neck, pulling me close. I wrap my large hands around her slim waist and thrust her down on my cock; she throws her head back and lets out a moan. I buck my hips upward, hitting her hard and deep. Her head rolls forward and she rests her forehead on mine as I slide her up and down on my dick. Her pelvis rolls simultaneously to hit her

G-spot. Selena tilts her head and plasters her lips to mine, kissing me roughly and feverishly as she rides me harder.

One of my hands tugs her blouse out from her skirt and slides up her torso to cup one of her breasts, slipping my hand under the lacy bralette she's wearing. Selena has a smaller chest; cute little apple breasts, and my large hands cover them completely. As I touch the soft skin beneath my hands, I miss the feeling of my hands being full, the perfect amount of breast resting in my palm. I squeeze Selena's breast hard before rolling her nipple between my fingers and pinching it. She moans into my mouth; I pinch her nipple again and I can feel her tighten around my cock briefly.

"Oh, Brandt!"

I've learned over the last few weeks Selena's biggest turn-on is getting rough with her nipples. I pinch her nipple repeatedly and she slams her tight pussy down on my cock, harder and harder. Her mouth moves against my ear as her hot, panting breaths tickle my earlobe, then she moves it to the sensitive spot behind my ear. She tongues it lightly, and I feel my balls tingle as a shiver runs up my spine. I thrust into her harder, moving both hands down to her perfect, juicy ass and giving it a good squeeze. My hand slides lower to gather some of her wetness on my finger. I trail it back to her small, puckered hole. Easing my finger into her hole, we're both breathing hard. As my finger gets deeper, her ass tightens around my finger. She is moaning so loudly that I bring my hand up from her nipple to cover her mouth to muffle the sound. I withdraw my finger before sliding it back in her asshole and slamming my dick into her hard. It's enough to push her over the edge. As her tight holes spasm around my finger and dick, I unload inside her, filling the condom while flashes of blue eyes, red hair, and creamy pale skin play on my mind.

Selena collapses on top of me, both of our chests rising and falling hard. I ease her off me, tug off the condom, and tie it up. I roll it into some tissues and dispose of it in the wastebasket. Selena is still sprawled on the couch, one leg hanging down, the other resting across the cushions. Her skirt is still bunched up around her waist and her legs are wide open, putting her pussy on display. Readjusting my clothes, I excuse myself from the office to give her some privacy, but also to head to the break room to get some coffee.

"Want a coffee?" I ask her. She grins and nods. "Find something to order while I grab coffee. I'll put it on the company's tab." Selena stands, adjusts her clothing, and follows me out of my office, heading to her desk to sift through the takeout pamphlets.

CHAPTER
TWO

BRANDT

At the end of the day, I order a car for Selena and walk her out of the building. I open the door for her and she lowers herself off the curb and onto the street with one foot as she leans in to kiss me. I turn my cheek slightly so she doesn't connect with my lips. Instead, she lands a kiss on the corner of my mouth. She sighs, disappointed.

"Good night, Brandt. See you tomorrow." I offer her a silent nod and close the door behind her.

I take off toward Rhys' apartment, and a few blocks later, I approach Riley's building, I am filled with rage when I think about how that was *Elissa and Riley's* place. A haze of red floats into my vision and my breathing becomes ragged. In the crisp November air, I no longer feel a chill as I continue walking down the street.

Fire burns inside me, and any time anyone mentions or makes me think of *her*, it stokes the fire. Every mention of her name is like another log being thrown on, making the fire last longer. If I'd truly known how she was, I never would have entertained the deal. Perfectly manicured hands tore my heart from my chest and then served it to me on a plate, raw, with a *bon appétite* note attached.

Oh, who am I kidding.

I would take the deal, over and over again, because the time with her was amazing. The only thing I would change is the way I left my heart unguarded. I dove in headfirst, with reckless abandon, and allowed my heart to run my emotions.

When I finally reach Rhys' place, I buzz up. I wait for a minute, and nothing. I buzz again. Again, nothing. I reach into my pocket and pull out my phone, thinking that calling him might be a better way to get his attention. Just as I'm about to press the green call button, a loud screeching noise echoes throughout the lobby of the building. There's giggling in the background and Rhys' voice is fragmented between heaving breaths. I grumble inwardly.

"Yeah?" My eyes drift toward the ceiling as I shake my head at his casual tone.

"It's me. But clearly you're busy tonight." Someone, I assume Riley, cackles in the background, then makes their way to the speaker.

"Brrrraaandtttttt," a plastered Riley shouts through the speaker. "Where are you? Are you here?" I mumble back, telling Rhys to get ahold of Riley and buzz me up for a moment. A minute later, the door clicks and a long buzz drowns out the silence of the lobby. I make my way toward the elevator and my phone beeps in my pocket. I extricate it from my jacket to see who messaged me.

Selena: *Baby, you seemed off when we left. Let me know if you wanna talk.*

Me: *Thanks. And please don't call me that.*

Selena sends an embarrassed-looking emoji, and a gif of Puss in Boots giving kitty eyes.

Selena: *Sorry. But let me know if you want to come over soon. I'll be up a little longer. I'm not wearing much…*

As I close in on Rhys' door, I look at the message Selena sent and chuckle to myself, knowing Riley would say something about her being "thirsty." The door flings open suddenly and a squeal jars my mind as a tiny body jumps on me.

"Oof." For a tiny girl, she sure can knock the wind out of you. "Hey Riley," I say flatly.

She happily greets me with "Oh, Brandty," but her mood changes when my phone's text message alert sounds twice in quick succession.

"Who the hell is texting you so much?" She rips the phone out of my hand and scrolls through the messages. Riley's brows furrow and her cheeks redden. The grinding of her teeth ruins the stillness in the air.

"*Selena?*" Riley sneers. "As in, your assistant?" I make a noncommittal noise in response and avoid her stare. "Are you fucking joking, Brandt? Elissa—" Riley and I both freeze, our eyes darting to find each other's as the blood drains from our faces at the mention of *her* name. She shakes off the frost before me and changes the direction of the conversation, clearing her throat as she hands me my phone.

"I mean…damn, this girl is thirstaaay." Riley turns to Rhys, pats his shoulder, and stumbles into the bedroom. Rhys gives me an apologetic look and gestures for me to come in. I take off my shoes while shrugging off my jacket, tossing it over a kitchen chair as I make my way to the living room before collapsing on the couch. My sprawled body takes up the length of the couch, and I close my eyes and drift off for a moment. Suddenly, cold glass rests against my cheek and I shiver from the abrupt sensation. Rhys is pressing a beer bottle to my face.

"I was just resting my eyes," I say.

"Mmhm. So, why are you here so late?" Rhys asks me. I falter for a second. I haven't been sure what to say to him as of late because of Riley, who is in the next room, probably listening to our conversation. The bottle of beer hovers in front of my lips before I take a long pull, still debating on what I should tell him.

"Just didn't want to go straight home. Had a long day and hooked up with my assistant again, but now she's getting clingy. I told her it was just casual," I say to Rhys with a long sigh. "She wants more, and I just can't give it to her. Elissa fucked me up, and I'm not ready for anything… more." Rhys nods his head in understanding. This thing with Selena started a few weeks ago, out of necessity—I needed to try and erase Elissa's skin, body, and taste from my mind. Her being is burned into my brain like a searing brand, leaving her mark on me forever. But, as great as Selena has been, she's just a temporary distraction, and one that's not working very well, either. It's not her fault—it's Elissa's, for fucking me up.

"Maybe you need to get out and hook up with someone else, and break it off with her," Rhys suggests. I contemplate his words. *But is another random hookup going to help this aching, suffocating feeling I have in my chest?*

"Sure, easier said than done when all I do is work until 11 PM. When or how am I supposed to see anyone when I'm always at the office?" My mind meanders to Lori, who had been Elissa's assistant. She's a solid eight with a great, voluptuous rack and an ass for days. She rarely wears skirts, but the dress pants she wears with her pumps make her ass look fantastic. I shake off the thought, slightly disgusted with myself. *Is this how businessmen usually act when they're sleeping with their assistants?* I decide to message Selena to break it off, and I look over at Rhys and ask him what I should say. He shrugs.

"Just say something like you had fun, but you should break it off before it gets complicated."

With every tap my fingers make on the screen, I feel as though an immense pressure is being lifted off me, but at the same time, a slow, sinking feeling creeps into my stomach as my heart pangs. I'm finding it increasingly hard to believe I'll ever get over *her*. Even when I'm not actively thinking about her, I'm still thinking about her; I see her everywhere I go. I can't get her out of my system. She's stuck onto me like a tiny, prickly burr on the cuff of my pant leg.

"How's Riley doing with everything?" I ask, Rhys shrugs and rakes his hands through his hair.

"I don't know man, she…she just won't talk about it. It's like she's pretending everything is okay, or like Elissa is just on some vacation," Rhys mutters. My lips thin and I nod my head, not quite sure what to say. My mind still wrestles with Elissa's abandonment of us daily and it's been three fucking months. *Get over it, dude. But it's easier said than done when my heart aches for her every damn day.*

"How are you holding up with everything? Sorry I've been so absent at CGC." Rhys' head falls forward and he sighs.

"It's all right man. A lot of fucking work. Doing your job and mine, it's exhausting. But I know it's only temporary, so get out of there fast," he growls. A sympathetic chuckle rumbles out of me, and I feel for him, I do. He's been a great sport for letting me lean on him and stepping up to the plate to take on all the extras that I can't do right now.

I keep the message with Selena open, and the three dots pop up and disappear a few times, indicating she's typing a reply. The anxiety of awaiting her response bubbles in my gut. But, after half an hour, there's no response. I finish my beer as Riley walks out into the living room in nothing but a small tank top and cheeky pink underwear. Rhys' eyes bug out and a small drop of sweat forms on his brow. He's clearly embarrassed that his girlfriend is walking around practically naked in front of me. It hardly matters to me. Riley is a gorgeous woman, no one can deny that, but there's really only one woman who's ever caught my attention. My hands twitch, and I'm itching to feel her in my arms again; to feel her silky creamy skin under my fingertips again…

However, as my eyes linger on Riley's form, I notice something different about her. As long as I've known her, she's always been petite, but now she's so small I can see the faint ridges of her ribs through her skintight tank top. Her midriff, and even her cheeks, look especially hollow. I make a mental note to talk to Rhys about this when we're alone. Riley grabs a beer cap from the counter, twists it in her hand, and tosses it onto the coffee table. She takes a long pull of Rhys' beer and tries to wrestle the remote out of his hand. When she's unsuccessful, she moans and licks his ear.

"And…that's my cue. See you guys later." I stand up and walk out of the apartment, not looking back. Before I close the apartment door behind me, I hear Riley say, "Yes!" I assume she won control of the remote by distraction. Riley: 1, Rhys: 0.

Back at my apartment building, as I walk out of the elevator and down the hallway, I loosen the tie around my neck. I yank my apartment door open I start removing clothing as I make my way to the bedroom. I'm too revved up to sleep, so I decide to change into my workout clothes and make my way downstairs, to the building's gym. Once there, I hop on the treadmill and zone out as I start to jog.

"Haven't seen you here in a while," a smooth and delicate voice murmurs into my ear, and the hairs on the back of my neck stand up. I turn down the treadmill to a brisk walk. I don't need to look to know that it's Lexi, the petite, busty blonde who asks me out constantly. I nod in her direction.

"Yeah, work's been killing me." *Work, Elissa. Same thing. They both suck.*

"You don't say," Lexi drawls. "And here I was thinking you moved to another place, so you didn't have to evade me asking you out." A playful smirk stretches across her face. My face heats and my heartbeat quickens at her insinuation. She steps onto the treadmill beside mine and the air thickens; tension radiates between us. Our eyes lock and the heat creeps down my face to my neck, swirling the contents of my stomach. I break our connection, turn off the treadmill, and stalk to the bench press to set up the weights.

I'm doing quick presses of two hundred pounds for about ten minutes when I hear the beeping of Lexi's treadmill, signalling the cool-down period. Keeping my focus on the presses and my form, I don't realize she's come over to me until she materializes above me, staring at me upside down. Droplets of sweat glisten on her forehead as some roll down the length of her neck.

"Need a spot?" She extends her tiny hands so they hover under the bar, following my movement. I puff my chest and cheeks simultaneously as I keep pumping my arms, letting small puffs of breath out in between.

"Not an imperfect form there, Collins." My mind falters at the casual nickname, throwing me off. Typically, she'd flirt a bit more, or coo my name, trying to seduce me at every chance. I've obviously pissed her off, even though I've done nothing. I quirk my brow at her, and she lets out a small chuckle.

"What? That is your last name, right?" she taunts, her mouth upturning on the right corner. I nod and return the bar to its resting position. I sit up and she walks around the bench, now facing me, toe-to-toe. She cocks her leg and plants her hands on her hips.

"You gonna move? My turn," she says, rolling her tongue against her bottom lip before pulling it in. I bend over, grab my towel, and wipe some sweat off my brow before I stand up. We're millimetres apart. She's still got her bottom lip between her teeth, only now she's nibbling on it nervously, like she's debating something.

Two small, but firm, hands push against my chest, slamming me back down onto the bench while Lexi's legs wrap outside of mine, straddling me. Startled, I stay frozen as her fingers lace into my damp hair and she pulls me into her, pressing her soft, enormous chest into my collarbone. Her lips descend to mine, slowly, like she's giving me a moment to stop this, but right now I'm not thinking straight. For the first time, I realize I'm fighting to keep from getting hard for someone who isn't her. For the first time since Elissa left, I find my mind blank. I lean in, not stopping her, and her lips are full, but a little rough from all the nibbling she must do; a small habit I can tell she has by the feeling of her lips against mine.

Her tongue sweeps against my mouth, parting my lips. I let her tongue explore my mouth as my tongue finds hers. Her hands slide down my torso, and she tightens her grip around the bottom of my shirt and tugs. My hands grip her wrists to stop her as I break the kiss, both of us panting.

"Not like this," I say, heaving for air.

CHAPTER THREE

When the door buzzer goes off at Rhys' apartment, I am pissed. He's on top of me, and when he pauses at the sound, I shoot him a death glare.

"Don't you dare answer it," I growl at him. Since Elissa vanished, my emotions have been all over the place. I think I've received maybe three text messages from her? So, like, one per month.

"I have to! It's almost midnight. There's only one person it could be," Rhys whines. He smirks playfully, and I realize that he thinks I'm joking. I lock my legs around his waist, refusing to let him leave.

"We're going to finish first, so you better bring it." Rhys sighs and pulls back to pump into me again. He rolls his hips to grind into me, just the way I like it, so he can hit that sweet, sweet spot that makes my toes curl. It takes a few moments, but my head is finally back into it, and I start to feel lightheaded as tingles roll through my body. One more hard thrust and he pushes us over the edge and my body relaxes into ecstasy. Rhys only relaxes for a moment before the buzzer goes off again, and he jumps out of bed. He hops into a pair of jeans and runs to the buzzing box at the door.

My buzz now waning, I throw on some undies, pajama pants, and a tank top and slink into the kitchen to grab a shot of something, anything, to numb the pain. My stomach rumbles and I suppress the urge to eat with another shot of this shitty-tasting liquor. The warmth washes over me, staving off my hunger and a growing sense of irritation and anger.

My buzz returns almost immediately, and I skip to the door to find Rhys. As he presses the entry button, I slide my arms around him from behind, and my hands find their way into his pants. He tenses and wriggles around, trying to avoid my wandering hands, and a boisterous giggle escapes me. Rhys' finger finally releases the buzzer and he points me to the bedroom. I brush him off and head back toward the kitchen for another shot.

I tip back the alcohol and feel it make its way to my brain. A moment later, I feel that familiar wave of haziness washing over me. I decide it's a good idea to bound down the hallway and throw open the door, knowing that Rhys just buzzed Brandt up. Sure enough, when I open the door, Brandt is standing there. I throw myself into him, loose limbs akimbo. "Oh, Brandty" I say happily. He lets out a small grunt as I collide with him.

"Oof. Hey, Riley," he says flatly. I hear a muffled dinging sound, twice in quick succession, and I look down to see Brandt's cell phone in his hand. I am just drunk enough to obnoxiously rip the phone out of his hand. The screen is still open to a text conversation. *Selena? As in, Elissa's assistant? Are you fucking joking?* I guess I say as much out loud, because when I look up at Brandt, his face looks how I feel — hollow and drained. I catch myself and say something stupid instead.

"I mean…damn, this girl is thirstaaay." It's not Brandt's fault Elissa left; he's free to bang whoever he wants. Still, a sharp pang ricochets through my gut when I think of him with someone other than Elissa. I turn to Rhys, pat him on the shoulder, and decide to hide my drunk ass in his bedroom for a bit.

I lay back on Rhys' bed, staring up at the ceiling and shimmying my pajama pants off to get more comfortable. Despite my best efforts, my thoughts wander back to Brandt and how fast he seemed to shack up with his assistant after Elissa left. I thought he was really into her, but I guess he really is just some closed-off playboy. It's hard to judge him, as I imagine Elissa has probably kept her bed warm with random men over these last few months too. But still…I thought there was something there.

A sharp pang rumbles through my stomach, and I can't tell if it's from the pain of Elissa's abandonment or because I'm drinking on an empty stomach. I decide to go into the kitchen and find something light to eat. I hear Rhys and Brandt mumbling in the living room as I search the fridge, finding a beer and a yogurt cup. I try to listen to their conversation, but they're talking so damn quietly, I can't hear much.

I'm mentally tallying the yogurt's calories in my head as I wander into the living room, when I feel a burning, uncomfortable stare lingering on me. I glance toward Brandt and his eyes meet mine, full of unsure concern. The way he's looking at me makes my skin burn cold, like frostbite setting in. I feel exposed, judged. Desperately needing to take back control, I pop off my beer cap and take a large swig before jumping into Rhys' lap, making moves on him to win the remote. Hopefully the PDA makes Brandt uncomfortable enough to leave, or at least to stop looking at me.

When Brandt excuses himself from the awkward scene, I relax enough that Rhys is finally able to shove me off his lap. He jumps up and tries to walk Brandt to the door. Rhys returns a moment later, his eyes narrowed and levelled on me. He looks pissed.

"What the fuck was that, Riley?" *Uh oh. My full name — I'm in trouble.* I plaster on a flirtatious grin and crawl along the couch, fluttering my lashes coyly at him.

"I'm not sure what you mean," I say, feigning innocence. My body sways as I sit back on my haunches before getting to my knees to pull Rhys in closer. He brushes me off and takes a half-step back, staying just out of my grasp.

"C'mon Riley. You know exactly what. Something strange is going on with you lately. Your moods are all over the place. One minute you're happy, the next you're irritable. And now you're piss drunk." He waves his hands at me. I try to suppress an eye roll, but am unsuccessful. I climb up off the couch and stand, trying to get on his level, but Rhys towers over me.

"First off, you know I drink. You met me when Elissa and I were partying. Second, you know what's going on. My best friend is going through something, and she left me. She. Left. Me. With nothing more than a note to say goodbye. I've only gotten three messages from her — just enough to let me know she's still alive. I haven't heard her voice or seen her in three months; this is the longest we've gone without seeing each other or talking since we were born." I bite back the tears brewing inside. My frustration and anger rise, and I know I'm unfairly directing these feelings at Rhys, but I can't help it. He stepped on a fucking hornet's nest.

I give Rhys a long look, anger and pain flashing at him in my eyes. He looks...defeated. It hits me that this is the first time since Elissa left that I've really *looked* at him. His crystal blue eyes seem duller, and there are bags underneath. His face is pale and, thinking back, I don't think I've seen him *really* smile lately. I heave an enormous sigh, scrub my face, and pull Rhys into my arms. "I'm sorry, babe," I whisper. My arms squeeze his waist and I rest my head on his chest. His arms stay at his sides for a few beats before he wraps them around me, squeezing me back just as hard, and I feel thick underneath the weight of his arms, but I try to push the thought aside.

"What's going on with you? I'm sorry I haven't checked in with you for a while. I know I've been absorbed in my own shit."

Rhys' shoulders droop as he rests his chin on my head, and he heaves a deep sigh. "I know you've been having a hard time, Riles. But so have I. I've got the entirety of CGC on my shoulders while Brandt tries to figure out how to remove himself from Black & Wells," he explains. "I know that's not the same as feeling abandoned by your friend, but it's still a lot of stress. And I also feel like my best friend has abandoned me. Brandt isn't the same; he's more reserved and closed-off than usual. I'm also pissed as fucking hell at Elissa for what she did to you and Brandt…" He heaves another gigantic sigh and wraps me tighter in his arms. "I'm sorry too, baby. I love you."

My heart instantly warms at those words and one of the tiny cracks in my heart slowly stitches itself back together. After what feels like forever, I finally wriggle out of Rhys' arms and stare at him with soft eyes. I flick my silky raven hair out of my face, wipe my eyes, and place a gentle kiss on his cheek.

"I think I'm going to go home tonight. I haven't been home in a while," I say. Rhys' brow rises and his eyes fill with worry.

"No, Riles. Please, stay —" I raise my hand to cut him off and rest it on his chest.

"It's okay, I'll take a cab. No worries. Besides, I think we could both use a night apart to recharge. I'll come over after work tomorrow." I pull him in and leave him with a long, deep kiss, as a promise to return tomorrow. I dart to the bedroom, pull my regular clothes on, and slip out the front door. As I leave, I hear him shuffle to the living room and the sound of the TV turning on.

When I finally exit the elevator, my heels click across the tile floor. One heel catches a hole in the grout and I wobble. I lurch forward, my hands smashing against the lobby door as I catch myself. *That was close. Almost broke my ankle.* I straighten up, and as I do, I catch my reflection in the glass. A shudder rolls through my body. I shake my head, head outside, and order a car on my ride share app.

As the car glides silently through the streets of Toronto, my thoughts wander. It's getting harder and harder to keep Elissa off my mind without getting angry or sad. At first I thought I understood where she was coming from; I grew up with her. I know her parents weren't there for her and her like like she simply didn't exist most days. Hell, she practically lived at my house when Lana was busy. But when Elissa didn't come back after a few weeks, I started getting sad and resentful, especially when she didn't reach out to me to let me know what was going on. I've spent weeks agonizing, wondering if she's okay.

Slowly, that resentment and sadness changed into anger and depression. It's like I lost a part of myself. My heart aches to have Elissa in my life again. It feels like losing a sister, because that's who Elissa was to me. My sister, my family.

Thirty minutes later, I'm walking through my front door, into the apartment I shared with Elissa. Everything is dark, quiet. Suddenly, I feel a tidal wave of loneliness and depression hit me. I grab the bottle of whiskey that Elissa left behind from the top shelf in the kitchen and stumble off to my bedroom, taking a big swig as I walk. I kick my bedroom door shut behind me and strip off my clothes, curling up in bed and cradling the bottle in my arms like a baby. I allow my body to sink into the soft mattress that surrounds me like a cloud.

CHAPTER FOUR

BRANDT

I push Lexi off me. Her face flushes, with what I assume is embarrassment for throwing herself at me. She steps back and her hands fly to her face, hiding her eyes. I reach over to her, and my fingers gently wrap around her wrists and tug her arms down. Her lower lip quivers and her eyes fill with tears as she looks at me through her lashes. I pull Lexi into an embrace, and her tiny body curls into mine. She doesn't fit as perfectly as Elissa, but she fits well. Thinking of Eli makes my heart and body ache for her, and it feels like another tiny crack appears in my heart.

"Let's go out," I murmur into Lexi's hair. I press a kiss into her earlobe. She stiffens in my arms.

"Really?" There's hesitation in her voice. "Like…an actual date?" I feel her suck in a breath and hold it. Her lungs deflate only when she hears my answer.

"Yep. You and me, a fancy restaurant. What do you say?" Lexi pulls away slightly, studying my face to see if I'm serious.

"Aren't you seeing someone?" she asks me. Anger and pain flash through me as I try to keep a calm exterior. It should probably throw up a red flag that she tried to make a move on me while she thought I was seeing someone.

"Not anymore. So…do you want to go out?"

She beams at me and seems to be rendered speechless, because all she can muster is an enthusiastic nod. I place a soft kiss on the corner of her mouth, take out my cell phone, and pass it to her so she can add her contact information. While she taps away on the screen, I can't help but think about how fucked up everything has turned out.

Elissa really did a number on me. I truly thought there was something special between us. Was I just fooling myself? *Of course you were fooling yourself. Your entire relationship started based on lies and secrets. No wonder it all fell apart; you don't even know if she knows the truth.* Fuck me.

"Uh, Brandt?" Lexi's voice pulls me back to reality. She's nervous and chewing her lip again, and I feel my lips tug slightly.

"Sorry," I say, taking my phone back. "I'll text you tomorrow and we can make plans. Sound good?" Lexi nods her head and steps into my arms, giving me one last hug before I leave the gym, her strawberry scent lingering on me.

The next morning, while I'm getting ready for work, Rhys decides it's a good time to call me.

"Dude," Rhys groans. "When are you coming back to our office? Everything is fine, but we need to get you out of the Black & Wells building and into ours. We need to separate you from the drama of that place." *Well, fuck me. You don't say.* I put my phone on speaker and set it down on my dresser as I stroll into my closet to find a tie. I roll my eyes at his obvious statement and decide to change the conversation.

"How's Riley doing? Last night she seemed pretty toasted." I hear another groan from over the line. Another unpleasant topic? Shit, we're really killing it at this conversation thing today.

"I don't know, man. She's been real moody, and it's not hormonal. Trust me, I regrettably asked." I nod to myself like an idiot, then realize he can't see my actions.

"Oh, I see," I say. "She's doing all right with everything though?" A deep sigh echoes through the speaker.

"I suppose so. I mean, how do you feel? So take that, multiply it by one hundred, and you'll have an answer. Riley's known Elissa forever, and this has destroyed her. She's all over the place. Happy one minute, sad the next. She's drinking a lot more too…" He trails off.

"I only ask because she seems…petite. Smaller than normal."

"Meh," Rhys retorts. "I haven't really noticed anything different. She keeps talking about a fad diet she's doing, but I haven't really been paying attention. I feel bad for checking out of our conversations, but she only has one topic lately — Elissa. And I'm trying to be sympathetic, but it's getting to be too much. I love her, I do. But…"

"But what?" I ask, feeling a slight panic rise for him.

"I don't know, man," Rhys replies, exasperation clear in his tone. "I just don't know how much more I can take with these mood swings. She wasn't like this before Elissa left." I don't really know what else to say, and I get the feeling that Rhys might be at his limit in this relationship.

"Well, before you do anything rash, maybe try talking to her." He scoffs at my suggestion.

"I do try to talk to her, but lately it's like I can't say anything without setting her off. She's either in tears or snapping at me. The only time Riley is remotely herself again is when I'm fucking her." I sigh and tell him to try talking to her again. "Yeah, man. Anyway, are you coming into the office today? There are some numbers I need to go over with you."

"I'll try to take off around lunch. We'll see how my morning goes. If not, wanna grab dinner tonight, maybe a quick game beforehand?"

"Sounds good. Text me if you're not coming by at lunch." After my call with Rhys, I head into the office. When I get there, I collapse into my chair and toss my cell across my mahogany desk, leaning forward and scrubbing my hands against my face. Suddenly, I'm interrupted by a knock on my door. I look up to see Selena in the doorway.

"What can I do for you?" I ask. She scoffs and crosses her arms over her chest. She's wearing a tight blouse that leaves little to the imagination, with her perky, voluptuous cleavage cresting over the neckline. My eyes follow the buttons on her blouse down to her tapered waist, which is wrapped in a tight, black pencil skirt that curves around her hips nicely. My eyes flick back to hers, and a vindictive smile of victory appears on her face. She wore this outfit on purpose.

"You can stop eye-fucking me and try keeping it professional," she sneers. "Since, you know, you called it quits. By text message." There's a definite bite in those last three words. I let out a sigh and loosen my tie.

"Is this how it's going to be? You knew what this was, and now we still have to work together. Can you do that?" I ask her. A bit of a chill frosts my words. Selena's face hardens, and she gives me a stiff nod. I allow myself to relax a little and ask her again what she needs.

The next time I look up from my work, it's getting close to lunchtime. I message Rhys to let him know I can't make it to the office, but that a quick game and bite after work should be okay if he's still down. Suddenly, Lori, Elissa's old assistant — now mine and Selena's secretary — buzzes through the intercom.

"A Ms. Lexi Gardner is here to see you," she says, her voice crackling through the system. I press the button to respond and tell Lori to let Lexi in. A few moments later, Lexi strolls into my office wearing a long-sleeved floral wrap dress. The deep neckline allows her cleavage to peek out, and the waist cinches in to show off her hourglass figure. When she walks into the room, she casually tousles her hair, which is styled in soft blonde ringlets that reach almost to her waist. Her lips curl into a flirtatious grin as her heels click toward me, her bright blue eyes locking onto mine.

She circles her arms around my neck and presses a soft kiss to my cheek, but only one of my hands embraces her, just below her shoulder blade. Her shoulders slouch briefly, but she quickly composes herself and beams at me as she pulls away. I return the smile.

"Hey Lexi. What a surprise. What brings you here?" Lexi bites the corner of her lip before answering. "Hopefully it's a pleasant surprise?" she quips. "I just realized that my studio is near your office building, and I was on my way home after my morning class. I thought maybe you might want to grab a bite to eat?" Her fingers reach up to twirl a lock of hair nervously when I don't immediately respond.

"I know you said you'd text me to set something up, so I'm sorry if this is too spontaneous for you. I just figured 'what the hell,' since it's lunchtime, anyway," she says in a rushed breath. My mouth twitches as I try to hold back a smile.

"Sure, Lexi. I wasn't planning on taking a lunch, but since you're here, let's go." I grab my jacket from the coat rack in the corner of my office, shrug it on, and place my hand on the small of her back, escorting her toward the elevator. As I pass the front desk of my floor, I can feel Selena's eyes throwing daggers into my back. I feel a cold chill roll over my body, almost like a premonition of how my afternoon is going to be.

Lexi and I walk a few minutes down the road to a small deli around the corner from the Black & Wells Publishing and Press building. I haven't been here in roughly three months, not since Elissa disappeared — it hurt too much to come back. It's the only place close enough that has a decent lunch menu though, and I'm short on time for lunch, considering how Lexi showed up randomly. I turn to Lexi and hold the door open for her. She mumbles a "Thank you."

I step around her as I lead us to a booth by the back of the deli. I stand to the side until she chooses what side of the booth to sit on, and I slide into the other side. The waiter comes over a moment later. I order a coffee and a BLT, and Lexi orders a water and a garden salad. I cock my eyebrow at her after the waiter leaves.

"You can eat something more than a salad. I won't judge you." Lexi's face flushes.

"Yes, I know. But I genuinely like salads. I typically eat lighter lunches; it's easier on my body for the afternoon fitness classes I teach," she replies in a proud, firm voice.

We sit for a stretch of awkward silence until the waiter brings us our food. I begin eating, but Lexi picks at her plate without actually taking a bite, all the while nibbling on that damn lip again. I suppress a sigh, put down my sandwich, and grab her attention by clearing my throat.

"If you don't stop biting that lip, I just might have to do it myself," I grumble, which seems to throw her off her axis. Her collarbone and neck flush. "I was thinking — tomorrow night we should go out for dinner, if you don't have plans." Lexi immediately perks up with a wide grin. A playful look flashes across her face.

"My, my. How the tables have turned," she says coyly. "Is Brandt Collins actually taking the initiative to ask me out?" I feel the left side of my mouth quirk up.

"Indeed I am. So, tomorrow night?" I ask again. She rolls her eyes back and forth, like she's contemplating the offer, and not like she's been hounding me for a year to go on a date. "I mean, I suppose I could rearrange my schedule," she replies playfully. She throws another giant smile my way and nods her head.

"Yeah, I think I can fit a date in tomorrow night." She stabs at her salad and shoves a gigantic bite into her mouth, clearly more relaxed now. A sad pang ripples through my body as I remember the last time I was here with Elissa. She would have never ordered a salad. She would have ordered the greasiest sandwich on the menu and fries with gravy. I push the thought away and try to focus on the gorgeous woman in front of me, who isn't Elissa.

CHAPTER
FIVE

ELISSA

I've settled into London over the last three months fairly well. After everything that happened between my father and Brandt, I just needed to escape. Running around downtown Toronto barefoot just didn't cut it. Instead, I cleared out my bedroom, loaded up my car, and hauled ass out of town. I wasn't sure exactly where I should go, so I just got on Highway 401 and headed west. I drove all night until I ended up in London. It's a pleasant city; close to my hometown, but not a place my father would think to look first. I'm also only a forty-five minute drive from Lana.

I've even considered changing my name to make it harder for my father to find me, but it just seems like way too much work to change everything. And, if he really wanted to, he'd find me. Instead, I just go by Elli in London.

"Elli!" a gruff voice booms from the back of the room. "Where are the new chapters from Will Burke?" I cringe and turn around to see Gary Nicholson, my boss, stomping over to my desk. He's a middle-aged man, probably around my father's age. He's a bit scruffy looking; the kind of man who probably looked good when he was younger, but the years have caught up to him. When he reaches my desk, he folds his arms across his chest and stares me down. I sigh.

"I'm sorry, sir. He said he was sending them last night, but he must have forgotten." I know exactly why he'd forgotten to send them to me. "I'll get ahold of him and get him to send them over ASAP." Gary grunts at my response.

"You're damn right you will. If I don't have Will's new chapters in my hand by the end of the day, it's on you." He turns and stomps away, shaking his head. I suppress the urge to tell him off because here, I'm not *Elissa Black, daughter of Harold Black, heiress to Black & Wells Publishing and Press.* Here, I'm just Elli Black, junior editor at Wellington Drive Publishing. I grit my teeth and pull my cell out of my purse to text Will.

Me: *Hey*

Will Burke: *Hey babe. What's up?*

I groan at his little pet name but decide to ignore it.

Me: *Gary needs the new chapters by end of day.*

Will Burke: *Oh shit. That's right. Sorry, I was a bit tied up last night and forgot. Well, I had someone tied up, I suppose.*

I feel a flush creeping up my neck and a warmth start to brew below as I think back to last night. Will's large hands binding mine together with his soft silk tie, securing me to my metal headboard. His warm lips pressing kisses and soft bites into my wrists, trailing down my arms, to my neck, down the valley between my breasts, and then rolling his tongue over each nipple before descending further…

I press my thighs together and force the thoughts out of my head. I message Will back, feeling my face burn, as I ask him to email me the chapters so I can review them before passing them on to the chief editor. Five minutes later, I have a new email with the new chapters and a date for later tonight. I bite back a smile as I print out the chapters.

Later that night, I'm in my cozy one-bedroom apartment getting ready when Will knocks on my door. I shake my head; he has a key to my apartment and could just let himself in. I pull up the sleek dress that's some shade of green and wrap my arms around my breasts to hold it up, then run on my tiptoes to the door and swing it open. I greet him with a small smile as his face lights up with a goofy grin.

"Is that dress just going on, or coming off?" Will asks in a deep, gravelly voice, darkness swirling behind his eyes. I swat his arm playfully.

"Just going on. You came at the perfect time; I need you to zip me up." I turn around and use one hand to sweep my hair off the back of my neck. He grasps my waist with his massive hands for a moment before using one hand to slowly zip me up. His finger trails up my back, drifting along my spine and sending shivers to my core. When he's done, his hand returns to rest against my waist, and I let my hair fall as I turn to face him. I loop my arms around his neck and pull him in for a kiss. "If you're good tonight, I might just need help getting out of this dress later," I tease. I feel the tension grow in his pants.

"Fuck, yes. I'll be the best damn date ever." Will flashes his perfect white smile at me and I try my hardest to keep my knees from buckling underneath me. Will Burke is everything a woman could want. He's handsome, witty, a gentleman, and excellent in bed. Is it unethical for me to be sleeping with one of the authors I'm editing? Probably. But he's just so charming, and I really did try my damn hardest to resist him for a month. But he proved too much to resist, and I couldn't deny that I had the strongest urge to run my hands all over his muscular arms. He's got the best arms I've ever seen, and one is covered in ink. *So. Damn. Hot.* But that's it. We both know this thing between us is just passing time. I made it abundantly clear this time: no feelings. I won't ruin a good thing again without making the rules clear.

My heart pangs whenever I think about Brandt. I feel terrible for how I left, but what else was I supposed to do? He loved me, as Lana pointed out to me, and he actually seemed interested in marrying me. Marriage? Hell no. I didn't sign up for that, and I refuse to let my father push me into a marriage I don't want. Forcing me to work for the company to eventually take over, sure. But arranging a marriage, and not even clearing it with me first? Nope, not happening. Pressure in my chest starts building and my eyesight starts to tunnel. I feel my breathing starting to become laboured. Will's deep voice and a gentle embrace pull me back to the surface, preventing me from drowning.

"You good?" he asks. "Do you want to postpone and go for a run?" This man, I tell ya. He doesn't even know what's going on, but he knows I get these panic attacks and running is my only escape. Now he's telling me to breathe, simulating the breaths I need to take so I can follow along. He's calming me down, but it's not enough. I look at him with pleading eyes and he chuckles as he grabs my hand and pulls me back toward my bedroom.

He unzips my dress and I let it fall into a pool at my feet. Will pulls my running gear out of my dresser and tosses it to me, then moves to the closet, where his duffle bag of extra clothes lives. He extracts his own running gear and tosses it onto my bed before he starts stripping his clothes off. Once I'm dressed, he walks over, gently pushes me to sit on the edge of my bed, and starts lacing up my runners for me.

It's not lost on me that what Brandt probably wanted with me is what I have with Will; or at least what it looks like, but more permanent. But what Will and I have going on is so far from that idyllic scene of two people sharing their lives together. We fuck and spend some time together, but that's it. Basically fuck buddies — no strings, no feelings. If Brandt was in love with me, he was going to want more than that.

I run my fingers through Will's thick, cocoa-coloured hair, lean forward, and place a thankful kiss on his forehead. He smirks, and when he's finished, he laces his own shoes, stands, and offers me a hand. He pulls me into an embrace, then leads me out into the hallway of my apartment building and out to the street. He squeezes my hand before letting go to jog ahead of me. I watch his form and how his shorts swish and bunch to the rhythm of his gait. He turns around, jogging in place and giving me a shit-eating grin, knowing full well that I'm standing here just blatantly checking him out. He jerks his head in a "come on" motion, and I do.

When my heel strikes the cement for the first time, I instantly feel the stress shedding away from me, like a snake shedding its skin. I quickly catch up to Will, nudge him with my elbow, and take off at full speed. I hear him laugh at my competitiveness, and I know he's now staying a few paces behind me, not because he's slower or letting me stay ahead, but because he's now returning the gesture of checking me out. Knowing this, I let my ass shake and sway a little more while I flex my thighs, really giving him something to watch and enjoy. I glance over my shoulder and wink, then blow a playful kiss at him.

With Will, it's so easy. There are no expectations, and we both know that when it comes time to end things, it'll be okay. We've discussed it at length, and he's never offended when I need to cancel plans or kick him out after sex. He also doesn't let this thing between us complicate our working relationship, either. He's almost like the male version of me back when I was in university. That, or he's just really good at hiding his feelings, unlike Brandt. With Brandt I was always hyperaware of him, and constantly caught myself holding my body a certain way, or acting a certain way, to make sure he noticed me as well. And when I noticed him noticing me, I would clam up and become nervous. Still, sometimes I find myself missing that feeling; the tingle and excitement I would get, the rush of hormones and longing, the way he'd set my skin and body on fire with a single look… A heaviness aches in my chest, and I try to breathe through it.

Will has finally matched my pace and we're running in tandem. I shake my head and laugh at him. He whips around and starts running backward, making goofy faces at me until he stumbles. Luckily, he catches himself and turns back around, and I laugh my ass off, hard enough that I need to stop and catch my breath. We've only made it two blocks from my apartment, but I'm already feeling much better. Like I said, things with Will are just…easy. I can let go of everything with him.

CHAPTER
SIX

Another week has dragged by, and I'm exhausted. I haven't been creating as many live videos lately, and have just been focusing on my posts. I've also been shopping for new clothes more frequently because nothing I have fits, but it's like everything I buy just makes me look…ugh. I also want to lose a few pounds from the drinking I've been doing lately; detox my body and whatnot. So, I've been keeping a food diary again. I know it can be a slippery slope, but I swear I will never go down that hole again. I just want to monitor my calorie intake and alcohol consumption. I know I've gone a bit overboard lately, but I was trying to numb myself from Elissa leaving.

Rhys has been shutting me out, and I think it's because of me. No, I know it's because of me, and how I've been handling the situation. But what am I supposed to do? My best friend just left me, without so much as a proper goodbye. I'm trying not to dwell on it because I can't control this situation, so instead I'm focusing on my health. I'm in the middle of writing down what I ate and drank for the day in my journal when Rhys walks into my apartment. My heart squeezes as I think of this place as just *my* apartment. Elissa's room still sits empty, with the door closed. I can't bring myself to move my stuff into her room. It feels too weird, and maybe I'm still holding on to hope that she will be back any day now. I hastily snap the book shut and shove it between the couch cushions.

"Hey babe," I call out from the living room, looking over my shoulder with a smile. Rhys is looking haggard. His icy blue eyes are rimmed with dark purple circles, his hair is mussed, and his face looks sullen. "Are you okay?" Rhys doesn't answer me; he just scrubs his face with his hands then walks over and collapses onto the loveseat. "Babe?" I ask again, still getting no response.

Rhys finally answers me after a few more seconds of silence, but he doesn't look in my direction. He keeps his eyes trained on the ceiling.

"Just a long day at work," he says on an exhale. "I don't want to do anything tonight. So, either we have dinner here and go to bed, or I'll just head home."

"We can do that. I'm not really hungry, uh, big lunch. So, we can go right to bed." He studies my face and shrugs.

"Sure," he says lazily. "Let's go." I stand up first and offer him my hand, then pull him toward my bedroom. I kiss him as we pass the threshold of my room and at first, he doesn't kiss me back. But after I peck his face a few times, he finally reciprocates and gives me lazy kisses. Insecurities start to flood my mind, as I wonder if I did something to cause him to act this way. I thread my fingers into his short charcoal hair and tug so his lips break from mine. I kiss down his jawline and place rough kisses on his neck, and he finally relents, allowing himself to relax.

I feel the tension melt from his body, like an ice cream melting in the summer heat. Rhys snakes his arms around my waist and pulls me in tighter, and my breasts squish against his chest. His hands drop to my round, toned cheeks and he squeezes them before he lifts me up. I lock my legs around his hips as he walks us to the foot of my bed and tosses me to the mattress, where I land with a small bounce. Rhys' corded, bulging arms tug his shirt over his head, tossing it onto the floor. He stands there for a minute, taking me in, as I do the same to him. My eyes roam all over his broad, toned chest, wide shoulders, and the six rock-hard abs that lead down into that sexy "V."

He braces into the bed with one knee and I sit up, closing the distance between us. My hands are burning with the need to touch his skin, his muscles, his body. I salivate at the thought of running my tongue in between the ridges of each individual ab muscle. My hands grip the back of his neck, pulling him down to meet my lips. I devour his lips, relishing in their softness, in his sweet taste. Rhys rolls us to our sides so that we face each other, then hitches my leg up on his waist as his hand plunges into my pajama shorts.

He traces little circles on my sensitive mound, dipping a finger into my wet entrance, and continuing the circles with my juices as lube. Rhys pushes his face off mine and savagely kisses and bites my neck as my head tips back. I'm moaning his name, jutting my hips toward him, begging for his fingers. He complies with hooked fingers, stroking inside me, thrusting in and out. I'm getting close, and I can feel the burning on my neck from all his attention. I open my eyes ever so slightly, and lift his head back toward mine, bringing him in for a kiss. My windows grow misty from the heat that is being created inside this room, as the snow dances on the other side of the glass.

I trail my hand down his chest, rubbing his amazing abs like my hands are clothing on a washboard, and I slip my hand into the waistband of his pants and boxers. As I sneak my hand into his pants, I notice a slight shift in his kissing. Rather than being passionate, it seems more… focused. More robotic. I try to shake the thought off, but when my hand finds his cock, he feels like he's barely at half-mast.

My heart quickens, but not for any good reasons. Dread floods through my body. Rhys has never had a hard time getting…well, hard. He tenses as I rub his cock, trying to get the blood pumping. A few moments pass and he's still not hard, and my heart plummets into my stomach. I roll him onto his back, undo his pants, tug them down, and expose his dick. It's only slightly more rigid, so I decide it's time to put my tongue into action.

Still pumping his cock with one hand, I swirl and flick my tongue on his impressive crown, slowly sucking it into my mouth and pulling him out with a little *pop*. His member has a slight reaction; not what I was hoping for, but we're moving in the right direction. I get both hands going now; one pumping, one playing with his neatly trimmed balls while my mouth completely sheaths him, sucking and rolling my tongue against his sensitive crown. Trying to let go of all the negative thoughts pinging through my head, I buckle down and give him my best blowjob tricks.

What is going on? He's never like this. Finally, after what feels like an eternity, I let his dick fall from my mouth, and I sit back on my haunches and look at him. He's flung his arm across his face, shielding his eyes from me. "Rhys?" I whisper into the quiet room, noticing he's making no noises. My skin breaks out into a cold sweat as panic sets in.

"Baby?" I whisper shakily. He lets out a heavy sigh as I watch his chest rise and fall. Instead of answering me, he rolls over, puts his back to me, and tucks himself under the blankets. I stare at Rhys, willing him to turn around, to crack a goofy smile and pretend he's playing a prank. A terrible prank, to say the least, but a prank. When he doesn't respond or move a muscle, I slink off the bed and out of my room, closing the door with a soft thud.

I wander to the living room in a daze, grab my phone and one of the throw blankets off the ladder, and open the door to Elissa's room. I lay on Elissa's old mattress, sans sheets or pillows, and twist my body into the fetal position. I'm snuggled tight under the blanket, facing the windows. My eyes follow the snowflakes that flurry and dance in the sky as my eyes and nose prickle with unshed tears. I unlock my phone, my face glowing in the light of the screen, and

I pull up the messaging app. When I find Elissa's name, I open the thread and start pouring all my feelings out.

Me: *What the hell? Why can't you ever message me back? I'm worried about you. If you're worrying I'll tell anyone where you ran off to, then you don't know me very well. We've been best friends for years, and this is the longest we've ever gone without talking. It's been longer than three months, E. I need to talk to you. When you left, you fucked everything up. Brandt's a mess, I'm no better, and Rhys...well. He's been acting really weird lately. I just need my best friend. I need to talk to you. Fuck! Why can't you just answer me...*

Tears are now streaming down my face and my finger hovers over the send button. In a moment of clarity, I end up erasing the entire message, letting the rapid clicking of the erasing drown out my sobs. I can't let Elissa know how much her leaving like that affected me. She clearly doesn't care about how I'm doing, so why should I give a damn to try so hard to get her back?

I settle for a brief message.

Me: *I miss you... :(*

The three dots that indicate Elissa is typing a response pop up for a moment, bouncing on the screen, creating an awful suspense that makes me just want to throw my phone across the room. Suddenly, the dots disappear. When no response comes, I feel anger bubbling up inside me, and this time, I flip over and I really do chuck my phone across Elissa's room. It sails right out her bedroom door, into the living room, and out of sight. Suddenly, I hear a massive crash. I hear a door fling open a moment later, and Rhys appears in front of Elissa's door, looking between me and the living room.

"What the fuck, Riley?!" he yells. I pull the blanket over my head, and when I don't respond, he stomps away. A few seconds later, I hear him slam the front door shut, leaving me all alone, just like I feel. Alone.

Good. Fuck Elissa. Fuck Rhys.

CHAPTER
SEVEN

Thank God I don't have a regular job because I don't know how long I slept, but when I wake up, the sun is shining and streaming through the windows. I feel lighter this morning. I reach around the mattress to find my phone. *Oh, right…I threw it last night.* I immediately return to a grumpy state, remembering what happened the night before. I drag myself into the living room and take in the disaster I created.

The television has fallen over, its screen now flat against the ground. My phone must have knocked it over. I feel my gut churning. I gingerly tip the TV upright and millions of little shards clatter to the ground, sprinkling on top of my foot. *Well, fuck.* Amidst all the glass lies my phone, cracked to high hell. I try to turn it on, and the screen is a chaotic array of broken pixels and bright colours. Guess I'll be getting a new phone today.

A few hours later, as I'm leaving the Eaton Centre and about to step onto the subway, my new iPhone finally syncs with all of my cloud data, and I have three messages waiting for me from Rhys. My nerves get the better of me and I decide to ignore him for a little longer. We've never had a fight like that before. Was it even a fight? Because I don't think words were even spoken, other than his angry outburst. Besides, I'm still unbelievably upset and devastated by what happened, or *didn't* happen, last night.

Things have been tense between me and Rhys for the last few weeks. I know a lot of it is my fault. My moods have been all over the place ever since Elissa left. But that's not my fault; it's like a death in the family, especially the way she doesn't even respond to me. I feel broken, as though I don't have any control. She was always there to check in on me, and now? She's just…gone. At least I still have self-control. I've lost another ten pounds or so, but it's fine. *I'm fine.* Sure, I might get a little dizzy from time to time, but I'm eating enough. Besides, there's been a few nights of binging that I'm paying for now. Once the extra weight is gone, I'll go back to eating more. But like, a healthy more.

Another ding from my phone and I check to see the incoming message. It's from Rhys. I'm hesitant to open it, but I do anyway. The bustle of downtown Toronto rushes around me as I take my time opening the messages he's sent since last night.

Rhys: *Baby, we need to talk.*

My heart drops to my feet. Nothing good ever comes from that line. I hurry down the steps to the subway, people passing in a blur as I go. I delay the conversation a bit longer as the dread weighs heavily in my stomach. I stand and watch someone in the corridor playing on plastic bins with drumsticks, and it echoes through the space. He's really good. I can almost imagine what he could do with a real drum kit.

When I step onto the subway car, I risk the feeling and check the messages again.

Rhys: *I'm sorry about last night. Things took a weird turn.*

Rhys: *Riles. Please message me back. We need to talk about this. I'm sorry, babe. I love you.*

Instant relief spreads through my body at the last three words in his most recent message. He still loves me. I feel a glow emanating from my heart as the warmth repairs the cracks that were left over the last twenty-four hours. My fingers fly across the screen as I absentmindedly take a seat in the subway car.

Me: *Meet me at my place in 20?*

Rhys responds with a happy face. A fluttering awakens in my chest and my mood instantly lightens.

A knock sounds at my door roughly ten minutes after I get home. I open the door and there is Rhys with a bag of something that smells like Chinese takeout. My stomach lurches and churns at the smell, and it feels like a small worm of vomit wriggles up my throat. He steps around me and lets himself into my place. I watch him with careful eyes as he toes off his shoes and makes his way to the kitchen. He unpacks the food on the island as I grab some dishes from the cupboards behind him. It's clear Rhys and I both feel the tension in the air, as no words have been spoken yet. I reach into the fridge and grab two beers, twist the caps off, and place one in front of where Rhys is standing. He nods his head in appreciation.

"So…"

"Mmm. So…" If this were a movie, there would be crickets chirping in the background. The awkwardness is killing me. I just need him to say something. My gaze wavers as I look into his eyes, trying to get a sense of what he is thinking in that beautiful head of his. My eyes are pleading with him to say something, anything. He heaves a breath, rubs his hands on his face, and looks me in the eye again. My stomach gurgles, feeling like it's eating itself, and hungry for the steamy, scrumptious food sitting on the counter. But I just can't dive in. Even thinking about eating right now makes me nauseous.

"Riley…I'm sorry about last night. I've no excuse for you that suffices to explain my behaviour. I've been under a lot of pressure since Elissa left, and so Brandt has put almost all the company management on me while he figures out Black & Wells. And things with you have been, well, strained recently. I don't know if you've noticed, but something's going on. I know I haven't been the best these last few weeks, but there's something more going on with you than just Elissa being gone," Rhys says. Tingles erupt throughout my body and my heartbeat becomes erratic as

I wonder where the hell this conversation is going. Blood rushes to my head, and I feel light, airy.

"I know Elissa leaving has been hard on you, but you never want —" I attempt to cut in and defend myself, to say that I don't need to talk about Elissa, but he cuts off my attempt to cut him off. "Riles, you never want to talk about it. And it kills me that we have such a good thing here, but you won't open up and let me in. I'm not this guy, Riley. I'm not normally a guy who says things like 'I love you' or dates anyone. But there's something about you. I don't want to lose you, but I need to know what's going on."

Guilt and anger build simultaneously inside my body, fighting for dominance. I'm not sure which one will win out, but I wrestle with the turmoil overtaking my body, trying to keep my emotions in check. My thoughts stop filtering, and I can't focus on anything. My breathing grows ragged. But as Rhys' voice continually hammers at me to open up, I only retreat further into myself. I feel the walls around the room shaking, cracking, and crumbling. His voice pounds in my ears, and I try to muffle the sound with my hands, but that only seems to make him more furious.

His hands are gripping my shoulders, and I can see the worry swimming in his eyes. When his lips finally stop moving, my hands slowly fall from my ears, both of us breathing hard. Rhys' head does this expectant wobble, as if to say "*Well?*" I feel lightheaded. Something has shifted in me, something doesn't feel right. My heart was beating fast a moment ago, but now it seems like an eternity passes between beats. My fingers and toes all seem a little tingly. I'm looking at Rhys, and he's started talking again.

I can't quite make out what he's saying, except for a few choice words: can't, this, anymore, over, and sorry. I fight my tongue and mouth, trying to force them to make words come out.

Static clouds my vision and I think I'm getting a migraine with the way my vision is tunnelling. I try and grab the counter for support as my legs turn to jelly.

"Rhys, stop. I can't do this right now. We can talk in a few minutes, I just need to sit down for a…" Suddenly, everything goes black as the ground is rushing up toward me.

• • •

Soft beeping wakes me from my sleep. It gets louder as I come to. *Wait, sleeping? I don't remember going to bed. Fuck, my head hurts.* I brace myself to try to sit up but my arm gives out on me, both from fatigue and a sudden searing pain pinching my wrist. I finally open my eyes to see a bright white room surrounding me. I look down at my wrist and notice an IV is taped to it. *How did I get to the hospital? The last thing I remember was fighting with Rhys.* Rhys! I wriggle and twist, finally managing to sit up and look around for him, but he's not here. My eyes are dry and blurry, and I blink the grittiness away.

Rhys might not be here, but in the chair beside the foot of my bed is a huddled, hunched over form. A mess of brown hair sprawls across my ankles, but it can't fool me — I see the red peeking through. She's slouched forward, sleeping at my feet, and a rush of emotions overcomes me, breaking down all the painful walls that have corrupted my heart. Tears swell in my eyes and a sob breaks through the soft beeping of the hospital machines before I pass out again from the lingering effects of the sedation.

She's here.

CHAPTER EIGHT

Seeing Riley lying there like a lifeless doll leaves me shattered. How could I have left her for so long? How did I stay silent, answering hardly any of her many text messages and calls? Why did I stay silent? Why didn't she tell me she was struggling again with her eating disorder? All these thoughts rush through my head, and all the answers point to me. I did this. Me leaving made her relapse. I made her relapse.

I don't deserve to sit here as family, but when I got that call from Lana saying that Riley was in the hospital, I got in my car and sped to Mount Sinai Hospital. I've been beside her ever since. Her parents are on a cruise and won't be able to get here anytime soon, so for now, it's just me.

I lean in, stroking her raven hair, and let my eyes roam over her, taking her in bit by bit. My heart cracks into a million pieces. Her hair, once silky and soft, is now dry and brittle. Her cheekbones are prominent and bony, her eyes are sunken and rimmed with dark purple rings, and her once-perfect rosy pout is now chapped and shrunken.

My eyes trail down her form. Her collarbone is hollow, her veins are dark against her translucent skin, and her narrow wrists look like they'll snap if she puts any pressure on them. I trace small circles along the inside of her wrist before placing a soft kiss there while a tear trails down my cheek. More tears burn my sinuses as I blink back the dam threatening to burst. *I need to stay strong for Riles.* My phone beeps and I'm silently thankful for the distraction.

Will Burke: *How's Riley?*

I smile when Will's name lights up my screen. Will has been so great with our arrangement. He makes everything so easy, and when I told him I had to leave, entirely unannounced, he made it so uncomplicated.

Me: *She looks awful. I feel terrible and it's all my fault. I should have been here for her.*

Will Burke: *It's not your fault. You didn't know, and you're there now. Has she woken up?*

Me: *No, not yet. The doctors said it would be a while still. They're keeping her sedated to pump as many fluids into her as possible. I just don't know how I'm going to handle this, Will. I don't think I can come back to London, not with her like this. This is all my fault.*

The three dots of Will typing a reply bounce on my last nerve as I wait for his response, but it never comes. I put my phone to sleep and toss it on the foot of Riley's bed, then grab the television remote and flick through the channels, trying to find something to watch. I catch a whiff of something a little musky and realize it's me. I've been sitting here for six hours waiting for Riley to wake up, and before that spent over four hours in the car, non-stop, to get here as soon as humanly possible.

I look at my watch — it's only 9:30 AM. I push myself out of my chair, grab my phone from Riley's bed and tuck it into my purse. I find a pad of paper inside the nightstand and extract a pen from my purse to scratch a quick note on it for Riley, in case she wakes up, before I exit the hospital and make my way back to my old apartment. *Hopefully the key still works…*

Relief floods me as my key turns in our apartment door, but the relief is quickly chased away by guilt at the realization that Riley didn't change the locks on me. I'm swamped with more guilt when I continue down the hallway and see that she kept her room, which means my old room is still empty. I shuffle through the apartment to my room and slowly press open the door.

My bed, dresser, and closet are all in the exact same state they were left in almost four months ago. I walk over to my bed, plop my suitcase and duffle bag down on the mattress, and collapse beside them, staring up at the ceiling. I close my eyes and take a few steadying breaths. The last time I was in this apartment, I was rushing around in a formal gown, tossing things into boxes and suitcases to flee this place. Now, three months later, I'm back.

It feels like a lifetime ago that I was here, and yet it feels like it was yesterday.

My stomach twists and I suddenly feel queasy as my heart pangs. *Brandt…* The last time I was *really* here was with Brandt, before the gala. Memories flood me — of my hands winding through Brandt's golden-brown hair as he braced my thighs, hoisted me up, and locked my legs around his hips. His teeth, dragging along my neck, leaving goosebumps in their wake, little nips and sucks, and his name spilling from my lips.

My groin tingles and warmth spreads throughout my body. My breathing quickens and I press my thighs together and clench, trying to suppress the building lust. Something inside me aches for him. To go back, and have things be like they were before, before everything got messed up. Before I messed things up.

I strip down, fling my clothes across the room, and bolt toward the washroom. I turn on the shower but keep the water cold. I need to stifle this raging heat inside me before I do something stupid. When I step under the spray, the chill immediately pierces my skin, sending all my nerve endings directly into a wintry tundra. I rake my fingers through my hair, tousling the wet strands without any shampoo or conditioner. My shoulders sag as I heave a deep sigh, releasing all the pent-up stress and wanting.

I think I hear the sound of a door closing, but I brush off the thought that it could be Riley. Because it isn't — she's still in the hospital. As I step out of the shower, I realize I've forgotten a towel, so I tiptoe toward my room only to slip on a wet tile and come crashing down. I land on my back, with my legs spread wide open.

"Shit!" I yelp. Footsteps come running, and I'm definitely not imagining them. I wince as I open my eyes and there is Brandt, standing in front of me, and I can feel his eyes crawling all over my naked, wet body. I don't even have the energy to yell or cry. I throw an arm over my eyes, feeling the heat creep up my body, but this time it's not from lust.

"Don't just stand there gawking!" I cry. "Help me find a towel." I risk a peek and see Brandt snap out of his daze and he tugs on the closest thing to him — one of the sheets I left behind in my closet. "Thanks," I mutter when he tosses it to me. It lands on me in a heap. He's now turned around with his hands covering his face and his ears are bright red, as if he hasn't seen my naked body before.

"S-sorry," he stutters. I roll my eyes as I stand up and wrap the sheet around my body. It does little to hide anything because my dripping wet skin immediately soaks through the white fabric. I bunch the sheet up, trying to get more coverage. Brandt hazards a glance over his shoulder to see if I'm decent before turning back around to face me. My core heats up again when we lock eyes. My knees feel weak, and all my nerves start to tingle. I forgot what just one look from this man does to me. I almost forget about everything and rush to him so I can feel his lips against mine. Almost.

"So, what are you doing back?"

"What are you doing barging in here?" We speak at the same time, our questions clashing. Brandt's thick, perfectly sculpted eyebrows furrow and his mouth presses into a thin line as mine lifts into a cocky smile.

"Well, technically I live here."

"Technically, you don't," he responds. "You haven't lived here in almost four months." When he says that, it feels like an arrow's been shot through my gut.

"Yeah, well. What are you doing here? This isn't your place either, and I doubt Riley is comfortable with you just entering her place," I snipe back. Brandt heaves a sigh and scrubs his face before responding.

"Rhys told me she was taken to the hospital — from what he said it sounded like she had some kind of episode as he was breaking up with her, but I'm not quite sure. He thought it was some sort of dramatic ploy, in his words, to get him to stay, but apparently it was the last straw for him. I guess things have been weird between them for a while. Anyway, he gave me her key and asked if I could grab her a few things, like her charger and some clothes, before giving her key back."

"Fucking coward. He should have done it himself," I say through gritted teeth. Brandt shrugs nonchalantly. "Well, you can give the key to me and go. I'm going back to the hospital after this, so I can take her everything she needs." Brandt hesitates before handing me the key. Our fingers brush and electricity sparks between us. I feel my heart glow as my body reacts and aches for more of his touch. I try to shake the sensation off.

"Is she…okay?" he asks tenderly. His eyes search mine for an answer. My lips quiver, and I'm at a loss for words.

"Honestly, I'm not sure. She's still asleep. They've had her sedated for the last six hours I've been at the hospital, and only the nurses come in to check vitals. I haven't seen the doctor since I arrived…" My voice breaks. I try to blink back the tears as two strong, muscular arms wrap themselves around me, instantly obliterating the sadness taking hold. His familiar wintergreen freshness invades my senses. I inhale deeply, wishing I could bottle up his smell. Like they have a mind of their own, my arms wrap around his waist and squeeze. Accepting his tenderness is so easy. The hug may be a nice and comforting thing he's doing, but it means the world to me…

My body grows rigid as my mind finally catches on that we're embracing. I start to panic. My breathing grows rapid and I step out of the embrace and clutch my sheet, feeling all the more aware of the fact that I'm essentially naked. A flush creeps its way up from my chest to my cheeks.

Brandt clears his throat and shifts his eyes away, and I nibble on my bottom lip, thinking of something to say.

"Well, I guess I should go, since you have everything under control," Brandt says. Something inside me falters as I nod slowly. Brandt starts to turn around, but halts.

"How long are you back for?"

"I'm not sure."

"I see," he says shortly. He rolls his shoulders and stalks out of the room, then out of the apartment, without another word.

CHAPTER NINE

The steady beeping of the machines and monitors grates on my nerves as I sit in Riley's hospital room, thumbing through the latest chapters of Will's manuscript. I've been back at the hospital for an hour and can't get my mind off Brandt, or our unexpected reunion after I disappeared almost four months ago. He walked in on me. Naked. Spread-eagled on the floor. Oh. My. God. I mean, he's seen it before, but come on — it's still super embarrassing.

After nearly four months, I finally see him again and he's standing there, right in front of me. All perfect, golden Greek god, with his chiselled jaw and a slight amount of scruff that just makes him more ruggedly good-looking.

The way his eyes crawled all over my body, like tiny scorching fire ants, leaving a blazing trail. And when his arms wrapped around me…

I'm pulled away from my thoughts as my pen scrapes across the page, leaving a long, red line through the manuscript.

"*Shit,*" I whisper. Wishing I used the kind of pens that erase, I toss the manuscript into my black Kate Spade purse, along with the accursed red pen, and lean down onto the bed, folding my arms underneath my head.

Sitting here and waiting for Riley to wake up is hard. It's harder still to look at her and see just how much weight she's lost in these last few months. She tried to reach out to me a bunch of times since I've been gone, but not once did I stop to give her any kind of *real* response. I can't help but think that this all could have been avoided if I had just answered her. But I couldn't. There was too much guilt. I also didn't want to put her in the middle of my drama with my father, or have her feel like she had to lie to Brandt, or Rhys. After very little sleep over the last twenty-four hours, I eventually allow myself to drift off to sleep, hopefully to banish the drowning thoughts of negativity.

A soft, light touch strokes my shoulder. I take a few moments to regain semi-consciousness as the stroke becomes a more vigorous shaking, and I hear someone chanting my name.

"Elissa…Elissa?" A soft, dry voice repeats my name. I rouse enough to remember where I am and snap upward. I stare into a pair of sparkling chocolate eyes while my own eyes flood with joyful tears.

"Riley?"

"You're here?" Riley asks, weakly. I bark out a laughing sob.

"Of course! Where else would I be?" Riley's beaming face falls at my response. "Lady, you know I'm always here for you," I plead. At that, her eyes shift away, but not before I see the flash of pain in them. My heart sinks in my chest and it hurts to breathe.

"Honestly…I really don't think you're always here for me, because if you were, you would have at least answered my calls and messages. Instead, you left me to pick up all the pieces you left behind, shattered Brandt's heart, and wrote me off like I was some sort of lost baggage, left unclaimed."

A pang of guilt ricochets through me at the mention of Brandt, and at how I left her all alone. Riley's cheeks redden and she squints her eyes like she's trying to figure out what to say next.

"Where's Rhys?" she asks. My stomach drops. After all she's been through, I have to tell her about Rhys. The fucking coward couldn't even stay around long enough to tell her himself. "Elissa…where's Rhys?"

I clear my throat awkwardly.

"He's…not coming."

"What do you mean, he's not coming?" she asks. I avert my eyes from her pleading gaze for a moment and glance around the room, as if trying to find an exit.

"He said that when he brought you to the hospital, it was his last straw. Apparently, things have been weird between you two and he's moving on. He said he tried breaking up with you, but you collapsed, and he thought it was some dramatic ploy — his words, not mine!" Riley wipes a tear from the corner of her eye.

"Well, fuck him," she says, after a moment of silence. I grab her hand and squeeze, letting her know I agree.

"Lady, when you're feeling better, we're gonna get all gussied up, hit the town, and find you a new man. I promise," I say. She looks at me with hopeful eyes.

"Does that mean you're sticking around?" My mouth opens, but nothing comes out. How can I tell her I'm planning on leaving again? Instead, I close my mouth and give a soft nod.

A few hours later and the doctor is in the room getting ready to discharge Riley.

"It's imperative that she attends all the meetings with the support group and stays consistent with them. Another relapse like this could be catastrophic to her health," the doctor says with a stern look. "It's also important that someone stay with her over the next few weeks to help monitor her food intake. Would that be you?" Both the doctor and Riley look at me. I swallow the anxiety bubbling up in my throat and give a slight nod. Riley exhales a breath of relief, and the doctor's face stretches into a warm smile. "It's so good to see that Riley has a strong support system. She'll need it during her recovery process." Another heavy wave of guilt crashes into me, making me feel sick to my stomach.

A few moments later, the private room's washroom door swings open and Riley steps out, fully dressed in her regular clothing. If I thought the hospital gown made her look sickly, her regular clothes make her look deathly. Her soft grey t-shirt hangs off her, like she's a child wearing an adult's shirt. Her black leggings, once skin-tight, now sag and bunch loosely. Every few steps she stops to hike them up so they don't fall off her waist. She was already a size two. How much smaller could she have gotten in four months?

My heart breaks as she hobbles around the room, collecting her things and packing them away. She's lost most of her muscle mass and is literally skin and bones. Just moving across the room is hard on her body. Even the light activity of packing has her out of breath. I carefully step toward her to start helping her pack her things, and zip the suitcase of things I brought her closed. She gives me a grateful smile and I take all of her bags and carry them out, so she only has to worry about herself.

"Thanks, Elissa," she says, pausing at the door before we leave. "Thanks for coming back." And just like that, as we lock eyes, I am forgiven for everything that has happened between us over the last few months. My entire being swells with happiness, and I know Riley and I are going to be okay.

"Of course, Riles. And truly, I'm so sorry. I shouldn't have cut you out like that. This is all my fault —" Riley waves her hand in the air, cutting me off.

"Let's go home. We'll talk about it later," she says. I smile at her and link our arms as we head out of the hospital to the parking lot.

"Elissa?" she asks.

"Hmm?"

"Can we stop and grab poutines on the way home?" Our eyes connect, and part of me worries that this is a slippery slope when it comes to her binging habits, but I decide to support her decision right now. I give her a gentle push and nod my head, and we both break out in giggles.

Back at the apartment, I help Riley settle in and set our food down on the kitchen island. Before I sit down to eat, I go into my room and change into my Roots track pants and dusty rose Carhartt hoodie. When we've both changed, we sit together at the island and start eating, waiting for the other person to break the awkward silence.

"So," I say. Riley looks at me, eyes wary. "Brandt saw me naked this morning." Her mouth drops open, and her eyes bulge out of their sockets.

"Wait, what?!"

"Yep. He apparently had your key from Rhys and walked in to grab some things for you and didn't know I was here. I had just gotten out of the shower and since I forgot a towel, I slipped and fell. He walked in and I was flat on my back, with my legs spread wider than a centrefold Playboy Bunny."

Riley drops her fork and howls. Tears start cascading down her cheeks from laughing so hard. I groan, and my cheeks burn as I bury my face in my hands.

"Oh my God. That is…amazing. So, did you guys just do it?"

"Uh, no. It was hella awkward. He also seemed very indifferent to me…until he hugged me because I broke down in front of him about you. It was so weird. I had a white sheet wrapped around me, but I might as well have been naked since it was soaked and see-through."

The more I say, the more Riley struggles to control her laughter. I decide I'm done being in the hot seat, so I change the direction of the conversation.

"So, what happened Riles? Why the relapse?" Riley immediately stops laughing and freezes in place. Her eyes lose any kind of happy emotion and tears well up as she looks down at her hands. She picks up a fry and starts dragging it around in the gravy.

"I needed to feel in control..."

CHAPTER

TEN

Five years ago

RILEY

I'm running late for Mrs. Wilson's Grade 12 first-period calculus class when I'm stopped by my reflection on the way out
the door. The foyer of our house is expansive, with a crystal
chandelier that drips from the ceiling like water. The grand
entrance of the stairs is rounded, and it's very '80s prom mov-
ie-esque. A gigantic mirror on the wall catches my attention.

*It must be new. Mom's been on a redecorating kick because
of the fighting her and dad have been doing lately.* But as I
draw closer to the mirror, unease slowly ripples through

my body. I'm standing here, trying to tell myself that it's just the mirror, or the lighting, or *something* that's making me feel like this. But I don't know why it took me so long to notice. It's like all the negative comments on my social media are suddenly made real to me, all at once. My heart sinks. My cheeks look puffy, like a hamster, my eyes are too far apart, my raven hair looks like it's a Halloween wig, and the way my navy, white, and royal blue kilt cinches at my waist…I suddenly feel sick.

Why have I never noticed this before? A rising panic spreads through my system. My palms are sweating, my breathing is ragged, and my heart is thrashing around in my chest. My mind rolls back to last night and what I ate for dinner. I pull out my phone and start googling the calories in baked potatoes, a chicken breast, and a salad. I won't get the exact calories, but it's a start.… Wait, approximately 658 calories? *For chicken, salad, and a potato?!*

I was thinking about grabbing something to eat before leaving for school, but I think I'll skip breakfast today. As I'm debating, I hear a honk outside, letting me know that Elissa's here to pick me up for school. *Well, that solves that. I don't have time to grab something now.* I toss my backpack over my shoulder, grab my calculus textbook off the entry table, and head outside, sucking in my stomach and adjusting my kilt as I go.

When we pull into the parking lot at our high school, the football team is running drills, and the track team is running around the track. Just as I'm about to unbuckle my seatbelt, my stomach makes this awful grumbling sound. Blood rushes to my face, and I awkwardly chuckle.

"Did you not eat this morning, Riles? Jesus, that was a nasty rumble," Elissa asks. My face is burning now, and I shake my head.

"No, I didn't have time to grab anything. Besides, I want to try a new diet and lose a few pounds." Elissa sighs. "Not this again. Why are you listening to those bitches on social media? You don't even know who they are. They're just nameless trolls who are jealous of you because you're becoming popular, just from sharing your life. You're a size four. That's tiny! I'm a six, and I'm happy with how I look."

I groan. "Yeah, but you're all like…athletic and stuff."

"What the hell does that mean?"

We're walking along the path across from where the footballers are scrimmaging, and a few of them stop to whistle and catcall as we walk by. I suck my stomach in more, wrap my arms tighter around my textbook, and pick up the pace. My heart sinks in my chest, knowing that they're catcalling for Elissa, and not me. She's toned, muscular, and trim. Yeah, I may be thinner than her, but I have more fat compared to her toned body.

"It just means that you're in better shape than I am, and you look good. Me, I just have flab…" Elissa rolls her eyes at me, and I feel ashamed. Ashamed of my body, ashamed of my feelings, ashamed of myself. *She doesn't get it.* Shaking her head, Elissa continues into the back entrance of our high school. She enters before me, and the way she's oblivious to the eyes that roam over her body is insane.

"Hey Riley, hey Elissa," random people say as we pass them. I nod my head or offer a small wave as we pass. I toss the ends of my two French braids over my shoulders, and they fall against my back with a light thump. Squeezing my textbook closer to my stomach, we walk down the hallway until it opens into a gigantic foyer with the school office to the right. A large crucifix hangs from the vaulted ceiling, and a Canadian flag stands proudly in the corner by the main entrance. As clumps of students gather, waiting for the morning bell to ring, we try to weave our way through the crowd.

Passing the students proves difficult. The whispers and indistinct chatter tease my inner thoughts, and I tell myself they're not talking about me. I *know* they're not talking about me. But still, I can't stop thinking that they're all standing there judging me. Just like the nameless people on my social media who leave nasty comments. I know they're just jerks, but their words hurt.

We finally reach the opposite end of the hallway, where there's still a payphone hanging on the wall. *Does that thing even still work?* With Elissa still leading the way, we turn left toward a bank of lockers. Ours are right beside each other. Elissa and I both spin our locks until they click open, and we pull the doors open simultaneously. I grab a few books from my locker and shove them into my backpack while I pull my lunch out of my bag. I start to put it in my locker, then hesitate. I lean back and surreptitiously look over at Elissa. She's busy talking to Liana, one of the girls on the dance team, so I turn and quickly toss the brown paper bag into a garbage can about four feet away. I glance over and Elissa is still talking to Liana, so I slam my locker shut, interrupting their conversation.

"Well, I'm off to class! See you in second period 'Lissa," I say brightly, with a wave to her and Liana. I speed walk down the length of the windowed hallway, where I can see a bunch of students gathering on the quad, past the doors to the cafeteria, and around the corner to the stairwell. I take the steps two at a time, holding my kilt down with one hand so people can't see up my skirt, until I make it to the third floor.

I settle into my seat in the far back corner of the room, next to the window, and set my textbook on the desk. I pull out my notebook and a pencil and start scribbling on the last page — everything I ate yesterday. Then, I look up the calorie counts for each item online. Finally, the bell rings to start class, and I look at my notebook before the other students pile into the room. *2,000 calories yesterday. Not bad…but not great.* Mrs. Wilson enters the classroom and a hush falls over the room. The way this woman commands respect is amazing and admirable. However, my thoughts drift away from calculus, and I write a meal plan for me to follow that shaves off a good chunk of calories a day, which should totally be doable.

The next few months pass, and I'm thrilled with the way my body is looking. *Just a bit more, though. I'm almost there.* I'm getting more compliments in the hallways, and someone has asked me out every single day over the last few weeks. Even so, I find it's not enough. No matter how little I eat, there's still something missing. Whatever I do, I can't quite achieve the image I have in my mind. I've started exercising whenever I have a chance, mostly downstairs in our home gym, and into the early hours of the morning.

I know it's not healthy to only get a few hours of sleep a night, but I need to counteract whatever I eat.

Elissa is constantly hounding me. She says she's "concerned for me," as she likes to put it. But part of me thinks she's just jealous that I'm getting so much attention now. Not that it's ever been an issue before. We both always get a lot of attention. So maybe she is concerned, but I'm fine. Really. I'm still eating. Some days, I can't stop eating, and I'll eat until I puke. Those are the days I feel most disgusting.

My social media followers have really turned over a new leaf, too. There are barely any negative comments, and people are loving the workout videos I've been posting. Sure, there are some comments that my boobs are fake, but that's only because they look so big compared to my slim body. I feel most in control when I'm keeping my food diary. It gives me peace of mind that I am making progress, even when I have a "bad day" with a high caloric intake. I may not be able to control all the negative comments, but I can control this.

Elissa and I pull up to our favourite dress store in London so we can find our winter semi-formal dresses. We come shopping here a lot for dresses for the social family functions we have to attend, so when we enter the store, the manager knows us and greets us with a flute of champagne each. Elissa and I both turned eighteen earlier in the year, so luckily for us, we can actually enjoy the champagne.

"Welcome ladies," the manager coos. "I was so glad when I saw your names on the appointment list today!" Cheryl is a wonderful, cheerful woman. She's always the kindest and most honest salesperson. She'll tell us if something doesn't look right, which we always appreciate. "Let me pull a few of our new items in your sizes."

I clear my throat and stop her before she takes off into the back. "Actually, my size has changed, from a size four to a size two," I say proudly. Cheryl beams as she congratulates me, but I can feel Elissa's stare burning a hole in my face. When Cheryl disappears, Elissa grumbles at me.

"Losing that much weight in only a few months can't be healthy, Riles." I scoff and roll my eyes at her as I perch on the edge of a cushy bench.

"'Lissa, I know…you've only told me about one hundred times now. Seriously, can you drop it?"

"No, Riley. I can't just drop it. I'm seriously worried about you. I never see you eat anymore, and when I do, it's always something simple, like a salad, and you barely finish it!" I feel the burn of a flush crawling up my neck and spreading to my face. My blood boils.

"Just stop, Elissa. I. Am. Fine. You're worrying over nothing. I'm taking care of my body, okay?" Bringing the glass to my lips, I tip the flute of champagne back, downing it in one gulp. A few seconds later, my head goes light and fuzzy.

Cheryl returns with a bunch of dresses draped over her arms and sets them up in the changerooms. I stand and my head spins. *I guess I drank the champagne a little too fast.* Cheryl tops up my glass with bubbly and passes it to me, and I take another gulp, draining half the flute. I make my way into the dressing room and shuffle through the dresses she's hung up for me.

The first one I try on, I instantly love. It's a black Gucci dress with feathers dancing at the cap of the sleeve, but it also has intricate black floral lace sleeves. The smooth fabric drapes to mid-thigh. I step out and Cheryl oohs and ahhs. I love the way this dress gives me a delicate silhouette. Elissa looks pleased, but her tone is a little tight as she compliments me. No doubt she's still mad about our conversation a minute ago.

When I step back into the changeroom, I marvel at the golden Chanel evening gown. It's a shimmery, floor-length dress that loops around the neck and has an open, plunging back. It's gorgeous. The way it hugs my narrow hips and makes my ass look plump…I actually have an hourglass figure, and this dress is perfect for me. I even love the cut-outs along the ribs. I twirl around in the dressing room, feeling like a golden Roman goddess, especially with the way my long, black hair swoops over one shoulder.

My head spins again, probably from the champagne I drank. It may have been a dumb idea to drink two flutes of champagne when I've had nothing to eat yet today. *Oh well*. The tipsy feeling spreads throughout my body, making everything feel light and airy.

CHAPTER ELEVEN

Five years ago

ELISSA

The curtain shielding the dressing room slides open and Riley steps out. She's wearing a shimmery golden dress that flows and gathers in heaps on the floor. The shiny material curves and clings to every slope and contour of her body. She looks radiant, and you can see the sparkle in her eyes that tells me this is the dress she's going to be wearing.

As she spins, I see the dress has a beautiful looped neck with a plunging back, but my eyes catch the cutouts on the side of the dress. Tiny little jagged bumps are prominently sticking out of her side, and I realize that those bumps are her ribs. My heart sinks, and I almost drop my flute of champagne in shock.

As she continues to turn, I notice the hard bumps of her spine jutting out of her back, and that's when I realize how thin she's really become. I know she's been on some fad diet, and I've made my thoughts on it very clear, but this is just insane. My heart breaks looking at her skinny body. It looks like if she sneezed too hard, she'd snap in half. Guilt settles into my stomach, making me wonder how it took so long for me to notice. My mind reels as it reviews all the things you learn in high school health class about eating disorders, and that's when it really clicks.

Why hasn't she said anything? I mean, she eats in front of me *sometimes*. It's always something really healthy, sure. And some days she even eats piles of junk, so I never thought anything of it, not until there were days that she didn't eat at all, and then she'd just brush me off. Saying it was a "fasting diet." Staring at her now, I wonder how she didn't lose so much weight in her ass and breasts.

Riley continues to spin until she's facing me again, and I try to mask my concern with a supportive, happy face, but it's hard. The longer I stare at her, the more I notice the little things. Like how her eyes seem sunken in, her cheeks are hollow, and her fingers are bony. Her skin tone is typically a glowing creamy olive, but now she appears pale.

Her sharp brown eyes find mine and they slowly narrow. It's hard to hide my worry and I know she sees it.

"What's wrong? Do you not like the dress?" she asks shakily. I sigh and let my body relax into the bench a bit, to make myself seem more approachable.

"No, that's not it at all. It's beautiful, and you look gorgeous in it." I try to sound assertive, but my voice is weak. Instead of sounding certain, the statement just sort of trails off.

"Then what?" she snaps. That's another thing that I've failed to really notice. Riley's temper has been all over the place lately. Sometimes she's downright miserable and bitchy, and other times she's whiny. Her emotions are all over the place, and the shame I feel for not noticing before smothers me. The corners of my eyes soften, and I feel tears welling up as I plan what to say.

"You look beautiful in that dress. It makes you look really thin," I say cautiously, but her eyes shine with pride. "Don't you think maybe a little too thin, though? I mean, Riles…your ribs are sticking out like a starving dog's."

Riley's eyes scrunch and harden. I see the flames licking behind her stare; she's getting ready for a smackdown. The walls of my chest tighten and my heart races as I wait for the bomb to go off. Her bony fingers curl into fists and quiver momentarily before she relaxes and anchors them to her hips.

"What the fuck does that mean? You just said I look beautiful. How the fuck can I also look like a starving dog? Those two things don't go together." I shift in my seat, trying to find a comfortable angle for me to take this fight head on.

"I just mean…have you been eating enough? And before you say anything —" I cut off her attempt to blow a gasket. "I'm just concerned because I love you. I don't mean anything by it. Just making sure you're doing okay." I think

I've managed to soften the blow as her sharp shoulders dip, and she seems to relax. She shuffles forward, grabs the bottle of champagne, and drains almost the rest of the bottle with a few chugs. She places the bottle back on the table beside me while wiping her face on her forearm. Her eyes find mine, and for a moment I feel relieved.

"Fuck you, Elissa."

RILEY

The galloping beat of my heart makes my chest ache, and I wonder if she can physically see my heart beating out of my chest. *How fucking dare Elissa judge me! Who the hell does she think she is? Everything is fine. Oh shit…how many calories are in a bottle of champagne? Fuck. I really should have read the back of the label or something before drinking that much.*

The world around me whirls and I squeeze my eyes shut, trying to shake off the dizziness. My fingers tingle and a cold sweat breaks out on my brow. Taking deep, measured breaths, I try to steady myself and calm down.

"I don't know what you want from me," I snap. "What the fuck is this really about, E? So, I've lost a bit of weight. So fucking what. What's this really about?" The champagne I drank gurgles in my stomach, threatening to come back up. My stomach pinches and cramps from the sweetness of the bubbly. My head swoons again, and I'm finding it hard to focus, but my mind keeps going back to the fact that I need to write down the calories of the champagne in my journal.

I step off the pedestal, making my way toward my purse, when my foot gets caught in the long glittery skirt pooling at my feet, sending me flying forward. I put my hands out to stop myself, and they catch onto my purse on the bench, and it comes clattering down with me. With this all happening at once, I'm not paying attention to where I'm careening to. Suddenly, my head connects, hard, with the table where I placed the champagne bottle, and everything goes black.

My head is throbbing, and I squeeze my eyelids tightly before letting them flutter open. A bright light immediately burns my eyes. I look around and my mom's face is hovering in front of me.

"Oh God, Riley!" she cries. My dad rushes into view and they both collapse on top of me, embracing me tightly.

"Uh, can't breathe guys…"

My mom scoffs. "If you think you can't breathe now, just wait and see. If this ever happens again? God dammit, Riley. Just what were you thinking?"

My thoughts are cloudy, and my mind is foggy. *What are they talking about? Where the hell am I?* The sound of mechanical beeping finally breaks through the fog, and I can hear people calling for "Dr. So-and-so" over an intercom system. *How did I get to the hospital?* Then it all comes crashing back, and I remember everything. *Fuck.*

"Mom," I croak. "I'm fine. I guess it was the champagne we had at the dress store." I try to lie, but I'm worried they will see through it. Sure enough, they do.

"Riley Mikayla Jaimeson," my mom says. Her eyes narrow, and her lips pull into a tight line. "How dare you act like this? As if your dad and I aren't doctors. We know exactly how malnourished you are. Baby, this is serious. You have a serious eating disorder." I squirm in the bed, and my skin crawls with the need to run away.

Suddenly I notice Elissa in the corner chair. She slowly gets to her feet, her eyes brimming with unshed tears. Her footsteps are quiet as she crosses the room and drops my journal on my lap. She releases a heavy sigh. "I thought you were just journalling. But when you passed out, this dropped out of your bag as it hit the floor, and it fell open…" My heart stutters in my chest and my breath catches in my throat. I feel like I'm being suffocated. I reach out and my hand smooths the leatherbound cover. As I flip the journal open, my fingers run along the numbers and calculations I pored over, hour after hour, day after day.

"We're going to get you the help you need, sweetie," my dad says, his baritone voice breaking. His brown eyes, so similar to mine, are full of emotion. I've never seen my dad so…broken like this before. He looks scared, and worried. My own tears threaten to spill as I take a deep breath. I tilt my head up and my eyes roll back as I close them. I try to force my body to relax, and when it does, all the tears I've been holding back just fall. My mom lays down beside me, cradling me into her chest, stroking my hair, her chest heaving as she cries along with me. My dad's hand curls into mine and squeezes tight as he sits there silently.

"I-I don't know what happened," I confess. "I don't know h-h-how to stop." I stutter my words out between sobs. Shame, grief, and anxiety all swirl around inside me as I try to navigate what to do. I never wanted to let it get this far, this bad. *I thought I was doing fine. I had everything under control. I thought I had it under control.*

"We're here, baby. We'll get you the help you need."

CHAPTER TWELVE

BRANDT

She's back. Elissa is here. I should have known when Rhys called me to say he took Riley to the hospital that Elissa would show up. Riley is her best friend, but what kind of best friend just drops you and leaves with nothing but a note? A self-absorbed party girl with commitment issues, that's who.

But God damn if she didn't feel like coming home when I wrapped my arms around her. Her frame had gotten smaller, but it only made her breasts even more noticeable when she pressed up against my chest. When she tucked her head underneath my chin, I noticed that she still smells like warm vanilla, and although her hair was darker, the dye couldn't hide the familiar cinnamon tones to her hair. And that sight when I walked in — holy hell. If I hadn't spun around right then, she'd have seen just how much she still affects me. I'd have given her a salute for her return.

Oh, and all that soft, creamy skin. I wanted to lick all the water droplets off her body until goosebumps covered every inch of salty-sweet skin, instead of passing her a sheet to cover herself. To trail my tongue down until I reach the sweet spot of nerves that makes her writhe underneath me and scream my name. *No, Brandt. Don't let her being back get into your head. She won't stay.* I need to talk myself down and steel myself for when she decides to leave again.

I reach into my pocket and pull out my cell.

Me: *Thanks for the heads up. SHE is back, dickhead.*

Rhys: *Whoops. Sorry, dude. There was enough on my plate as it was. Just be glad she won't be sticking around for long.*

I toss my phone across the kitchen counter in my apartment and scrub my face, sighing deeply. Rhys is right. She won't be here for long, so I need to let it go. I need to let her go. I grab my phone again and text Lexi to see if she wants to get dinner.

One hour later and we're walking down Wellington Street West to a tiny French restaurant called Petite Bistro. It's a cozy little place with deep burgundy leather chairs and rich mahogany wood throughout the entire restaurant. Lexi slides her hand into mine and locks our fingers together. Her hand is small in mine, and something about holding her hand doesn't feel right. I tell myself it's because I've just run into Elissa unexpectedly. It's only because of that encounter that I'm comparing Lexi to *her*. Lexi's palm is clammy as she gently squeezes and looks over at me with worry in her eyes. I try to relax my expression, with little success.

"Is everything all right, Brandt?" Lexi asks. My eyes find hers and I nod. "Are you sure? You've been quiet the whole walk here. I know you're a man of few words, but you usually give me at least some conversation."

I take a deep breath and exhale, allowing the tension in my body to dissipate.

"Sorry. Someone I wasn't expecting to see showed up today, and it threw me off," I explain. A small thread of guilt weaves through me over not telling Lexi everything, but we've only been out a few times over the last few weeks. I just don't think it's necessary to tell her anything about Elissa.

"Oh, okay," she says, sounding a little dejected. I squeeze her hand for reassurance, and her body seems to relax a little.

When we reach the restaurant, I hold the door open for her. She brushes by me and I catch a whiff of her perfume — a sugary, bold caramel lingers in the air. *Not as nice as Elissa's vanilla. Wait, shit. Where did that come from?* I feel the hairs on the back of my neck prickle. I shake it off and redirect my attention to Lexi.

I stare at the back of her sleek, bleached blonde hair. My eyes trail down, taking in her sexy, defined shoulder blades, which look spectacular in her black strapless dress, as she shrugs off her fiery red peacoat. She glances over her shoulder at me with a wry, knowing smile. My eyes follow down her narrow waist to her thick, round ass, and to the hem of her dress, where her deliciously toned thighs peek out.

My mind drifts off and I question myself why it took me so long to notice Lexi, or any woman for that matter. Eight years of pining for Elissa, and when I finally had her, she left. Eight years. *What was wrong with me?* I know school and work was always my focus, but to only have one woman star in every one of my fantasies? Who does that? *A stalker, that's who.*

A perfectly arched eyebrow lifts in my direction as Lexi tries to get my attention. Her eyes find mine and I'm brought back to the moment. With a soft smile, she reaches out to grab my hand again as the waiter leads us to our table. For the umpteenth time tonight I try to banish all thoughts of Eli out of my mind.

There's a trio of thin tapered candles sitting in the centre of the circular table, which is draped with a luxurious burgundy tablecloth. There are two place settings, each with a white porcelain plate, water goblet, and gleaming silverware that sparkles in the candlelight. Soft instrumental music floats quietly through the air as we sit down.

"How was work?" I ask Lexi. She perks up and her eyes brighten when I start the conversation, asking about her workout studio. She's an animated talker, and uses a lot of hand gestures.

"It was good, and busy. All my classes were full. I was turning people away. Also, all my clients showed up today for their one-on-ones," she replies happily. I zone out, letting her voice fade into the background. I feel my eyes glaze over as she talks, but I nod along and make random 'hmm' noises as my mind drifts back to Elissa.

It took nearly four months, but I finally got her out of my head...well, almost. I'd finally stopped thinking about her constantly, and what I could have done differently to make her stay. Stopped beating myself up for the stupid deal I made with her father, and for how I handled it all and hid it from her. Beating myself up for thinking things were going well when I knew she was a flight risk.

And damn, did she look good. I'm not just saying that because her beautiful body was splayed across the floor, giving me a private show of her most intimate places. Memories of her earthy, mild musk linger in my sinuses from when my head was buried between her legs, my tongue parting her moistened lips. My mouth salivates at the thought.

"Brandt?" My name shakes me from my reverie. I blink my eyes a few times to refocus as my eyebrows inch upward.

"Mm, sorry," I say. "Still distracted, I guess."

"Is everything really okay?" she asks. Her voice is quiet and full of concern. I grumble inwardly, knowing full well I am treating her like shit. Fucking Elissa. Fuck her and her perfectly kissable lips, her beautiful swelling breasts, her dusty pink nipples that pucker when she's aroused, and her tight, heavenly pussy. My jeans tighten as I curse under my breath and wriggle in my seat.

"Yep. Everything is good. I don't want to talk about it and ruin the mood."

"Well, you're kind of doing that anyway. So, you might as well talk to me." I flinch inwardly at her terse words.

"Not tonight, please. I don't want to talk about it yet." Lexi seems satisfied with my response because her body relaxes as she reclines back in the chair and the corners of her lips turn up.

After dinner, we head back to our condo building, and I walk her to her apartment. She lives four floors beneath my condo. When we reach her door, she lingers, twirling her keys in her hands. She nibbles on the corner of her lips as she unlocks the door, then she turns and trails her hand down my biceps to my forearm and grasps my hand. She rubs her thumb across my knuckles nervously.

"Do you want to come in for a drink?" Her voice is breathy and quiet, but the look in her eyes is full of wanting and hope. I hesitate for a moment, wondering if I'm making a mistake by following Lexi into her apartment while I still have Elissa on my mind. But my feet move on their own, crossing the threshold. As I step in, her hands curl into the collar of my coat, and my mouth has a mind of its own as it crashes down on hers. My tongue flicks against her lips, diving into her mouth to explore. The tip of her nose is cold when it brushes against my cheek, as she accepts my tongue and tangles hers with mine.

My hands raise to cup her face, tilting her chin upward for a better angle before one of my hands slides into her hair and grabs a fistful. I firmly pull on the bunched hair to keep her head tilted up while I pepper kisses down her jaw and along her neck as I use my heel to kick her front door closed.

Her chest rises and falls as she exhales a breathy moan. "Brandt..."

I separate my lips from her neck briefly. My name on her lips sounds weird. Like it shouldn't be there. But if not there, then where?

"Bedroom?" I mutter.

Her head bobs hurriedly as I press my body into hers, pushing her against the wall. My hands firmly grasp her ass, lifting her so she can secure her legs around my waist as I carry her down the hallway. Lexi kisses the soft spot behind my ear and nips at my lobe, and I notice her apartment is like mine, but smaller. Where I have a generously sized two-bedroom loft apartment and two washrooms, hers is a simple one-bedroom, one-bathroom apartment.

My footsteps echo down the hallway as I stomp toward her room. I toe open the door, take a few steps in, and drop her onto the bed. I kneel down, kissing her legs as I pick up each one to take off her shoes. I grab her ankles once the shoes are off and flip her over onto her stomach. Her hair whips through the air as she gasps. I brush her hair off her shoulder and take my time unzipping her dress.

CHAPTER
THIRTEEN

As I stare at Lexi from behind while I unzip her dress, Elissa resurfaces in my thoughts. *Damn it.* It's like her presence in Toronto is haunting me. I try to shift my attention back to the sexy woman in front of me who actually wants me. As the zipper splits open, I notice her cherry red strapless lace bra. Using my forefinger and thumb, I flick open the clasp and tug Lexi to her feet by wrapping my hands around her waist. As she stands, her bra and dress fall into a puddle on the floor, leaving her covered by only her matching red lace panties.

Her face and body are flushed, and her skin is radiating her burning desire. My cock stirs. Her large, supple breasts look absolutely delicious. As I stare, her nipples tighten into little buds. I bend down and take her right nipple between my teeth, giving it a little tug before running my tongue over it. She moans. She tastes like smooth coconut butter, but it doesn't compare to the warm vanilla my senses yearn for.

My hand finds her free breast, cups it, and massages it as I flick over the nipple with my fingers. Her back arches to jut her hips into my torso, pleading for attention down south. My hand trails from her breast and, with a feathery touch, continues down her stomach, tickling the spot that dips into her hipbone, jarring her desire momentarily. When my hand reaches the apex between her thighs, two fingers creep past her panties and part her lips so my middle finger can lightly skim along her clit. Her breath hitches as she writhes and presses her pelvis toward me greedily to get more pressure.

I oblige and spread her wider for my finger to glide across. Slowly, I make my way down her body with my mouth, leaving a damp path that invites goosebumps when the air hits it. My tongue dips into her belly button as I suction my lips around it. A shiver rolls across her body. My mouth hovers over her pubic bone, millimetres away from her sweet spot. I know she can feel my hot breath above her opening. I tilt my head up and search her eyes.

"Please," she begs. "Please, Brandt. I need you." Those are all the words I need to hear. My tongue slithers along her lacy undergarments and my nose nudges them to the side so my tongue can access the puffy little mound of nerves. My tongue flickers in and out like a snake, teasing her desire.

"Brandt, please," she moans breathlessly. Her fingers wind through my hair and grasp firmly, pulling my face closer to her body. "Now," she demands.

My tongue flattens as I run it along her clit, and she tenses as she sucks in a deep breath and holds it. She finally exhales. I clamp my mouth around her mound and nibble on her clit lightly as a gasp echoes through her room. I release her clit only to create a vacuum seal and start sucking her clit hard. Every muscle in her body constricts, and she begins to pant. As I suck, my tongue teases her clit, flicking over and over.

My two fingers roll around and wipe the saliva leaking from the suction. Once they're wet, they find her opening and thrust inside. Another moan, louder now. I press in and out a few more times before I hook my fingers and find the raised G-spot and stroke it. Lexi's body is now rocking in rhythm with my thrusts, and every time my tongue brushes against her clit, her body jerks. She's inching toward the finish line, and I bring her just to the edge. Her pussy clenches around my fingers, ready to let go, and I withdraw.

She freezes. "What…" I stand up, unbutton my shirt, and let it fall off my shoulders to expose my broad chest. The ridges of my abs harden as I feel Lexi's eyes roam over my body, a stunned and appreciative look on her face. I feel her focus on the "V" that leads into my pants. I grab a small foil packet from my wallet before slowly undoing my pants and letting them drop to the floor as I step out of them.

Flashes of my first time with Elissa play in my mind as this scene with Lexi unfolds. A sharp pang in my chest catches me off guard. I stop moving for a moment, close my eyes, and push past the hurtful memories. When I reopen them, Lexi is staring at me with dark, hooded eyes, biting her bottom lip. I remove my boxers and I'm at half-mast. I crawl across the bed to her, then kiss her deep and hard. Our tongues clash as her small hand finds my dick and grabs it, giving it a few long, firm strokes.

I bring the foil packet up to my lips and tear it open, then sit back on my haunches to roll the latex down my thick, hardened shaft. I lean over Lexi and brace myself on my forearms as she hooks one of her legs around my hip. I draw closer, line myself up against her entrance, and pause. I search her eyes for permission. Her hands lace together behind my neck, bringing my face toward her, and she hungrily kisses my lips. "Yes," Lexi whispers. In one swift movement I am inside her to the hilt, and she inhales sharply. I stall, giving her time to adjust to my size before I start moving inside her.

"Oh God, Brandt," she mumbles as I start to move. My hips roll, making long, deep strides at an angle, so my pelvis is grinding against her clit. It's hard to stay focused every time my name is on her lips because my mind keeps going back to the feisty, cold, auburn-haired woman who stole my heart eight years ago and completely shattered it four months ago. Visions of her hair wrapped around my fist as I took her from behind fill my mind.

I pump harder, taking Lexi's leg off my hip and throwing it over my shoulder to get deeper.

"Yes, yes. Brandt!"

I bottom out, hitting her cervix with my hard, throbbing cock. "Fuck," I moan. Her pussy feels good — not quite as good as *hers,* but good. I crash my lips against hers, biting her lip and sucking her tongue, trying to get her out of my head. "L-Lexi." I drink in her moans with my mouth. I feel her pussy clenching; she's right on the precipice, ready for me to push her over the edge. I sink my teeth into her collarbone as I throttle into her.

Lexi grips me hard and her nails dig into my neck, creating a burning sensation. It hurts so good. "Brandt," she chants my name, over and over again. Suddenly, her pussy erupts around me, rippling on my dick, clenching harder with each spasm. I follow her, and a tingle runs through my body down to the base of my balls, tightening as I get ready for release. And, with one final thrust, an explosion of colours clouds my vision as I empty into the latex sheathing my throbbing cock.

I collapse beside Lexi, both of us heaving in euphoria.

"Mmm, that was…" Lexi is at a loss for words, obviously satisfied with my performance. "Amazing. Oh my God, Brandt." She rolls over onto her side and lays across my chest, an action I am unfamiliar with, but always longed for with Elissa. My body tenses at the gesture but relaxes after a few moments. My arm threads around her shoulder and my thumb traces circles on her skin. I let out a small chuckle, proud of myself for satisfying this blonde bombshell of a woman, who could have anyone she wants, but wants me.

A warm beam of light cascades across my face, stirring me awake. It takes me a few moments to remember where I am as I blink the sleepiness out of my eyes. I look down to see a fan of platinum blonde hair sprawled across my muscular chest, and remember the events of last night.

Flashes of auburn hair mix with platinum blonde as memories clash together in my mind, and separating the two seems almost impossible. Guilt crashes into me like a brick wall, for both comparing Lexi to Elissa and having Elissa on my mind as I was fucking Lexi. Lexi doesn't deserve this. I just wish I knew why Elissa had left. Maybe then I'd be able to get her off my mind.

Lexi stirs, whimpering in her sleep, "Mmm. Morning, baby." Her hand slides up and down my chest as she nuzzles closer into me. She places a soft kiss in the golden chest hair between my pecs. "Did you sleep okay?"

If I'm being honest with myself, I actually did sleep well beside Lexi all night. I didn't dream about Elissa at all. *Huh.* Which pleasantly surprises me. "Actually, yeah. I slept well," I say. I lean in to kiss her hairline. "I need to get up and get ready for work. I'll see you later?" Lexi looks up at me, uncertainty flooding her eyes.

"Uh, sure…" she says quietly. I kiss her on the lips before sliding out of her bed and tugging my pants on. As I'm buttoning up my shirt, I glance at her. She's sitting up, knees hugged to her chest, and the blankets are wrapped around her breasts. "Will I see you tonight?"

My lips twitch upward in a small grin. "Sure. Let's get dinner again," I suggest. Her face brightens like the sun streaming through her window. I walk over to her side of the bed and bend down as she circles her arms around my neck and kisses me hard, sliding her tongue across my lips. Her tongue teases mine as they dance together until she breaks the kiss.

"Now that's a good morning kiss," she said. Lexi playfully smacks my ass when I turn to leave her room, and with a grin I exit her apartment.

CHAPTER FOURTEEN

ELISSA

I'm standing in the kitchen washing dishes when my phone rings. I look over to see who it is, and it's my father. I groan and let it go to voicemail, but that doesn't silence him. He calls two more times before I finally pick up.

"Yes?" I say in a snarky tone.

"Wow, you finally picked up, after all these months," he grumbles on the other end. I stay quiet, waiting for him to say what he needs to. "Does this mean you're back for good?"

"I'm not sure what you —"

"Don't play coy, Elissa. We both know you're in Toronto. There's no way Riley being sick wouldn't bring you back. Stop being childish and let me know if you plan on staying. I know your job in London is waiting for an answer too."

Of course, he knew where I was all along. I'm only surprised he didn't hunt me down and bring me back of his own accord.

"I'm not sure, Father. There's a lot to think about." My father's grunt suggests that he doesn't like my answer. Too bad, he's not going to get a better one.

"I'm sure Will Burke will follow wherever you decide to land, and I don't care if you continue to finish editing his book for Wellington, as long as you get your ass back to work tomorrow."

"Wait, how did you…? Of course. You had me followed, didn't you?"

"I'm not about to let the *heiress* walk around creating chaos in her wake for the stakeholders of the company. We need to show a united front, so I kept tabs on you and spun it like it was my idea. Getting your toes wet with experience and whatnot." What a self-righteous asshat. I'd like to say that I can't believe he'd do something like this, but I'd be lying. He's just the type of arrogant asshole who would take this and spin it for his own gain. Not caring about me or what I'm going through, or even wanting to know why I left to begin with. The answer is him. And maybe a teensy bit because Lana pointed out how Brandt felt about me. I only spooked a little. Okay, fine, a lot.

But what was I supposed to do? He's this amazing, magnificent guy who seems to like me, and can deal with my detached disposition. But if he fell in love with me, that's just a landmine waiting to explode, and it did. He wasn't supposed to fall in love with me, but he did. He deserves to be with someone who can actually reciprocate his feelings. Even if I did eventually feel for him what he feels for me, I'd never really be able to give him what he wants.

"Elissa, did you hear me?" an angry, gruff voice barks at me. I huff.

"Yes, Father. I heard you. And I don't think I'll be there tomorrow. I already have a job, so thanks, but no thanks."

"If you're not at work tomorrow, Riley has a week to get her ass out of the place I paid for," he says coldly. The line goes dead — he's hung up on me. *Fucking prick.* I unlock my phone and tap out a message to Will, seeing where he is. I thought he mentioned he'd be in Toronto the next few days.

Will Burke: *At my hotel. Why, what's up?*

Me: *Come over?*

I send him my address and he responds, letting me know he'll be there in half an hour. I sigh, dragging my feet toward my bedroom to freshen up before Will gets here. *Back to Satan we go.*

The next morning, I'm standing in front of the never-ending skyscraper of Black & Wells Publishing and Press. I flick my left wrist to check my platinum gold and diamond Rolex, dreading the moment it ticks over to 9 AM and I have to be inside. My father knows how to pull me back in — by leveraging Riley and using her vulnerable state to get me to do as he wishes. I'm not ready to go back in there, but I'll do it for Riley.

I try to think about this morning — waking up next to Will, and how nice it was to be able to be relaxed and wake up peacefully before the dread set in. My thumb finds its way into my mouth and I start chomping at my nail. *Take a deep breath. It'll all be okay. Yeah, keep telling yourself that.* My black Jimmy Choos click across the cement as I make my way toward the doors.

Inside, I pass the familiar front desk and security guard, nodding as I go. When I get to the elevator, I feel a dozen pair of eyes on me, burrowing into my skin as I wait. The bell to the elevator dings as the doors clang open. I step in hurriedly and mash the button to close the doors, trapping myself in this giant metal box, alone, free from questioning stares.

The elevator stops at my floor, and it instantly feels like the air has evaporated from the elevator. The doors slide open in slow motion; I step out. There are phones ringing in the distance, but other than that it's quiet. My heels are the only noise echoing through the corridor. As I near my office, I notice only Lori is sitting at her desk. When I approach, she looks up and all the colour drains from her face. Her mouth drops open in shock.

"M-M-Ms. Black! You're back?" I wave her off and continue to my office, only to stop abruptly when I notice Selena has taken up residence in there. *Huh, a lot has changed.* I knock quietly on the door, and Selena's shoulders sag as she lets out an exaggerated breath.

"What is it now, Lori?" she says, irritation tinging her tone. When I don't respond, she glances up and then back down at her screen. Then her head shoots back up and she jumps to attention, sending her chair flying across the floor behind her. "Ms. Black! You're here. Oh, wow. Um, this is only temporary, me being here. Brandt — I mean, Mr. Collins — said it was all right if I used this space as I took over some of your duties while you were away, and…" she pauses when she notices my hand held up to stop her incessant rambling. I blow my faded brown bangs out of my eyes, and level my gaze with hers. She's as white as the snow outside and is shivering.

"That's fine, Selena. Just point me to another office, please." Selena nods at my request and rounds the desk, taking control and showing me where the next available space is. It's a little further down the hallway, closer to the boardroom and washroom. Selena starts stammering again.

"Again, I'm sorry. I can have all your stuff arranged to be in your original office for tomorrow morning, and I can resume working at my reception desk. It's no problem."

"It's fine, Selena. Really. You've probably earned that office and whatever you're working on, so keep doing it for now. We'll figure out everything as we go. I'm certainly in no rush."

Selena's eyebrows are perched high on her forehead and her eyes are brimming with questions.

"Does this mean you're back for good?"

I let out a sigh and shake my head noncommittally. "I'm not sure yet. We'll see." She relaxes a bit at my answer.

"Listen, about Brandt. It was a casual thing, and when you left, I didn't know if you were still engaged or not, but he assured me he wasn't…" I stop short and my head turns sharply to face her. My fingers curl into fists and my nails bite into my palms.

"Excuse me?"

"Uh…um…" Selena stammers, unable to come up with anything else to say.

"That is all, Selena. Thank you for showing me to my new office. Please go."

Selena is clearly unsure of what to do, because she looks away and back at me a few times before turning to head back to her office — *my office* — with her head sagging as she walks away briskly. Just as I'm about to turn and enter my new office, the boardroom door opens and out steps Will, my father, and Brandt. They're all chatting, and my father is doing his obnoxious fake laugh that he uses with potential partners and clients. My father spots me first and a Cheshire-like smile curls his mouth as he rubs his moustache, a conniving glint in his eyes.

Brandt remains focused on Harold's face for a moment before he looks in the direction Harold is looking. When Brandt's eyes and mine lock, we both still. Everything around us melts away, and it's just us. Time seems to stop, giving us the silence we need to process this encounter. My eyes plead for forgiveness, but his lose all sense of emotion, and I watch as they freeze over and his stare turns cold and unrelenting. One of his eyes twitches as his hands and the papers he is holding slowly find their place at his sides.

When Will turns curiously to see what the two men are looking at, his entire demeanor changes, lightens, and he bounces over to me. He wraps an arm around my waist, pulling me in for a tender kiss on the lips. His face tinges pink when he realizes he's kissed me in front of my father.

Brandt is the first one to break the awkwardness with a clearing of his throat.

"So, I take it you two already know each other?" he says coldly. My heart squeezes and I forget how to breathe. Seeing him stare at me with such disgust and hate in his eyes breaks something inside me.

"Yeah, we've been seeing each other for a few months now. We met when she was working in London," Will answers. He turns to me. "Babe, I didn't know you were coming here today when you said you were going into work. I thought you left to head back to London!" He kisses me again, behind my ear, and I watch Brandt watch the exchange between me and Will. I can't think of anything to say. My tongue goes numb, and I can't remember how to work it.

CHAPTER FIFTEEN

Who the fuck is this guy? Will Burke is sitting across from Harold and me, telling us about his next big idea — a collection of short stories set across Canada and told from different perspectives. One of the perspectives? A cat. A. Fucking. Cat.

Harold, however, is eating this shit up. He's sitting here looking like Will is the next big thing in publishing, almost looking at him like he's in love. I shudder. There's something about this guy that doesn't seem right. Will swivels his chair in short bursts as he talks. He's cocky, and completely at ease. I study him. He seems to be my opposite. Wavy chestnut hair, bold ocean-blue eyes, and an open and talkative demeanor.

I zone out for most of the meeting, unable to shake the feeling that something seems off. Harold hasn't said much to me yet, and generally he's pretty chatty, even if he's grumpy. Lori, my assistant, bustles in and out of the boardroom with refreshments and documents. When she enters the room, the aroma of freshly brewed coffee steams through the air, along with the buttery, savoury scent of croissants. My mouth salivates a little and my muscles relax. Maybe I just need something to perk me up, and that's why I'm feeling thrown off about Will.

Nope. I hate him. It turns out that I didn't need food or caffeine. When the meeting is over, we exit the boardroom, and all the air rushes out of me. I'm stuck in place, rigid. My hands drop to my sides as I clench the papers I'm holding and anger takes over my body. My eyes find hers instantly. Elissa is here. She's frozen in place, and her eyes are wide and uneasy. Clearly she's uncomfortable. I glance at Harold, and he looks pleased. Giddy, almost. There's a sparkle of something in his eyes. Mischief, maybe?

That's when this dick makes my entire day worse. He saunters over to Elissa and devours her face in front of me and her father. "So, I take it you two already know each other?" I say in an icy, sarcastic tone. Plus, he calls her babe. My fists clench harder, crinkling the paper between my fingers. I don't think I can work with this guy. Harold and I are going to be having a long conversation about this, I'm sure. This guy is a joke.

And how Elissa is with him, I'll never understand. I thought she didn't do relationships. She just uses men to keep her bed warm for her — I was an exception, but only out of convenience. And now she's with this smug prick? Anger and resentment bubble inside of me, causing sweat to break out across the back of my neck. Oh, and they've been together a few months? I grit my teeth. I can't believe she'd rather be with this guy than with me. And just who the fuck is he? I make a mental note to look him up online later.

"We met when she started editing my manuscript for Wellington Drive Publishing," Mr. Smug-Prick says. "We were working late one night, one thing led to another, and things just sort of happened." Ugh, enough of this.

"Yeah, we don't need a play-by-play, Mr. Burke," I say curtly. I shoot Elissa a sideways glance and she looks as white as a ghost…and remorseful? She turns to Will and whispers something to him, then disappears behind the office door and shuts it behind her. My vision blinks in and out in my right eye, and my jaw is sore from clenching. I excuse myself from the other two men and stalk off to my office, slamming the door shut behind me.

I lean back against the door and bang the heels of my palms against it. Fuck. Why is she here? Is she staying now? There's a rap on my door and I push off it to open the door. Selena is standing there, her eyes shifting around as she whispers, "Can I come in?" I step aside, letting her into my office, and she closes the door softly behind her. I settle down at my desk and open my laptop, feigning a work ethic. My mind keeps running, chasing the questions of why Elissa is here.

"What's up?" I ask Selena. She looks nervous, twiddling her fingers.

"Well, so…I ran into Elissa, and I may have let it slip that we were sleeping together for a bit while she was gone, and she seemed angry. I mean, I think she was angry. She didn't say much and brushed me off." Her whispers are hurried. "I thought you said you weren't engaged!"

I roll my eyes and groan. "It's a long story, but I'm not engaged. I know Harold announced it at the gala, but that was only a PR move on his part. Fucking idiot. And who cares what she thinks? Elissa and I weren't together, so she has no say in who I fuck." Selena flinches at my cold words, but eventually relaxes. I try to relax my clenching jaw, which feels like it's about to break.

I can't be bothered with the drama that Selena has created with Elissa. I doubt Elissa even cared I slept with her assistant. There are women that want me, and I'd been celibate for too long before Elissa. Since all hope of having her as mine was lost when she left, I moved on…or at least, I'm trying to. Shame permeates me as my thoughts are once again stuck on the woman that up and left me with only a line in a note, and not on the woman who actively wants me. I resolve to push Elissa out of my mind and focus on Lexi. She deserves that much from me.

Deciding I need a caffeine fix, I exit my office and head to the breakroom, instead of calling Lori to get my coffee for me. I need the walk to clear my head. That must be wishful thinking though, because when I walk into the breakroom, a familiar head of wavy, albeit more brownish, hair gleams in front of the coffeemaker. As if a simple box of hair dye could hide her beautiful copper hair. An ache to bury my hands in that hair pulses in my fingers. I clear my throat in hopes of clearing my thoughts, to no avail.

Everything slows down as she twirls around, her hair swooshing over one shoulder and cascading around the other, like a shampoo commercial, and a whiff of vanilla drifts through the air. My eyes involuntarily close as I drink in the scent. I shake myself back to reality and allow the anger to take over and settle in my face.

"Oh, Brandt. I didn't see you there, sorry," Elissa says softly, with a shimmer in her beautiful jewel eyes. It takes everything I have inside me not to crack at her sweet, lilted voice. It sounds like honey and home. My jaw clenches again as I steel my resolve.

"It's Mr. Collins at work, let's not forget that," I say in a deep, frosty tone that cools the room by twenty degrees, snuffing out the chemical fire that burns naturally between us. I glance at the empty coffeepot. "And if you finish the pot, you need to make a new one — or do they do that differently in London?" A second later I realize I've made a fool out of myself as the coffee machine starts gurgling and percolating new drips of coffee into the pot. My cheeks warm as I try to keep a cool exterior.

Elissa's lips tug into a smug smirk. "Of course, Mr. Collins. Wouldn't want people to get the wrong idea about our relationship, like your little assistant — she might be the jealous type. And the coffee wasn't that great, so I'd already planned on making a new pot. So, you can hold your hostility because I remember breakroom decorum." She blows her bangs out of her eyes and struts out of the breakroom, shaking her perfect round ass as she leaves. No doubt she's doing it on purpose because she knows I'm watching her walk away. Fuck.

• • •

I manage to avoid Elissa, and any unnecessary drama, for the rest of the day. I hear giggling outside my office, and I peek to see what's going on. Both Selena and Lori are standing there flirting and giggling with Will Burke. My blood thickens and my eyes start to cloud red. Everything about this man irritates me, and not because he's with Elissa. I could care less. There's just something about him that is…I don't know. Wrong.

The clicking of heels rings through the hallway and the two ladies scatter back to their desks, which tells me one thing — Elissa is headed this way. She's like the Wicked Witch of the West to these women. Will straightens up, adjusts his belt, and cements a wide smile on his face. When Elissa grows closer, Will steps forward to encircle her into a firm embrace. Elissa looks slightly uncomfortable with the affection in the office as she hugs him back with rigid arms. He interlocks their fingers together and places a kiss on her cheek.

I grab my briefcase off my desk and stomp toward them, accidentally grazing my shoulder against Will's as I pass by, causing him to stagger slightly. I smirk to myself as I continue toward the elevator, but it quickly evaporates when I hear footsteps echoing behind me. Great.

The three of us step into the lift and the air is thick with tension. My jaw continually clenches as I try to bite back every vicious thing I want to say to both of them, but also biting back everything I want to confess to Elissa. Like how much she hurt me, how much I miss her, how much I still need her, crave her. She's only three feet away from me and she's with another guy. Some sleazy, flirty, fuckboy. This elevator brings back so many memories. The heated passion that was shared on this lift multiple times. Memories of pressing her against the wall, of my hand threading in her hair while the other hand lifts her thigh, of digging my pelvis into hers, flood my mind.

I clear my throat and expel the thoughts, literally biting my tongue until I taste metal. I adjust my waistband and belt. How I wish for another elevator ride with Elissa like that, rather than the one I'm having right now. Will stands beside her, possessive and smug. His eyes flicker toward mine as if to say, "She's mine, back off." I can almost hear his silent and demanding voice telling me he knows everything and he's not about to lose her to me. Little does he know that she couldn't have cared for me like I did her. I wonder if he really does know everything. I doubt she opened up to tell him anything; she doesn't let people in.

After an eternity, the elevator slows to a stop, and I bolt the second the doors slide open. Not very manly, maybe, but I can't take standing in that elevator with those two another minute. I stalk toward the front door but when I look up, I notice blonde hair covered by a black toque with a brown pom on top. She's wrapped in a tight black peacoat with a dusting of white snow on the shoulders, and a white infinity scarf circling her neck. Her legs are firm and toned in colourful tie-dye tights, with combat boots on her feet.

When Lexi turns to see me, she brightens and skips over to me, snaking her arms around my waist and planting a kiss on my lips. I press my tongue into her mouth, making a statement in front of Will and Elissa: I've moved on.

CHAPTER
SIXTEEN

ELISSA

When Brandt embraces Lexi and gives her a passionate kiss, something inside me bubbles up; a vicious, scorching green bile travels up my throat and burns. I think Will notices my shift in energy because his arm snakes around my waist, spinning me around to face him. He cups my face.

"Let's go, baby," he says, smooth and grumbly. His hand finds mine and he tugs me along, leading me out of the building and leaving Brandt behind. It takes everything I have not to turn around and look back, to see if he's watching me leave — but I know he is. I can feel his stare burrowing into me.

On the cab drive back to my apartment, Will talks enthusiastically about the meeting he had with my father and Brandt, and how my father offered him a book deal once the book we're working on with Wellington Drive Publishing is finished. I nod absentmindedly, pretending this conversation interests me. I stare out the window of the cab, watching the late November snow sprinkle past the moving vehicle, and think about Brandt's cold demeanor today.

He's never been a huge talker. "Strong and silent type" describes him well, but he's never truly been cold like that before. Lana must have been wrong when she said he loved me, because there's no way someone who loves you could treat you this way. Well, at least, I'd assume so — I don't know much about love. But from watching Lana with her husband, Tiago, there's no way that Brandt loved me. Maybe that's the operative word: loved.

If he did love me, it sure took him no time at all to move on. Men are all the same. I know, I shouldn't judge, not with my history of one-night stands — but he certainly moved on fast. I bet it wasn't even a week before he buried his dick in another warm, wet pussy. I should be happy he's moved on, though. It means that we should be able to fall into a professional working relationship, without the drama or baggage. Still, I'm struggling with why this is bothering me so much.

How is it even possible that every time he's near it's like all the air has been sucked out of the room? It makes me feel like my body is suffocating under the pressure. Like I'm being held underwater, and I can only breathe if he's touching me.

God, why is it even bothering me? It's not like things with Brandt were serious. I don't do serious, I don't do relationships, I don't do commitment. I don't even do the same partner multiple times — usually. But there I was with Brandt, repeatedly, and now Will. I don't think I've had a random lay since before Brandt.

Will's voice shakes me from my inner turmoil.

"Hmm?"

"Where'd ya go?"

"Huh? Oh. Sorry, just thinking about how weird it is to be back. I thought I'd finally escaped my father's reach. I guess I really can't outrun him."

Will studies my face, like he's debating asking me something.

"What? Just say it," I say to Will. He looks unsure. His brows are creased, and he bites the inside of his cheek.

"Does this have something to do with Brandt? I noticed some tension between you two." God, why is this guy so perceptive? Or are Brandt and I just that transparent?

"Nope. I don't really know him well, and only worked with him for a bit before I left." He looks at me in disbelief, but doesn't say anything else as the cab comes to a stop in front of my building. He pays the cab driver, opens the door, and steps out first, then extends a hand to help me out. I take it as I slide my ass across the seat and my skirt bunches up my thigh.

My heeled boot sinks into the slush along the curb as I step out of the cab. I holler a thank-you to the driver as Will closes the door. His warm hand takes mine and he intertwines our fingers as we walk toward the lobby of my building, bringing our hands up to his mouth and kissing my knuckles. We stomp our shoes to get the snow off as we enter the lobby, and as I'm twisting the key in the lock Will is behind me. His arms wrap around my waist and he nuzzles my hair away from my neck as he presses wet kisses along the nape. The tiny little hairs along my back and neck stand up when his hot breath lingers on my skin in between kisses. His lips search out the lobe of my ear and nibble it. My pussy clenches to stave off desire until we're in my apartment, but truthfully, my mind is elsewhere. I'm wishing this was with someone else, that someone else's lips were caressing my body.

We barely make it onto the elevator when Will pins me against the wall and pushes his tongue into my mouth, our tongues tangling together. My hands slide up his chest, grasping onto his jacket to tug him closer. He sucks my bottom lip and gives it a rough bite. I whimper, feeling heat seeping into my panties.

The elevator comes to a gradual stop, and we continue making out while we walk out of the lift and to my door. He presses me against my door and I fumble with my keys before he takes them from me and grinds them into the lock, opening the door with a click. He pushes past the entrance of my apartment and starts pushing my coat off, letting it fall to the floor. He kicks off his shoes, grabs my ass, and squeezes as I circle my arms around his neck. He lifts me and locks my ankles around his waist. I holler out Riley's name. When there's no answer, he carries me to the living room, sets me down, and bends me over the armrest of the couch.

His hands skim along the curve of my ass before he gives it a sharp smack. He tugs me into a standing position by grasping my throat while his other hand makes quick work of the zipper on the back of my skirt. He lets the skirt fall to my ankles and pulls me back against his chest, so that his hard shaft is resting at the top of my crack and lower back. Using his hand on the back of my neck, he bends me over the couch once more and rips my panties down around my knees. I motion to step out of them.

"Leave them," he demands in a low growl. I comply and the area between my legs convulses. He nudges one of my legs open a bit wider, like a cop getting ready to do a pat-down. A wet pop comes from behind me and his hand slides between my legs. He spreads my lips with moistened fingers, then slips them in and thrusts hard. The immediacy shocks me and I let out a sharp gasp. Another biting slap of my ass and he slips a third finger in, rubbing the spot inside that makes my knees weak. He leans forward and reaches around with his other hand to rub my clit, then whispers in my ear, "Your pussy is so wet for me." But truthfully, it's been wet since the moment I laid eyes on Brandt again.

He withdraws his fingers, and I hear the jangle of his belt and then his zipper, then a soft thud as his pants clunk to the floor. I'm so turned on, and ready for his swollen cock to fill my channel, but then suddenly the hard look on Brandt's face when he watched Will kiss me at the office floats into my memories. My heart sinks. I hear the tear of a foil packet and a few moments later I have a hard cock slamming into me. A familiar fullness greets me, but something feels off. Hollow, almost.

Will's hand is still rubbing my clit as he rolls his hips hard, thrusting into me at maximum depth. He may not be as large as Brandt, but he sure knows how to use all seven inches he's been given. He starts circling his hips, and at the top of the circle, he slams into me deep and slow, changing the pace. "Fuck," he barks. "Your fucking pussy is such a hungry little cunt, isn't she? She's devouring my cock like she's been starved for too long."

Will has one hell of a dirty mouth, and a twitchy hand. Another smack. "Answer me. She's fucking hungry for me, isn't she?"

"Yes, she's hungry for you."

"This is my little dirty cunt, isn't it?" he demands. I whimper, struggling to agree that my pussy is his because my mind keeps going back to the clenched jaw and ice-cold stare I got from Brandt. *Smack.* "Answer me."

"Y-yes, it's yours," I say, jolted as he rocks into me, harder and harder.

"Good girl," he purrs. He pulls out and spins me around, then lifts me off the ground and carries me to my room, tossing me on the bed. I bounce and my hair splays across the mattress. He climbs on top of me, and he smells like musk and sweat as he grabs my arms and holds them with one hand over my head, pinning me down. "Look me in the eyes," he demands. Reluctantly, my eyes lock onto his. He lines up his cock with my hole and slowly rocks inside of me.

I have a hard time re-entering the headspace to let go, as this feels too intimate for me. Will pumps into me with long, deep, purposeful strokes, his eyes never wavering from mine. He begins to pick up the pace and I try to let myself go. I try to focus on the pleasure I was feeling just moments ago, before this position change.

"Elissa," he whispers. "Elissa…Elissa." His hips start bucking in erratic, jerky movements, and with one last deep thrust, he's over the edge, and his hot seed is warming up the condom in my pussy. I clench around his dick, simulating an orgasm, and let out a porn star-worthy moan, faking my orgasm for the first time in years.

He rests his head on my chest, breathing heavily. I feel sweat rolling down his back. He releases my arms and kisses me along the valley of my breasts and collarbone. He snuggles his head into the crook of my neck before rolling me over and spooning me, tangling our legs together.

"Good night, baby," he whispers, kissing my ear as he drifts off to sleep. Me, on the other hand? I'm miles away from sleep. My chest feels heavy, and I'm struggling to breathe. I look over to the alarm clock beside my bed. It's 10:05 PM. I carefully slip out of Will's embrace once he starts snoring, and quietly pad over to the bathroom. I splash cold water on my face and tiptoe back to my room. I slide open one of my dresser drawers and find some spandex pants and a purple tank top with a built-in bra. When I'm dressed, I grab my coat, duffle bag, and keys, and head to the gym a few blocks away.

The weather is freezing, but I decide to walk the three blocks, giving me time to cool off and decompress after that too-intimate encounter with Will. My heart starts to race as I go over how he suddenly went from fucking me to making love. I don't make love, I fuck. Somehow, tonight, he changed the rules, and I let him.

•••

The gym is empty, except for the handful of people that probably work night shifts, so they're here on their days off. Or maybe they're like me and can't sleep. I grab the first locker in the changeroom and shove my stuff into it, then pull out my phone, headphones, and runners. I sit down on the bench behind me and tie my shoes, then make my way to the bank of treadmills.

I hop on, turning the treadmill up to a quick pace, starting me off in a jog. I open my music app and select one of my more angsty playlists for my run. I'm about an hour and a half into my run when a devastating, hard-faced man walks into the gym and catches my attention. His golden-brown locks are damp from the falling snow, and he has a shadow of dirty blonde stubble on his jaw. When his familiar eyes meet mine, my heart stops. Or time stops. Or both. I'm not sure, but suddenly the air feels charged, like if someone were to strike a match, the gym would explode. He disappears into the men's changeroom and I push him out of my mind, focusing on my pace as I turn up the treadmill's speed. *Focus on running.* I switch my playlist to something harder so I can outrun the tempo; outrun my thoughts.

Out of the corner of my eye, a tall, muscular form comes into focus, and I'm scared to look over because I know it's him. I can tell by the energy I feel and his smell — his minty, wintry, pine needle scent. It intoxicates me. I take a deep breath with the pretense of regulating my breath, but in reality, I'm inhaling every last bit of his scent that I can before it escapes me. A pool of warmth ripples between my thighs.

I break down and look over at him, then take out one of my earbuds and give him a weak smile.

"Couldn't sleep either?" I ask him. His lips are pressed together in a tight line, and he shakes his head.

"Nope. I didn't know you came here," he says. My mouth falls open and I wordlessly look away for a moment, thinking of what to say without making it awkward. Then I realize — it doesn't matter, it'll be awkward no matter what.

"My apartment complex in London didn't have a gym, so I had to sign up for one, and I guess I just got used to going to a gym late at night." I glance at my phone to see that it's almost 12 AM, I start to wonder why he's here so late. So, I ask. "What's got you here so late?"

He turns his icy stare toward me. His jaw flexes, then relaxes. "Same," he says, offering nothing more. Same what? That he couldn't sleep, or that he likes going to the gym late at night? This man is infuriating. He glances at me from his periphery, like he's debating saying something else. I can feel the wheels turning in his head.

"Yes…?" I ask him. He slows down his treadmill and turns his head to me, so I follow suit. The pregnant pause slowly kills me as I wait for him to speak.

"How long are you staying? Are you here to stay?"

CHAPTER SEVENTEEN

ELISSA

I blink at Brandt a few times before answering.

"I'm not sure how to answer that. It's complicated. I don't want to stay, but my father has given me an ultimatum, so here I am." He nods his head once at my answer. "So, who was that woman you were with? She was pretty." Brandt shoots me a glare, and if looks could kill, I'd surely be dead.

"Yeah, not talking about that with you."

"Understood. I get it. Will and I are just casual. Just kind of fell into bed with each other," I nervously ramble. Brandt stiffens at the mention of Will. "Sorry, just nervous. Didn't expect to run into you here."

"What's there to be nervous about? You left, came back, and now we need to work with each other," Brandt dead-pans. His cavalier tone stings, and I don't know why. I take a long look at him from the corner of my eye, and he looks just as devastatingly gorgeous as he did when I left, but he seems somehow bigger now. His arms seem to have more prominent veins and are bulkier, his chest is broader and more expansive, and I can see his waist taper thanks to the tight t-shirt he's wearing. There's sweat dripping down his temples and it's all I can do not to grab his head and lick away the salty beads of water.

I want to say something, but I'm at a loss for words. He looks at me with expectant eyes. Expecting what, I'm not sure. My phone starts ringing and I look at the caller ID. It's Will, probably wondering where I am. Brandt's eyebrows are raised. "You going to get that?"

I bite my lip and nod my head. "Yeah, it's Will. He's probably wondering where I went." Brandt clenches his fists around the metal handles of the treadmill until his knuckles turn bright white.

"Oh, so he stays over."

"Uh, yeah. Sometimes." Another awkward silence stretches out the moment between us, and the clanging of the workout machines and the ringing of my phone fill the space. The phone call goes to voicemail, but Will's name lights up my phone screen again. "I guess I should take this. See you tomorrow, *Mr. Collins*." I turn on my heel, saunter away, and answer the phone call.

"Hey Will. Yeah, sorry…I couldn't sleep, so I went to the gym. Yeah, I'll be home shortly; I'm just leaving now."

With a final glance over my shoulder, I catch Brandt's eyes and hold them for a moment before turning around and walking to the changeroom.

• • •

My morning is a blur, as I barely got any sleep last night after the gym. I kept replaying the awkward conversation between Brandt and me in my head, over and over. Will ended up joining me on my commute to work because he has another meeting with my father. I'm not looking forward to today. I hope I can just hunker down in my office and get work done, without distractions or chaos.

After Will and I pass through security, he wraps his arm around my waist and escorts me to my office. We're walking by the front desks on my floor when Lori beams at Will. He reciprocates the gesture, making Lori's cheeks burn and causing her to drop the files she has in her hands. Will is your typical tall, dark, and handsome. He's got these deep brown eyes that swallow you whole when you're staring into them, and his chestnut hair is loopy and thick; you can see his Greek ancestry peeking through thanks to the hair and his hooked nose.

And, while he may be part Greek, he's built like a Roman. Thick, heavy arm muscles, those beautiful bumps where his neck connects to his collarbone, a perfectly crafted eight-pack with that delicious "V" snaking into his jeans…God, I could start drooling right about now, which is why I don't blame Lori for being taken by his appearance. Will drops his hand from my waist and links our fingers together. My pulse quickens as he does this intimate gesture, and I finally realize why my heart feels ready to pound out of my chest — Brandt is standing in his office doorway, his expression dark and brooding. His eyes are laser-focused on the point of connection between me and Will.

Under his dark stare, I fight the squirm of guilt wriggling through my body. I try to discreetly shake off Will's hand, but he only tightens his grip, making my joints crack and pinch under the pressure. I muster up whatever strength I have left to meet Brandt's gaze. "Good morning, Mr. Collins," I say, with a hint of condescension in my voice, as Will and I stroll past and continue to my office. Will's grip loosens a smidge as we near my office. When we're standing in front of my door, I can still feel a burning sensation on my back, but I can't bring myself to turn around. Will pauses outside my door long enough for me to walk through, then follows in close behind me and closes the door with a click.

"Was that necessary, Will? It felt like you were going to snap my fingers right off." Will shrugs at my comment.

"I don't like how that Brandt guy stares at you. There's something weird about it," he says. I chew the inside of my cheek. I still haven't told Will why I left. Or part of why I left, at least. I felt as though it was none of his business — nothing or no one before him should matter; it's all part of history. And Will knowing would do no good.

"Still, you don't need to go all caveman. What's next? Gonna lift your leg and piss on me like a dog would?" Will gives me a devilish grin and cocks an eyebrow at me. "No, no. Don't even think about it."

"I mean...if you're into that sort of thing, I'd definitely be open to discussing the possibility of it."

"Ew. Just no." Will chortles and steps closer to me, nestling his head in the crook of my neck. He pulls a handful of hair and inhales deeply before leaving a trail of feathery kisses behind.

"I have to go meet your dad," he mutters between kisses, and I tense at the term "dad." "I'll be back soon. Maybe we can have a rendezvous in your office at lunch, and..."

I inwardly groan at the suggestion. *What is wrong with me?* I normally wouldn't pass up an afternoon romp in the office. Will and I used to do it in London all the time. "I don't think that's possible. I wouldn't put it past my father to bug my office," I say weakly, grasping for the lame excuse.

"Or would it be the best way to debug your office?" he asks, waggling his eyebrows at me with dark eyes. I carefully step out of his embrace and press my hands against his chest. I give him a quick peck on the cheek and send him off to meet my father. A few moments later there's a light knock on my door and Lori pops her head in, a red flush creeping across her cheeks. She looks like she needs to talk about something private, so I wave her in and tell her to close the door.

"So...are you with Will?" Lori says with a girlish gasp. I stare at her, dumbfounded. When did we get to a place that we could gossip like this?

Confused with the conversation, I reply, "Um, I don't think this is an appropriate conversation for work. You shouldn't be discussing your boss's private life. Let's get back to work, shall we? I'm not sure how Mr. Collins was running things while I was gone, but I do not gossip." I shut that shit down fast. And honestly, if she couldn't put two and two together when Will grabbed my hand as we walked in, she's not as smart as she claims to be.

Lori clamps her mouth shut and retreats out of my office, closing the door behind her. A few seconds later there's another rap at my door, but this time it's singular. My heart starts fluttering as though it knows who is at the door before it even swings open. Brandt walks in, and he's wearing a light beige button-down shirt with the sleeves rolled up, showing off his impeccably muscular, veiny forearms.

My eyes wander all over his arms and I think about how good they felt wrapped around me, like they were made to fit around my waist perfectly. However, that image is instantly shattered as I remember the gorgeous, fit, busty blonde who was here last night. Just like that, I'm instantly irritated.

"What do you want?" I ask, trying my best to keep the haughtiness out of my tone and make the words sound pleasant. His icy stare softens momentarily as our eyes connect, but instantly freezes over again.

"Just wanted to make sure you're prepared for the meeting this afternoon. I know you've only been back all of, what? Two days?"

I sneer at him. "Yes, I am ready. Thank you very much, *Mr. Collins*. You can see yourself out." Brandt pauses and his face screws up, like there's something on the tip of his tongue that he wants to say. My head shakes slightly as I give him a questioning look. Brandt clears his throat and I run my tongue along the inside of my teeth, watching as his Adam's apple bobs in slow motion. I want to take a bite out of it.

"So, you and Will are a thing?"

I roll my eyes. Why does everyone keep asking this?

"You already knew this. I basically babbled it at you last night at the gym," I say, exasperated. His hand rubs the back of his neck, and his cheeks turn a light pink.

"Yeah, I know. But is it serious? He was holding your hand," he says quietly. Did he notice my discomfort when Will grabbed my hand? Or does he just know me so well that he recognizes that holding hands isn't something I do? I know we never used to hold hands, so maybe that's where he's coming from.

"Uh, it's really none of your business, Mr. Collins. We're not technically friends. I think it'd be best if we respect each other's boundaries, please."

CHAPTER
EIGHTEEN

RILEY

Three weeks have gone by since I was discharged from the hospital, and I'm finally feeling more stable. Having Elissa back has been such a big help for my mental stability. My therapist says that I need to learn how to cope without Elissa here, considering how she seems to be a flight risk. She's given me some exercises to practice, like tapping along the meridians of the body when I'm overwhelmed, breathing techniques, journalling my feelings, et cetera. That's just for personal growth and to rely less on others, like Elissa or Rhys.

She also wants me keeping a separate journal of my feelings when I feel like I need to cut or count calories. She wants me to recognize patterns and triggers, and when I have these feelings or urges, to eat something, rather than skip it. To force myself to eat. She said, "Even if it is only an apple, the point is to start healing your relationship with food when these negative thoughts strike."

Dr. Nadia seems legit, but I'm not totally sure about her techniques. She came highly recommended though, and I do want to get better. I want to be able to focus and put my life back together. Dr. Nadia even suggested I take a break from my social media accounts; to have a total blackout without telling my followers where I am. That makes me anxious, since I worked so hard to create a community, but I'm willing to do whatever it takes to get better.

Elissa has been great through all of this. She's been there to take me to my weigh-in appointments, she's cooking healthy, vitamin-dense meals for us, and she's making sure I'm taking my medication and going to my therapy appointments. Which I'm sure is counterintuitive to the codependence thing I'm supposed to be working on, but I also need support. So, where do I draw the line? Which is something I should ask my therapist, so I do.

I pull myself out of my thoughts for a moment to look around her office. It reminds me of a sterile hospital environment, probably because it's in the hospital. White walls, cool blue tones throughout the room, and a fuzzy throw rug in an attempt to make this room warm.

"How do I separate support from codependence? If I'm supposed to separate myself from Elissa so that I don't fall apart again *if* she leaves, how do I do that when I'm supposed to accept support?"

"That's an excellent question, Riley. Let's see…is what Elissa is doing for you something you normally wouldn't do on your own? For example, if she were to leave, would you stop following the routine she does for you?" It takes me a few moments, but I slowly nod. "Well, then that would be the issue. I suggest participating with her in the things she does for you, like the cooking of meals. Make it part of your routine so that it becomes a healthy habit for you."

After my session, I step out onto Queen Street and crash into something, causing me to fall over and slam into the slush-covered ground. My first thought is *thank God I wore pants today.* I look up and I'm temporarily blinded by the sunlight pouring around the silhouetted figure, but as my eyes adjust, the person's face slowly comes into focus. My heart stutters and falls.

"Sorry, I didn't mean to bump into you. I was kind of distracted…" his voice trails off. All the remnants of weeks past, love, and passion gnaw at my heartstrings. He's so oblivious to his surroundings, he doesn't even notice it's me he's knocked down. He finally tears his attention from his phone and extends a hand to help me up, still not registering it's me he knocked over. Then his eyes lock onto mine; my heartbeat slows.

"Oh, it's you," he says dejectedly. His words poke holes in my fragile heart. His once-shining blue eyes are now dull when they look at me. "Glad to see you're doing better."

"Yep," I say, rolling my lips to make the "p" pop. We stand awkwardly for a moment before Rhys continues.

"So, Elissa is back. You must be happy."

I roll my eyes and scoff at Rhys.

"You know what? Fuck you, Rhys. I'm sure my therapist would say something about me confronting you, but fuck it. You're an asshole. Instead of giving me space or having patience with me for what I was going through, you ditched me the moment things got hard. For your information, I struggle with anorexia and depression. I was going through an episode of dehydration and malnutrition when you so kindly dumped my ass, so don't stand there acting like you care, because you don't. You couldn't even stick around the hospital to see if I was going to be all right, or to find out what was wrong with me. So, fu —"

Soft lips surrounded by scratchy stubble crash down on mine. The taste of a mixture of Jack Daniels and an ashy, burnt pot lingers on his tongue as it slides between my lips and runs along my teeth. I open to allow him to explore my mouth. My heart swells until it feels like it's ready to burst through my chest. Tiny little fireworks are exploding throughout my body.

His hands weave through my hair and one hand grabs my neck, holding it firmly, while the other wraps around my waist, pulling me tightly to him. All my anger melts away as this kiss completely shatters any thoughts I had only moments ago. I revel in the sultry warmth of his kiss as his tongue clashes against mine, right here in the middle of the sidewalk, with snow falling around us like glitter and confetti.

My ass starts to burn from the cold air hitting the damp spot from where I fell, and it brings me back to clarity. I push off Rhys' chest and shuffle back slightly.

"No…no. You can't just kiss me to shut me up!" Rhys opens and closes his mouth, ostensibly trying to find some kind of excuse or explanation that will make it okay. I want to let it be okay, but I can't.

"Baby, I miss you. I'm so sorry," Rhys pleads. My knees buckle. *I miss him, too.* But I won't tell him that. He takes my hands in his massive ones and wraps them tightly, warming mine up. He kisses my knuckles. "Riles, please. Can we just talk? We can go to your place and just talk."

His eyes quiver as they look into mine. I missed those crystal blue eyes that drown me whole. I squeeze my eyes shut and, in a weak moment, nod my head. His shoulders relax and he drops my hands to hail a car.

CHAPTER

NINETEEN

RILEY

We're finally back at my apartment, and instead of talking, Rhys' mouth has descended on mine, sucking at my lips hungrily. His hard body is pressed against mine and I can feel the tension building against my stomach. I'm weak, I know. But I missed his lips on mine, and the way his body feels against mine. When we're together it's like two puzzle pieces clicking together; our bodies were made for each other. He buries his head in my neck and my fingers lace through his inky hair; the scent of warm coconut wafts toward my nose and I inhale deeply.

He devours every inch of my skin and I revel in the sensation. His mouth slides across my neck with little nips and sucks, setting my skin on fire. Goosebumps rise across my body as his tongue dances along my neck and down to the swell of my cleavage. I'm slowly getting lost in his smell, his passion, and his desire. I've missed this. I've missed him. *I wouldn't need to miss him if he had just stuck around.* He didn't stick around. We were supposed to talk.

"W-wait," I stammer. I try to wriggle out of his embrace. He hums into my skin, not stopping. "Rhys. We were supposed to talk, not do this."

"Baby, we'll talk after. I need you. I've missed your taste. I've missed your body. Please," Rhys says, his eyes pleading. His gaze locks onto mine and desire wrestles with his sincerity. I find my defences breaking, shattering apart. "Please, Riley."

I take a deep breath and tumble into the abyss, accepting the hazards that lay before me and my heart, because I love this man, and I need him. I crave him. He runs his fingers along my shoulders and tucks his hands underneath my coat to push it off. I let it fall to the floor. I let his hand find mine as he tugs me slowly down the hallway, giving me plenty of chances to stop this, but I don't. We're at my bedroom door and he pushes me against the door, taking over from where he left off at the entryway.

He kisses down my body and helps me out of my shoes. His fingers make quick work of my dress pants, unbuttoning and unzipping and tugging them down. As he stands back up, he fingers the hem of my blouse and slowly trails it up my body until he's pulling it over my head. I'm standing in front of him in only my silky pink panties and bra with black lace trim, thanking the gods that I chose to wear matching underwear today. Rhys takes a step back and sucks in a breath.

"God fucking dammit, Riles. You're so damn sexy," he says, before he dives back into kissing every inch of my body. "I fucking need you, baby."

His hand plunges into my panties, wasting no time in finding my sensitive mound. "Shit, baby. You're soaking wet already. This pretty cunt missed me," Rhys says, his voice gravelly. He pulls his hand out of my panties, scoops me up in his arms, and walks me to my bed, placing me down softly on the pillows.

He stands, towering over me as he takes his time undressing. "I'm gonna fuck you so hard, baby. I've missed your cunt." I need to squeeze my legs together to stop my juices from seeping out of me and making a mess all over my bed. With every dirty word uttered from his sexy mouth I pant harder and harder. His musky sandalwood scent envelops me as he tosses his shirt over to me on the bed. I grab the shirt and scrunch it into my face, taking a deep breath. My panties moisten a little more.

He crawls on top of me, stark naked, and his fingers hook my panties, sliding them down and off my legs. He nudges my legs open and indulges his tastebuds with the taste of my pussy. A small grunt bursts from him as his mouth connects with me. Rhys' tongue licks the length of my opening, savouring the moment and flavour. His hand parts me as his tongue flicks over my lips and clit, teasing me, making me squirm.

"Please, Rhys," I whine, looking down at him and lifting my hips, trying to ride his face. A dark chuckle vibrates against me down there before his tongue plunges deep inside me. His mouth locks over my clit and sucks me in repeatedly, making it throb and pulse even harder. His fingers find my hole next, and it's tight as he shoves three of his digits into me, hooking them to reach that heavenly spot. "Oh, Rhys. Rhys…Rhys…" I'm barrelling toward my climax when he stops.

My eyes flutter open and he's staring at me, watching me intensely as he lines himself up with my entrance. "You ready, baby?" I don't say anything, just give him a slight nod. I need him to fill me up.

He slides into me with one push, seating himself to the hilt. "Fuck, Riley. You're so tight." He pauses for a few minutes, allowing my passage to adjust to his size. It's only been a few weeks, but it feels like a lifetime ago that we last hooked up. Finally, I can't wait anymore, and I start moving underneath him, urging him to move. He chuckles. "You feel too good, I need a moment."

Slowly, he starts pumping inside of me, rocking into me, gradually picking up speed and force until his balls are smacking against my ass. Rhys hooks his hand around my knee and lifts it up onto his shoulder, allowing him deeper access. "Rhys," I whimper, as he grazes against that eye-rolling spot. He rolls his hips into me harder, his pubic bone grinding up against my clit.

"Come for me, baby," he says, moaning into my ear. "I want to feel your pussy clench around my dick." It doesn't take much after that. A few more hard, deep thrusts and I feel the tingle travel up my body. My toes fan out and I grip his shoulders, my nails digging into his back. Another good plunge and he hits that spot, and I'm pushed over the edge. My clit is fluttering as my pussy is clenching him in succession. Rhys' body grows rigid as I feel him growing inside me, ready to explode. I hear his teeth grit in my ear as he grunts and warm liquid fills me, his cock throbbing inside me.

He's still rocking into me softly as we ride the pleasure and come down. A mixture of his seed and my fluids leak out of me, down my cheeks and onto the sheets below. Both of us are panting. Rhys finally rolls off me, his chest rising and falling as he lays next to me.

"Shit, I needed that," he mumbles. A prickle of uneasiness ripples through me, and anxiety starts gripping at my chest. I hesitate to say anything, but decide to speak up.

"So, should we talk?" Suddenly, music fills the air, and it's coming from the floor. Rhys scrambles out of bed and searches for his phone in the heap of clothing. He silences the call, but it seems too convenient to be a phone call.

"Oh, shit," he whispers. I lean over, trying to see his phone screen, but he moves out of my line of view. "Sorry, babe. I've gotta go. It's an emergency." My heart plummets, and I feel like I'm suffocating. The blood drains from my head, making me lightheaded.

"We'll have to talk later," he mumbles. He grabs his clothes off the floor and plops them on the bed as he wrestles everything on, one item at a time. When he's finished, his hands slide through his black hair, smoothing out any signs of my hands tousling it.

"Wait, what? You're leaving? Just like that?" Suddenly, almost all too clearly, I realize that there was no call. *I bet the fucking prick set an alarm.* I steel myself, or try to, when I ask the next question. "So, what? This was just a pity fuck? Because you ran into me and felt guilty?"

He glances at me with some undiscernible expression. Guilt? Sadness? Nah, it can't be either. This fucker doesn't seem to have a conscience. Anger bubbles up inside of me. I feel nauseous. I should have just fucking said no, like I planned on doing at first. Fuck me. "So, that's how it is. Fuck you, Rhys. Just get out. I'm so fucking done with you, I don't even know why you're here. You probably have so many other bitches you could have called since dumping me. Don't come near me ever again."

He opens his mouth to say something, but I shut that down, throwing my hand up in the air. I scooch off my bed, dragging the sheet with me and wrapping it around me, leaving him standing there, hopefully embarrassed, as I march out of the room to the washroom. I slam the door behind me and sit in silence until I hear the front door click shut, and then I cry.

CHAPTER TWENTY

ELISSA

The next few weeks around the office are tense. Brandt and I try to keep to ourselves for the most part, but everyone seems to think something is going on between us. A hush would break out across the room if we entered together, or if one of us entered the room when the other was already there.

The tension between us is practically tangible. The air is thick and charged whenever we're together. Brandt isn't a chatty guy, but he's never been cold toward me. I used to catch him staring at me, or hovering close by, waiting for me. But now? It's like he can't get away from me fast enough. I know I hurt him, but we were never exclusive; I didn't think it would be like this when I returned.

"Well, it sounds like this Rhys guy is a fucktard," says a warm, familiar voice. I slump against the hallway wall and kick off my heels before walking into the kitchen, where something that smells delicious is cooking. Sitting at the island are Riley and Will, halfway through a bottle of merlot. Will stands and rounds the island to greet me. He slides his arms around my waist, tugging me into his chest, and plants a kiss on my cheek, then moves to grab me a wine glass from the cupboard and pours me a glass.

I graciously take the glass. "What smells so good?" I ask. Riley perks up and it's like hearts start pouring out of her eyes.

"Your man is a wizard. He made homemade lasagna and garlic bread. And when I say homemade, I mean even the noodles were from scratch," Riley said. Warmth blooms throughout my body as I see Riley light up about food. The last few months were hard on her body, but her mental health took a serious nosedive when her eating disorder reared its ugly head, mostly due to my abandonment.

"Well, I'm famished. Is it almost done?" I ask as I start pulling out dishes and silverware. They clink against the island as I set them down. "So, who's going to tell me what's going on with Rhys?"

Will nods to Riley, encouraging her to speak up first. She takes a deep breath before explaining.

"After therapy today, I kind of bumped into Rhys. He was a total asshat at first. Saying things like 'oh, it's you' and not even apologizing for knocking me over. But then he was sweet, or seemed to be, when he said he wanted to talk and that he missed me…"

I give her a pointed and confused look. Her face screws up for a moment before she continues explaining.

"So, he asked if we could talk here, and I was hesitant at first, but my heart just couldn't say no. I love him, even still. You know?" I nod my head in response and wait for her to continue. Her eyes begin to well with tears. "We came back here, and he just started kissing me and turning me on, and I tried to stop it, not really hard, but I wanted to talk. And he said 'after.' So, I thought that meant we were gonna talk about getting back together maybe. But once we finished fucking it seemed like he set his alarm to go off at exactly the right moment to leave without talking. Almost like he premeditated the whole interaction. He basically admitted it was a pity fuck," she says on a sob.

Tears stream down her face and Will is perched beside her on the stool, rubbing her back, trying to soothe her. My heart warms at the sight, seeing this man comfort my friend in a moment of need. I walk around the counter and cradle her head into my chest, stroking her sleek black hair.

"It'll be okay. Who fucking needs that piece of shit, anyway?" I say firmly.

Will lifts his glass and says, "Hear, hear." We all sort of giggle and grab our glasses to clink them together. Riley takes a few steadying breaths just as the oven timer goes off. Will gets up to take the lasagna out of the oven, and when he opens the door, a cloud of mouthwatering steam pours out, filling the kitchen air with the aroma of cheese, meat, and tomato sauce. Freshly baked bread also perfumes the air as he pulls a loaf of garlic bread out of the oven. I sidle up beside Riley, topping up her glass of wine while Will dishes out dinner. And, for the first time in a while, it feels like I'm home.

• • •

Getting out of bed this morning to get to work was a chore. Riley and I stayed up late gossiping and bitching about Rhys and Brandt while polishing off another two bottles of wine. When we finally went to bed, Will kept me up again for another hour *making love*, as he forces me to look in his eyes now. A shiver rolls down my spine at the thought of love, or making love, or anything to do with love. A pang of loneliness sends an agonizing stab through my body. I try to shake the feeling just as I feel a piercing, icy burn spread across my back. I don't dare to look behind me as I walk toward the elevator in the Black & Wells Publishing and Press lobby. I hit the button to go up.

When the doors slide open, I step in and shuffle to the back corner after pressing the button for the twenty-second floor. The door is slowly grinding closed when a giant, masculine hand pops between the closing doors. Brandt steps into the elevator and takes the corner across from me, but it doesn't feel like enough distance between us. I can feel the electricity crackling; every nerve in my body is charged and vibrating. I swear I can't be the only one feeling this. Yet, there is Brandt, standing cool, calm, and collected. Like I don't even exist; like it doesn't affect him at all.

"Morning," I mumble, braving the first moment of contact. His head turns slightly, and he nods in reciprocation. I grit my teeth into a tight smile. "How was your night?" I continue, trying to make pleasant conversation.

He rummages through his jacket pocket, pulls out his cell phone, and devotes all his attention to the little screen. "Oh-kay then. Nice talking to you, too," I mumble again.

Brandt drops his arms to put his phone back in his pocket, folds his arms, and with furrowed brows, he sighs. His feet shift apart slightly, as though he's bracing for an attack.

"What, Elissa? What could you possibly want to talk about? You've made it abundantly clear that we are not friends. So, what will idle small talk accomplish? Let's just stick to work topics and that's it."

I'm suddenly feeling three feet shorter than when I walked into the elevator a few moments ago. Brandt is towering over me, and I am the tiny little munchkin in the lift, feeling wholly embarrassed. I mutter an apology and we take the rest of the elevator ride in awkward silence.

When we reach our floor and the doors slide open, it only takes Brandt's long legs a few steps before he's already out of the elevator and halfway to our offices. I push myself off the back of the elevator wall and stroll forward, following behind Brandt. Lori and Selena are both at the front desk, watching with wide eyes as the two of us approach the glass doors that separate the hallway from the office area. Ever the gentleman, Brandt opts to hold the door open for me.

Unwanted stares burn into my back as I walk past my old office toward my new one by the conference room. I hear the women brightly greet Brandt as I continue to my office. I step inside and slump back against the door once it's closed. I kick off my heels and they tumble across the floor and land beside my desk. So not in the mood to wear heels right now.

I squeeze my eyes shut and my hands rest over my diaphragm as I concentrate on my breathing. It's going to be another long day, and the only way to make it through is to try and focus on my breathing and possibly sneak out for a lunchtime jog. I sit down at my desk and wake my computer to find a new instant message from Brandt on Microsoft Teams.

Brandt Collins: *Email from your father. We're supposed to have a full division plan by next week's conference meeting. He wants it finalized before the new year.*

Next week? My father's giving us three days to prepare for the meeting. He wants an entire plan for the year to be finalized in three days. Is he fucking nuts? Well, of course he is.

Brandt Collins: *I guess it'll be a long night. I'll have Lori order in some dinner for us.*

Elissa Black: *Sure. Chinese?*

Brandt replies with a thumbs-up emoji. I groan at the thought of having to work late tonight, and possibly losing my entire weekend to this division plan. My phone goes off and I check the screen. Will's messaged me, asking me to go out for dinner tonight. I slump down in my chair, fold my arms across my desk, and drop my head into my arms. This is going to be a long day.

CHAPTER
TWENTY-ONE

BRANDT

Elissa has been plaguing my dreams for the last few days. I've been trying to give Lexi my full attention, but it's getting harder the longer Elissa sticks around. When I'm lucky to catch a glimpse of her smile, her perfect heart-shaped lips have an exaggerated turn-out because of the braces she wore back in freshman year, and her straight white teeth peek out from a sliver of a gap between her lips.

I'm distracted by the way her curvaceous ass looks in any pair of pants or skirt, or the way it sways when she's wearing heels. The lilt of her laughter echoes down the hall and reverberates into my office, making my body ache for her to be in my arms again. But then I remember how she left, how she destroyed my heart, how she made it so hard for me to move on. I found some solace by diving into work and trying to forget her, drinking heavily with Rhys, and attempting to fuck her out of my system.

It took everything in me not to stop that elevator this morning and grab a fistful of her gorgeous cinnamon locks and inhale. It was even harder to act like an icy asshole when all I wanted was to push her up against the wall and feel her tender breasts in my hands. To hook her leg around my waist and hoist her up so she can feel just how hard she makes me. To thrust my tongue into her, tasting every corner of her smart mouth. To suck on her neck and leave my mark, so everyone knows that she is mine.

But then I remembered Lexi, and how that woman has chased me for well over a year. How this amazing, beautiful woman wants *me*. And then I remember that she isn't Elissa. No one will ever be Elissa. How do I fall out of love with someone who doesn't want me? How do I fall out of love with someone I've been infatuated with my entire adult life?

My skin crawls with anxiety and anticipation to be spending time alone with her working late; just us. I shoot Lexi a message to let her know I'm working late tonight and that we'll have to postpone our date. I gather my things from my desk, tuck them under my arm, and head toward the conference room.

As I approach, I notice Elissa is still in her office, talking on the phone. Her tone is clipped and irritated.

"No, Will. You can't come here for dinner…" Her voice trails off. She taps her foot on the ground and shakes her head, scrubbing her face with her hands. Her hip is popped while she stands facing the window, overlooking the busy downtown Toronto skyline. "No, listen. It's just work…" Another pause, then a sigh. "Fine. I will let Brandt know," she says defeatedly. She turns a fraction of the way around and tosses her phone on her desk, not realizing I'm standing in the doorway. I knock gently.

"Everything all right?" I ask, honestly intrigued by her conversation. It sounds like Will was picking a fight about something. Elissa's eyes widen as she turns around to face me. She folds her arms across her chest and rolls her eyes as she blows some hair out of her face.

"Yeah, just Will. He's coming to join us for dinner, I guess. He was adamant about it," she groans. "So, you might as well invite Lexi and make it a thing. It was Will's suggestion."

I'm not quite sure what to say, so I give her a curt nod and continue walking to the conference room to message Lexi.

A few moments later, Elissa arrives at the boardroom with her laptop, file folders, and a mug of coffee. Scratch that, a vat of coffee. She's got one of those giant Yeti tumblers that could caffeinate a horse. She sets everything down on the table beside my stuff, plugs her laptop into the boardroom television and drops down into the chair beside me, letting her limbs fly free, exhaling loudly. The picture of a drama queen.

I try to avoid looking at her in this low moment of hers. She's clearly frustrated and drained, but I can't bring myself to feel bad for her. Before I chide myself for not feeling any sort of remorse for her, I recall her strained relationship with her father. I can only imagine how he conned her into staying in Toronto. Elissa's eyes are closed, and she's humming softly to herself, her knee bouncing up and down.

Just as I'm about to give in and ask her what's wrong, she sighs, straightens up, and gives me a soft smile.

"Shall we get started, before Will and Lexi arrive?" she asks coolly. My mouth opens at first to say something, but my lips clamp together instead as I nod. Elissa reaches for her computer and the remote to the television and turns on the screen, her desktop now mirrored on the monitor. She scrolls and clicks around until she's brought up a bunch of files: budgets, presentations, emails, etc.

Forty-five minutes into the work session and Elissa grumbles something unintelligible.

"Sorry, I didn't catch that," I say, catching her off guard. She looks over at me, eyes wide, and chuckles.

"Ha. Sorry, I was just rereading my father's email and muttering to myself about how he's dumping this on us at the very last minute. I mean, we knew this was coming, but to have this completed in two days? He's a fucking nightmare."

I offer her a sympathetic smile, and my hand automatically reaches out for hers and squeezes. When our hands touch, we both instantly freeze, our eyes searching each other's. Elissa's eyes are quivering and glazing over with tears as she looks at me. My heart's beating erratically in my chest, and I wonder if she can hear it, or feel my pulse thundering as I hold her hand. The movement is ever so slight, but she squeezes my hand back as the corners of her lips curl softly upward.

A knock on the glass doors shatters the moment, and Elissa pushes her foot off the ground to create a chasm between us. Her head whips toward the door and blood rushes into her face. I grit my teeth when she fumbles to stand up and walk over to the door. I don't need to turn around to know who is standing behind me.

"Brandt?" A soft, gentle voice breaks the quiet of the room. Shit, I forgot Lexi was coming. I paste a smile on my face, stand up, and glide over to Lexi. I wrap my arm around her waist, pulling her in and placing a chaste kiss on her cheek. Worry swims in Lexi's blue eyes; I can see the confusion and tension on her face, her eyes begging me for an explanation. I glance over at Elissa and Will and realize they have exited the conference room and are down the hallway in what looks like a heated argument. His hand wraps around her bicep, his fingertips biting tightly into her flesh. She tries to jerk her arm away from him, but he won't let go.

"Is everything all right?" Lexi asks worriedly. I smile at her to reassure her and place another kiss at her hairline along her temple.

"Mhm," I hum. "Just comforting a…friend."

• • •

Elissa and Will have settled across the table from Lexi and me. Will's hardened stare burrows into me every time I talk or glance at them across the table. Lexi is oblivious to what is going on as she sits beside me, scrolling through her social media accounts.

"I think the first thing that should be finished before launching our new platform and division is to get all of our print archives digitized," Elissa says. "This should take roughly forty to sixty hours if we outsource the labour of data entry, then our tech guys can take that and put it on the new website's archive list." I start to respond and let Elissa know that I agree, but Will opens his dumb mouth.

"Actually, if you don't mind, I think that the best thing would be to attract new talent and projects to launch the division." My teeth clench together and Elissa is staring at Will in shock.

"Didn't think you had a say, Mr. Burke," I say icily. A slow, creeping smirk spreads across Will's face.

"It's something that I've discussed with Harold, and he seemed interested in my ideas." Will then turns his head back to Elissa. "I know it's ultimately your decision *babe*, but I think it's the smartest thing to do. You can always build the archives later and in the background. People want new and exciting. And this division isn't just going to be archives, so it makes more sense to cultivate the people you're going to have creating new content and products for this division." Elissa chews her lip as she looks between me and Will and gives me a "what do you think?" look. I grind my teeth, holding back the urge to leap across the table and punch Will in his smug face.

"I think that history is important to the division. It shows longevity and stability, not only to our customers and readers, but also to incoming new talent. It won't look like a completely new division. It's important for our future talent to choose to work with Black & Wells because of its history and reputation for news and everything media-related."

"But isn't this division more about branching out into the publication of more than just news?" Will challenges.

"Yes, but it comes down to trust and history, and I think achieving the *right* talent is in the details of history and longevity," I say through gritted teeth. I look to Elissa, imploring her to defend what we've been discussing for the last few weeks. Her nervous glance bounces between Will and me, and she finally looks at Lexi, who is blissfully oblivious right now. Elissa lowers her eyes to her hands and picks at her cuticles before answering.

"I…I don't know. I think you both make a lot of sense." *Well, that's a lot of help, Elissa. For fuck's sakes.* Will is searching Elissa's eyes with a hardened stare, challenging her to say something against him. "I…I think we should focus on building new content and talent, and maybe slowly work our way into building the archives. Maybe?" Elissa turns her head away from Will. They're both staring at me now. One face has a look of sorrow, and the other has a gloating smirk, with a triumphant sparkle behind his eyes.

CHAPTER
TWENTY-TWO

The room is charged with testosterone. The pissing contest that seems to be happening between Will and Brandt couldn't be missed by anyone other than Lexi. She's off in her own world, scrolling through her phone, seemingly quite bored. Every so often she glances up and flicks her hair over her shoulders, then returns her attention to her phone.

A worm of jealousy coils inside of me. To be that ignorant and oblivious to my surroundings would be wonderful. There was a time not too long ago where it didn't matter to me what happened around me. How I long to be back in school, or in London, out of my father's reach.

A buzz interrupts the men's competition and Lori's voice crackles over the intercom.

"Your food has arrived, Ms. Black." I press down the button and thank her. A few minutes later, Lori appears through the glass doors carrying the bags of Chinese food and sets them down on the far end of the room where there's a long, skinny table. She bustles in and out of the room, gathering plates and cutlery. She makes her final appearance carrying a bottle of wine and some glasses.

"That will be all, Lori. Thank you for staying. Have a good night," I say in a soft, grateful voice. Lori's face pinkens, and she inclines her head in acknowledgement and exits the room. Lexi suddenly becomes aware of where she is when the smell of food reaches her nose. Her stomach grumbles loudly in the room. My lips tighten as I suppress a laugh. Brandt's eyes catch mine and he seems to be biting back some laughter as well. We hold each other's gaze for a few seconds and his pupils dilate, his eyes shining as he looks at me.

My heart aches. Will clears his throat beside me and he grabs my hand. He stands up, tugging me to my feet, and guides us over to where the food is set up. Will takes his time dishing out food for the both of us. As he opens each of the containers, savoury curls of steam circle in the air, and I finally realize just how hungry I am.

I take my full plate of food from Will and grab the bottle of wine to bring it to the table. Will grabs a few glasses and follows me back to our seats. As I uncork the wine, my eyes drift over to Lexi and Brandt, who are over by the food. He is standing close behind her as she's piling her plate with food. Heaping mountains of food cover her plate, and I wonder where the hell she puts it all in her tiny, slim body. Her curves are glorious; her ass and breasts are both respectively large. A pang of jealousy hits me as I can see why men, and Brandt, find her attractive.

But it's not just her curves. It's her petite frame, her delicate, long lashes, and her perfectly pouty lips. The way her eyes glow and crinkle when she giggles, and her lilting, melodic voice. It probably helps that she likely has a healthy relationship with her parents, and doesn't have any commitment issues, unlike yours truly.

I don't notice that I haven't actually taken a bite, I'm just pushing my food around on my plate, until Will nudges me and asks, "Is everything okay? You should get eating." My eyelids flutter, and I'm brought back to the moment. I stab a chicken ball and pop it into my mouth, giving Will a tiny, sarcastic smile. I pick up the wine bottle, pour a generous helping of red into my glass, and chug it back.

Will's eyebrows lift suspiciously, but he doesn't utter a word. Brandt and Lexi are back at the table and Lexi's eyes are wide as she watches me gulp down my glass of wine. My eyes bounce between Will and Lexi, and I slowly set my glass down.

"What did I miss?" I ask the two of them. Will shrugs and keeps quiet, but Lexi speaks up.

"I was just surprised that you drank your glass so fast, that's all," she quips. My eyes narrow at her, and I toss my hair over my shoulder.

"I didn't realize that I would be admonished for my drinking habits," I bite out, offering her a cold smile.

"Excuse me." I stand up, saunter out of the room, and down the hall to my office. I slam my door shut, then walk over and rustle through the bottom drawer of my desk to find the bottle of whiskey I stashed in there when I came back. I twist the lid off, toss it onto my desk, and wrap my lips around the bottle. I take a swig and let the warm liquid burn my throat.

A pleasant and familiar warmth spreads through my body just as a single knock sounds on my door. A moment later, the door creaks open and Brandt enters. I let out a long, exasperated sigh.

"Yes?"

"Just seeing if you were okay."

"Why wouldn't I be?" Brandt gives me a look that says it all. I'm standing here, hiding out in my office, slugging back some whiskey from my secret office stash. My cheeks start to burn. "You know how much I can drink, and then Lexi pointed it out and made it awkward. As if tonight isn't awkward enough as it is. I need some liquid courage if I'm going to be stuck in that boardroom any longer." Brandt doesn't say anything, just offers a curt nod and exits my office.

I heave another sigh and replace the cap back on the bottle, then place it back in the bottom drawer of my desk. I walk over to the mirror in the corner of my office and ruffle my hair a bit, steeling my nerves to face the boardroom and its three very unlikely occupants.

• • •

After dinner, Brandt makes it known that Will and Lexi need to leave so that we can finish our work.

"We've been distracted enough for now, and at this rate, Elissa and I will never get this project done before the end of the weekend." Lexi pouts and wraps her delicate arms around Brandt's waist.

"Will you come over later? I don't mind how late. I just don't want to go all weekend without seeing you." Brandt mumbles something that doesn't quite reach my ears, and my dinner starts bubbling in my stomach. I turn to start walking Will to the elevators as one hand curls into a tight fist. Will shakes my hand and that's when I realize I am squeezing his hand a little too hard.

"Whoops," I whisper. I turn to Will to say my good-byes, and his expression is hard. He gives me a rigid hug and I can feel his jaw clench and hear his teeth grinding in my ear. He puts a few centimetres between us for a moment before placing a rough, lingering kiss on my lips. Heat travels across my face to the tips of my ears. I try to pull away, but he locks me in closer.

"Will," I mumble between kisses. I finally manage to break free from him when Lexi and Brandt approach us at the elevator.

"I'll see you tonight," Will says in a gruff voice, his dark brown eyes growing even darker. My heart sinks a bit, and a slow, creeping anxiety spreads over me.

It's not until both Lexi and Will step into the elevator that I feel like I can breathe. The awkward hum slowly fades away as the elevator doors close and it descends. Both Brandt and I sigh in relief.

"Shall we continue?" Brandt asks as we walk back to the boardroom. I give him a slight nod and stop briefly at my office to grab the bottle of whiskey.

"Now we can continue."

• • •

It's around one in the morning when Brandt and I decide to wrap up for the night. I've drank roughly half the bottle of whiskey while Brandt has been nursing the bottle of wine. We've managed to get a lot of work done and should only need a few more hours to finish up before the meeting on Monday. Brandt has elected for us to finish it tomorrow over lunch in the office.

"Yes, because I love nothing more than to come to work on a Saturday," I say sarcastically. Brandt's lips quirk.

"Better than spending your Sunday in the office."

"Touché, Mr. Collins." My words are a little slurred. It's been a while since I've drank that much alcohol — and to think, drinking that much whiskey four months ago would have been nothing. My alcohol tolerance has clearly gone down the drain. My ankles wobble slightly when I stand up from the table. I slip my heels back on my feet and collect my things.

Brandt is already halfway out of the conference room by the time I'm rounding the table. I look over my shoulder out of the bank of floor-to-ceiling windows and notice a small blizzard has started up outside. I resolve to take a cab home tonight, because me in heels plus whiskey on a freezing night doesn't mix. Brandt is standing in the doorway holding the glass door open for me. I try my best to avoid bumping into him when my ankle gives out. My heel skids and turns inward.

I lurch to the side and my body presses up against Brandt's. I feel his large, warm hand wrap around my bicep to steady me. His face is tilted down, facing me, and I'm suddenly very aware that our lips are only centimetres apart. Both of our chests are rising and falling rapidly. My eyes shift from his burning stare to his lips, and they linger there. I remember how they taste and feel against me. I suck in my bottom lip and bite down on it, holding back the urge to press my lips against his.

He clears his throat and I'm pulled from my thoughts. I straighten up.

"Uh, thanks for catching me," I whisper, feeling my ears burn.

CHAPTER TWENTY-THREE

ELISSA

The thudding of my heart is thunderous as it pounds against my ribs. My skin prickles from the surge of adrenaline running through me. As Brandt's strong, firm hand loosens its grip on my arm an immediate chill flutters over me. I swoon a little, wanting his hand to stay where it was.

Brandt takes his leave first, shuffling his large body down the hallway toward his office and disappearing through the doorway. I have a short walk, since my new office is just a few feet from the conference room. I walk in and deposit my stuff on my desk, then collapse back into my chair. The wheels of the chair drag across the hardwood floor. I take a few moments to collect my swirling mind, fidgeting with my cuticles as I do so.

There's a light knock on my office door. I glance up and Brandt is there, wrapped up in his charcoal wool winter jacket, with his messenger bag slung over his shoulder. One carefully groomed eyebrow perks up.

"Ready to head out?" he asks, flicking his head toward the long hallway leading to the elevators. I nod, swipe everything off my desk into my bag, and push off from the chair, tucking it snugly underneath my desk. I round the edge of my desk and stop to put on my long puffer jacket, then exit my office. As I'm passing Brandt I catch a whiff of his cologne. My eyes flutter closed as I savour the rich, wintry scent. I casually flick my hair over my shoulder before pulling out my toque from the pocket of my jacket and tugging over my head. My hands separate my hair at the back and pull it forward over my shoulders.

I shake my wrist, jiggling and rearranging my white gold Rolex, with its halo of tiny diamonds accenting the watch's face. Our footsteps echo through the quiet corridor as we near the elevator, neither one of us daring to say anything. With every step, the tension from the moment that passed between us in the conference room builds. My heels click faster down the hallway as my pace keeps me slightly ahead of Brandt. I hope he doesn't notice the heat creeping across my cheeks.

This whole night has been a disaster. First with Will and Lexi showing up, and then my drunken habits reappearing and making a mess out of everything. Had Brandt not cleared his throat after I stumbled into him, I think I might have kissed him. Fuck, I wanted to kiss him. When his hand touched my arm, steadying it, it was the most desire I'd felt from such a small gesture in a long time. The heat from his hand has spiked a fever under my skin.

Brandt gives me a strange look as he steps forward and presses the button for the elevator. My head jerks as I look around and notice we've come to a stop at the elevator. The heat in my cheeks grows to a burn, lighting up my whole face and drying out the saliva in my mouth, making it feel like the Sahara Desert. What. An. Idiot. Blood pounds against my ear drums as my breathing picks up, and in the reflection of the elevator my face looks like a pomegranate. *Inhale. Exhale. Repeat.*

After a few calming breaths, a slight chill rolls over me and I feel the colour fade from my face and my rapid heartbeat subsides. A low rumble, almost a chuckle, comes from my left. Straining to see out of the corner of my eyes, I try and glimpse Brandt to see if the noise came from him or if I dreamt it.

The elevator dings before the doors slide open and an arm waves in front of me, extending the invitation to step onto the elevator first. I murmur softly in thanks, and as I step into the car, my foot wobbles and lodges into the track of the door. Brandt steps around me, making his way to the back of the car as I step out of my heel. The doors start to slide closed, and I whip out a hand to stop them. I smack the door, hard, and my hand throbs with pain, but the doors do stay open.

I wiggle my shoe, trying to get the damn thing unstuck, as my head swirls and spins. Bending over like this with a belly full of liquor is not a great feeling. My cheeks

puff out and I exhale and grunt with the effort of shimmying my heel out. Finally, the heel gives way, and I go flying
backward. Unable to catch myself and off-balance thanks
to only wearing one heel, I stumble and lose my balance.
My heeled foot slips, twisting inward as my ankle rolls
underneath me.

I tilt backward, my arms flapping in the air like a chick-
en, and I fall on my ass, landing against something firm,
but softer than a wall. A sweat breaks out across my body
and heat surges through me. I lean to the side a smidge to
see if I actually did what I think I did.

Yep. It's Brandt. I landed on Brandt. His legs are
sprawled open on either side of mine, and he has one hand
bracing himself on the floor while the other is rubbing the
back of his head. When his chest rises, it brushes against
my back, and I feel a swirl of heat simmer below. Brandt
leans forward a bit, still rubbing his head as he winces and
exhales in pain.

"Are you okay?" I ask in shock, as I take in the beautiful
man behind me. I lean closer to him, and my eyes travel
to his lips. Longing pulls me in closer. I can smell coffee
laced with wine on his breath, hear the breaths he draws as
he moans slightly from hitting his head on the lift's metal
railing. I suck in my lower lip and bite down on it, debating
whether or not to give in to this urge to kiss him.

"Yeah, I'm fine. I just hit my…" he trails off, his sparkling eyes locking onto mine briefly before settling on my
lips. "Um…my head," he finishes the last word quietly as
our bodies pull us together, our lips inching closer. His
breathing grows ragged, as does mine, and the pounding

in my chest rivals the one in my ears. I don't know which one is louder. Or is it Brandt's I hear?

Our eyes don't break contact as we draw closer. His hand drops from the back of his head and trails down my shoulder, to my arm. Even through my thick, puffy coat, I can feel his warm, soft fingertips grazing me. Our eyes quiver; our lips are a breath away. My lids drift closed and my parted lips pucker. His lips brush mine, ever so lightly. I can't tell if it's in my head that I feel his lips brushing mine, or if it's real. I can't open my eyes and find out it's all in my head. It would crush me.

Then the elevator screeches, shattering the moment, begging us to push a damn floor button. Adrenaline spikes through my entire body, triggering every nerve ending, making my skin crawl. Brandt pushes away from me and staggers to his feet, then lunges toward the wall filled with buttons and hits the one for the main floor lobby. Something falls to the pit of my stomach, and a pulsing throb starts in my lower parts, like I've just fallen and landed on my tailbone. I brace myself against the floor with both hands and launch myself to my feet.

I toe around my one heel until it's flipped right side up, and stuff my foot back into it. Brandt clears his throat and stands facing the door, about as far in front of me as he can get. His coat is rumpled, his pants are creased, and he stands tall and rigid. He runs a hand through his golden-brown hair and rubs the spot where he hit his head.

Like it has a mind of its own, my hand stretches outward and reaches for the spot on his head, but stops a few inches away. Hovering in the air, my fingers clench and I withdraw, letting my arm fall to my side. A few moments later, the elevator dings and the doors open to the darkness of the lobby. Brandt exits first and stops a few feet away, waiting for me. I take slow, hesitant steps as I approach him. My fingers curl around the strap of my bag, clenching in the hopes of squashing the pulsing urge to grab his hand.

What is wrong with me? Is it because I've seen him with Lexi? I'm not a jealous person, but this has me all messed up. Seeing him wrap his arms around Lexi, with his lips touching her perfect pouty mouth, and the way her fingers interlock with his made my blood boil. But they match; they do look nice together, and I cannot deny it. Both look like Greek gods — bronzed, toned, and beautiful. Her blonde hair and big blue eyes with his golden-brown waves and defined green eyes…the pairing of their good looks will make everyone jealous.

My heart sinks as my mind plays through Brandt and Lexi's future together. An overwhelming sadness erupts in my chest, crushing the air out of my lungs. I'm drowning in the thoughts that come rushing in.

"Elissa?" Brandt calls out to me. I shake the thoughts from my mind, and my eyes search for his. His brows furrow as he looks at me with worried eyes. A soft smile plays on my lips.

"Coming," I say. My heels click across the deserted lobby as I make my way toward Brandt.

CHAPTER TWENTY-FOUR

My body is humming — vibrating. Every tiny, minuscule molecule in my body is singing to touch her, to feel her, to kiss her.

We left the elevator and I've had a minute to settle down. This evening has left my body charged and I'm ready to dive into the deep end and just go for it — to kiss her. But I can't. My head won't allow my heart or dick to follow their desires. Elissa is liquored up, wobbling like a baby deer in her heels, her winged eyeliner is a bit smudged, and her cherry red lipstick is smeared, with a dot of it decorating her front tooth. And damn if she doesn't look fucking beautiful as a mess. Her hair looks like ruffled reddish-brown feathers, soft and full and frizzy, like a burning cloud in an evening sunset.

Her slim form tapers in, then flares to her wide, athletic hips and ass. Her deep periwinkle skirt is wrinkled and mussed, her blouse is partially untucked at the front and a couple more buttons than normal are undone near her bust, leaving her cleavage peeking out from behind. Her puffer coat hangs off her shoulders, wide open, only cinched at the waist by the belt clasped together.

I turn away from her and bury my nose in my phone, scrolling through pages of nothing as I wait for her to catch up. Every click that echoes from her shoes steps on my nerves, pricking them like a reflex test. Whiskey, wine, and warm vanilla dance in the air as she bustles past me. I inhale deeply, letting the scent fill my lungs. I hope it sticks to every capillary, clinging on for dear life, so that I never forget this smell.

I follow her outside and step toward the curb to hail a cab to drive us home, but Elissa is not beside me. She's already staggering down the snowy December sidewalk. As she walks in the flurries, her head tilts upward, her mouth opens, and her tongue sticks out to catch the snowflakes. Her lips turn up into a soft smile. My heart squeezes. It's something so mundane and childish, yet I've never seen her happier. I slip my phone out of my pocket and snap a picture of her catching snowflakes.

I brace myself for the cold gusts of wind as I jog to catch up to her. Her feet stop abruptly, and her face is overcome with confusion.

"Thought I'd walk you home, since it's so late," I say, in a low, soft voice. Her cheeks and nose are a pinched red from the chilly air nipping at her soft skin. Her eyes never waver from mine as she silently takes in my words. They twinkle like sapphires under the tall streetlamps that are decorated with Christmas lights. The wind blows a gigantic gust of snow, and it dusts on her upper cheek, just under her eye. My leather-gloved hand cups her face as my thumb brushes off the snow. Her face reddens, and my groin grows tight. *Fuck, I want to kiss her. I need to kiss her…*

I clear my throat. "Let's go." I nod, and she falls into step beside me. I slow my pace so she can keep up with my long gait. It's a short twenty-minute walk, but it feels like eternity in the peaceful tundra of downtown Toronto. Very few cars slosh past us in the late hours of the night, and it is a quiet walk; just us, our footsteps, and the hum of electricity from the overhead traffic and streetlights. We walk in comfortable silence. I bury my hands deep in my pockets when the itch to hold her hand takes over, pressing my hands further into my pockets as if to trap them there.

When we reach her apartment, she spins on her heels to face me, her nose and face red and stiff from the icy wind; her eyes are shining though. Her tongue rolls along her bottom lip before she sucks the corner in and bites down. Her chin tilts and her eyes find mine.

"Good night, Mr. Collins," she mumbles in a soft, dulcet tone.

"Good night, Ms. Black."

I step backward, toward the curb, and flag down a passing cab. Her arms are loosely folded across her chest, and she raises a gloved hand, her fingers curling slightly in a wave. I nod my head and duck into the car, watching her enter the building before I tell the driver my address.

• • •

My phone goes off in my pocket as I exit the cab. I toss the driver two twenties and tell him, "Keep the change. Merry Christmas." I slam the door shut and pull my phone out of my jacket. Putting my middle finger between my teeth to pull the glove off my hand, I unlock my screen and see a message waiting from Lexi.

Lexi: *Are you still coming over tonight?*

I groan, hoping that she hasn't been waiting up all night for me to come over. Instead of answering, I slide my phone back into my pocket and head toward the elevator.

Once inside my apartment I lock my door, toe off my shoes, and toss my jacket on the leather stool that sits at the island counter. I swivel and loosen the burgundy tie around my neck and pop open a few of the buttons on my shirt as I make my way to my bedroom.

I strip off my clothes and toss them into the hamper in the corner of my room. Stepping through my walk-in closet to the bathroom, I grab my toothbrush and squeeze a little toothpaste on top. While I'm scrubbing my teeth the little plastic bristles dig into my gums, and my mind floats back to tonight and the elevator ride.

Seeing Eli's softened face, like she was letting her guard down, broke my resolve. It felt like this magnetic force was pulling me closer to her, inch by inch, until her breath was tickling my lips. The way she was nestled between my legs when we fell, and with her leaned into my chest, I could smell the lavender shampoo she's switched to. My hand twitched and ached to touch her face as we were sitting there.

My groin tightens for the hundredth time tonight. Still brushing my teeth, my free hand grabs my dick through my powder-blue boxers and squeezes to stop the throbbing, to no avail. My jaw clenches and my teeth grind together as my eyes roll back into my head. I make my final spit, rinse my mouth, and collapse into my bed, scooching my legs down so the silky dark blankets come up to cover my body.

I try to drift off to sleep, but all I see when I close my eyes is a tangled mess of auburn hair. Her soft, heart-shaped lips puckered and slightly parted, waiting for mine to press against hers. I imagine running my tongue along the rim of her lips before thrusting it in and thoroughly exploring every corner of her mouth, then sucking on her tongue; the feel of her lips between my teeth as they rake along the swollen skin, eliciting a moan from her beautiful throat.

I roll onto my back as a heavy sigh escapes me, concaving my chest. My restraint is chipping away with every breath. My hand snakes into my boxers and wraps around my engorged rod, giving it a little squeeze before leaning over to grab some lube out of my nightstand drawer. Squirting a generous helping of liquid into my hand, I slather it on my hardened shaft, taking my time as I tug up and down. I slide my hand from the base of my cock to the tip, running my thumb over the tiny hole where precum is oozing out.

A strangled moan erupts from my throat as I imagine beautiful, brilliant blue eyes blinking back at me. A lilting laugh echoes through my head as her head tilts backward, her mouth wide open. Then my mind flashes to the damned elevator again. *Why is it always to do with the elevator for us?* Her leaning back onto my chest, my body being pulled into her orbit. Her kissable lips parting, waiting for mine. But here is where I can change what happened.

My hand threads into her hair, cupping her nape and crushing our lips together. It's a clashing mix of lips and teeth as our mouths hungrily taste each other. Her hands slide up my chest and grab hold of the lapel of my jacket, tugging it hard, pulling me in, even though I can't get any closer. I lean forward, pressing her down onto the floor, my free hand supporting my weight as our pelvises press together, rubbing on the outside of our clothes. I can feel her dampened heat warming up to mine, and my name tumbles from her lips in broken breaths between kisses.

My hand slams harder and harder, squeezing as I near the tip of my dick, milking myself like an udder. Reaching over to my nightstand, I palm around to find the box of tissues, rip a couple out, and grunt as I pump myself to climax. My hips rock with the torrent of cum rippling out of me, and my mouth falls open as a bellowing moan leaves my lips.

"Eli…" my voice whispers on a dissatisfied moan as I stare up at the dark ceiling, waiting for it to cave in on me.

CHAPTER
TWENTY-FIVE

RILEY

A grumbling gurgle in my gut jolts me awake. A wave of nausea washes over me, dousing me in chills all over my body. I groan and roll over onto my side, clutching my tummy. I crack one eye open to check the alarm clock on my dresser. I still have an hour to sleep before I have to be up and at the Mode Hotel on Danforth to set up for a Christmas party I've been hired to coordinate.

Ever since the Black & Wells gala last summer, I've been getting all sorts of requests to host and plan events for big companies. I've been so busy lately; it's like I haven't had a chance to breathe. Companies and people have been contacting me around the clock, wanting me to plan their holiday parties for staff and big family gatherings. I've had to switch my phone off every night in order to get any sleep, or some kind of sleep at least, because I'm still not sleeping well. The incident with Rhys still has me fucked up. He fucked me and then fucked me good, so to speak.

My dehydrated mind screams at me to get some water and aspirin to quell this hangover. I didn't think I drank that much last night, but maybe my body is changing, and my alcohol tolerance is weakening. I groan and roll out of bed, my feet dragging against the hardwood floors as I head to the bathroom. Tiny bottles and lotions are displaced as I search the cabinet for the aspirin bottle, and when I find it, I pop the lid off and pour two pills into my hand before tossing them into my mouth.

I lean forward, allowing my head to hover under the matte black tap, and turn the water on, guzzling a few mouthfuls of water to swallow the pills. The back of my hand drags across my mouth, mopping up the dribble of water running down my chin. My eyes find my reflection and my shoulders slump as I sigh. I feel — and look — haggard. My normally sleek black hair is frizzy, knotted, and sticking up. My once-bright brown eyes, with their golden flecks of amber, are now dull and sunken, with purple-black bruise-like circles under them. My lips are dry and chapped, and tiny divots of skin are missing because of me chewing away at the dry spots.

The way things were left with Rhys is slowly eating away at me. Parts of myself that I felt confident about are slowly decaying away as negative thoughts cloud my mind. Tears bubble to the surface as I continue to stare into the mirror. Rolling my eyes back, I blink away the tears and take a cleansing breath before I exit the washroom.

My feet slap against the floor as I head back to my room. I glance at the clock again and groan. It's not worth it to try and get just forty-five more minutes of sleep, so I grab my phone off the charger, strip my clothes off, and wrap my cushy pink housecoat around my body. I make my way back to the washroom to soak under the boiling temperature of water that I prefer.

• • •

I arrive at the Mode Hotel about thirty minutes early, and thankfully so. The snow is falling in heaps, and I almost couldn't get a car to bring me here. The roads are slippery and covered in snow, and the plows aren't out yet. A couple of streets are blocked off because of the drifts and cars are piled off to the side, abandoned in the deep powder. I step out of the cab and tighten my scarf around my neck, creating a snug little pocket to keep my face warm. I close the door softly, and the car tries to speed off, but the wheels simply spin uselessly in the snow, going nowhere.

I step over a bank of hardened snow and nearly slip and fall on my ass, my legs sliding out from under me, stretching my legs into a starting split position. A gust of icy wind bites at my face as I slowly take my time wriggling my legs back together so I don't fall.

I finally make it to the door unscathed. My tiny hands wrap around the metallic handle, and the freezing metal sends a chill up my spine. I shake it off and pull the door open, whooshing the snow in front of it out of the way, and drag my wheelie suitcase, with its garment bag attached to the handle, behind me.

The lobby of the swanky hotel is expansive. Three large, expensive-looking, and dazzling chandeliers hang from the twenty-foot ceiling. They are dripping with little crystals, making it look like a waterfall. Floor-to-ceiling windows separate a small portion of the lobby, sectioning off the restaurant, Rn (pronounced "ern," or so they tell me). A clever little add-on to their hotel name — if you were to put the two together it would spell "modern."

The restaurant is more like a bistro-bar. There are tall, sleek, standing tables with white tabletops and black hardware, with a circular bar around the bottom third to rest a foot on. There are a handful or two of sitting tables that have tall black chairs that look like thrones, minus the armrests. The bar is the focus. At the far end there is a tapas and grill area where people can mingle over a selection of options. The surface of the bar is made of hearty, sturdy oak, stained dark and polished slick and lacquered. The knots in the wood are smoothed over with finesse and a small LED light track under the lip highlights the front of the long, intricately carved face of the bar.

Swanky low-hanging lights, similar to the chandeliers in the lobby, line the length of the bar every few feet, glistening in the dark ambiance of the room. Behind the bar are glass shelves lined to the ceiling with pictures, plaques, and bottles of liquor and glasses. A handsome bartender with broad shoulders, a toothy grin, a strong jawline that's peppered in stubble, and large, muscular arms is at the ready, wearing a black t-shirt and jeans.

My mouth waters as my eyes travel all over his body. His chestnut hair is coiffed with precision and he has piercing amber eyes, like the rich, deep whiskey Elissa drinks. His smile reaches his eyes as he bellows out a hearty laugh and my thighs clench together. I quickly turn my head away and almost move toward the lobby desk when I hear a familiar laugh coming from the bar.

My stomach lurches. The hairs on my neck bristle as the familiar sound vibrates to my core. A light sweat breaks out over my body and my hands curl into tiny fists. My insides flop and a fresh wave of nausea hits me like a ton of bricks. My legs carry me to the washroom in the lobby at lightning speed. Thoughts flash inside my head, and black and white static speckles my vision. Shallow, ragged breaths rush into my lungs.

I flounder over to the closest stall and the door smashes open against the stall divider. Clattering to my knees, I kneel over the porcelain toilet moments before a burn comes hurtling up my throat. Bile bursts from my mouth as I heave and grunt into the toilet bowl. Feeling like I've puked the lifeforce out of me, I finally wobble to my feet.

I stagger over to the sink, turn on the tap, and cup some water in my hands, slurping the water up and swishing it around in my mouth before spitting it back out. My shaking hands dig through my red Kate Spade purse and find some mints to suck on. I toss my hair over my shoulders, wipe the waterlogged eyeliner stains from the corners of my eyes and walk back to the main lobby.

I check in with the concierge, drop off my bags, and get my guest badge, securing it onto the bottom of my blazer, then follow the attendant back to the restaurant where I'll be spending the day setting up for tonight's event. When I cross the threshold, icy blue eyes meet mine, freezing me in place.

CHAPTER TWENTY-SIX

RILEY

The temperature in the room drops about ten degrees, but my body heats up rapidly, keeping me unbearably warm. My smile quivers as I'm aware of a hardened face as I enter the room. I do my best to ignore the stare that is burning into me and keep my eyes in front of me as I near the bar. I allow a smile to touch my lips as I greet the bartender.

"Hello. I'm Riley, and I was hired to set up the event tonight." The muscular bartender gives me a delicious once-over and his lips curve into a grin. A confidence-boosting energy shoots through me as I feel Rhys turn his burning stare to the bartender. Rhys puffs out his chest as his jaw clenches tightly. The bartender perches his arm on the bar top, leaning forward on a muscular forearm, and extends a hand to me.

"Dante," he says, his voice a smoky grumble. His words melt the ice frozen in my core left by the cold stare I received from Rhys a few moments ago. I slip my hand inside his, and his firm, warm grip envelops mine as he delicately shakes my hand. The harsh clearing of a throat interrupts the moment.

"Well, I guess I'll be off," Rhys says. His face is scrunched up and his brows are pinched together. "I'll see you after work tonight, yeah?" He directs his question to Dante who just tips his head in response, without taking his eyes off me. Rhys huffs, jams his arms into the sleeves of his jacket, and stomps off, leaving Dante and I alone. The corner of his mouth ticks up more once Rhys is gone.

"Rhys' ex, yeah?" A hint of an Australian accent swirls amongst his words.

A flush creeps up my neck until it reaches my ears.

"How'd you know?" Dante's smile stretches into a knowing grin, and he shrugs.

"Bartenders just know." A warmth in my belly stirs at the way he's looking at me. His eyes darken and grow predatory, like a hunter tracking his prey. His tongue darts out to lick the corner of his lip before it retreats, as if he held back licking his lips. "Shall we?" Dante asks, extending his arm to usher me toward the heaping pile of boxes and decorations in the corner of the restaurant.

• • •

Four-and-a-half hours later, I'm sliding my key card through the door reader to one of the suites the hotel is letting me use for the night in return for organizing the event, on top of my fee. I strip out of my business casual attire and toss it onto the hotel's California king bed, then trudge to the bathroom to get ready for the event. I scroll through my social media as I wait for the shower to warm up, but I'm not really paying any attention, it's just something for my hands to do.

My mind keeps racing back to Rhys standing at the hotel bar, all six-foot-three of him: broad shoulders, muscular arms, beautiful icy blue eyes, and shaggy black hair. His new beard, which looks annoyingly handsome and suits him perfectly, making his gorgeous face somehow more gorgeous. And the way he was glaring down the bartender, Dante. Excitement coils in my stomach, as though he was a little jealous.

The water is finally warm enough and steam starts to loop and swirl around me, fogging up the mirror. I set my phone down on the counter and step into the beautiful charcoal-tiled walk-in shower. It's a long and narrow alcove that's half wall, half window, with an opening near the end. The irregular tiles on the floor feel bumpy, yet smooth, underneath my feet.

I step into the stream of scalding water and let it run over me until little patches of red, raw skin are speckling my body. My fingers run through my wet hair and tiny strands get stuck underneath my acrylic nails as I scrub and lather my shampoo. Something in my gut twists, and I think I'm going to vomit again when I feel saliva pool in my mouth and burning creep up my esophagus, but it subsides. A rumble from my belly travels up instead, and I let out a small belch. Phew, just a burp.

My nerves have got me going haywire tonight. *I know it seemed like Rhys was friendly with Dante, but there's no way he'll show up tonight, right?* I turn off the shower and finish getting ready, drying and straightening my raven hair, then twisting two small plaits on each side of my temple into a half-updo. I put a little more sparkle into my makeup, just in case a certain someone shows up. A honey-yellow eyeshadow dusts the inner corners of my eyes as it blends outward into a darker earthy brown, topped off with a perfect swoop of eyeliner any makeup artist would be proud of. Just the right combination of colours to make my chocolatey eyes pop.

Rhys is going to wish he never dumped me if he shows up tonight. I slip on a black, shimmery cocktail dress that plunges deep, almost revealing my belly button. Peeking into the mirror, I swipe some cherry-red gloss across my lips. I slide my feet into my red slingback Louis Vuitton heels, pump one foot up in the air, and shoot a finger gun at my reflection in the mirror. I wink, trying to psyche myself up for the evening, then head downstairs.

Garland and twinkling lights are strung across the room, soft jazz Christmas music plays softly in the background, and festive smells of cinnamon and spice float in the air. I fiddle with and tweak all the decorations, making sure everything is lined up perfectly, before the first guests arrive. I glance over to the bar and catch Dante's eyes trailing down the length of my body, only stopping to appreciate the curves that are on display.

A giddy prickle of excitement flutters in my stomach as my face warms. I have to divert my attention, so I saunter over to the dessert table and rearrange a few things to make myself look busy. A shadow towers over me a moment later and a metallic, earthy scent envelops me. There's a soft clink and a martini with a lemon twist is placed on the dessert table. A low, silky grumble purrs in my ear, making the hairs on my neck rise.

"For all your hard work today." His Aussie voice rumbles in my ear, tickling every nerve in my body. A shiver rolls down my spine, and my mouth tugs into a smile. Rolling my shoulders back, I straighten my posture before turning to face Dante. I wrestle with my lungs to keep a steady stream of air flowing. I widen my smile to show a little teeth, running my tongue along the bottom of my front teeth as I take him in through lowered lashes.

Strong, defined cheekbones frame his face, sitting above hollow cheeks. Pouty, full lips pop from his face, and dimples dot the corners of his mouth when he smiles wide. His tousled chestnut hair brushes against the ridge of his ears and sweeps across his eyebrows when he moves. His eyes are a piercing amber with small, dark flecks of deeper brown woven around the pupil.

Tonight, he just might be the perfect distraction from Rhys.

CHAPTER
TWENTY-SEVEN

ELISSA

The soft murmur and flickering light of the living room television greets me when I enter my apartment. A thrumming in my pulse begins and my heart slides into my stomach. I slip out of my heels and wedge them between my fingers as I tiptoe down the hallway. A mess of brown curly hair peeks out from the arm of the couch, accompanied by gentle snoring. Will's eyelids flutter as he dreams, keeping a constant sliver of them open so I can see flashes of his brown eyes rolling around.

My heart sinks, knowing that I am about to hurt another great guy, but I can't let this *thing* linger anymore. Not with how things could have happened with Brandt.

There's just a pull with him I can't ignore. And I know he's with Lexi, but I can't keep things going with Will until I'm ready to admit I might have feelings for Brandt.

My chilly hand rests on Will's shoulder, giving it a slight jostle. His upper body raises and rolls and settles again, refusing to awaken from his slumber.

"Will," I say, shaking him more fervently. He snorts a breath in, then his eyes pop open and he jerks into an upright position. His eyes settle on me, a soft smile appears, and his shoulders relax as he reclines back.

"Hey, baby. Finally home?" His voice is gravelly with sleep. Anxiety grips my chest at the pet name, and a sinking guilt pulls me under. My hand waves at his hips, signalling for him to make some room, and he shifts over so I can perch my hip on the edge of the couch. He stretches upward, puckering his lips, but I don't move. Will's face twists. I bite my lip and lean forward to grab the remote from the coffee table and switch off the television.

Will pushes his body further upright and his eyes give me all his attention. My hands clasp together in my lap, my fingers picking away at my polish and cuticles.

"I-I don't know what I'm doing, so I'm just going to say it. Rip it off like a bandage," I say falteringly. Will's face darkens and his jaw pulses. "I need to end this. It's not working for me anymore, and it's not fair to you to keep stringing you along." Will scoffs, swinging his legs around me, then sitting up and planting his feet on the floor.

"This is because of him, isn't it?" Will growls. "I fucking knew there was something there. I fucking knew it." His hard eyes pin me down. My eyebrows pinch together, and I let my eyes soften while I pick at my thumb and chip off the paint.

"Regardless of whether this is because of Brandt or not, we both knew what this was. It was supposed to be easy; convenient. It hasn't been like that since I came back to Toronto, and I've let this go on for far too long. I should have ended it when I left London —" Will cuts me off.

"What the hell are you talking about? It is easy, fun, and convenient. I don't hound you about dates or spending time together. I make sure I'm available for when you want to fuck me." My eyes plead with him as my body heats up and my pulse races.

"It hasn't been fucking in weeks, Will. You've been *making love* to me, having me look you in the eyes. It's too much. And tonight, you insisted on having dinner with me when you knew I was working. You made me have Brandt bring Lexi, so it didn't look weird. But it was. It was weird. I just can't do this anymore; it's gotten too complicated."

Will's face falls and his jaw drops. His narrowed, beady eyes skewer me.

"*Complicated?* Complicated, really? You've gotta be fucking joking me. What's so complicated about our arrangement? So fucking what if I have feelings for you? Have I put that on you at all? No. I haven't mentioned it because I know you don't want that, not yet." Will shoots up and stomps over to the kitchen. He grasps the cupboard handles and rips them open, then tries to slam them shut. Unfortunately, his anger is thwarted by the soft-close mechanism of the doors. He's fuming — his shoulders are hunched, his chest is heaving, and his hands are curled into white-knuckled fists. He watches the stupid cupboards close softly, and doesn't continue his rant until they've shut.

"This isn't fucking complicated," he grumbles. His head jerks to face me, his eyes glinting darkly. He stalks over, jaw clenched, and steps in front of me, toe-to-toe. His fingers reach out to wrap around my jaw and then abruptly his grip tightens. He yanks me to my feet. I wince as my mouth pops open, and my heart's beating in my throat.

His eyes are devoid of any emotion. Will's arm snakes around my waist and squeezes, pushing the little oxygen I have left out of my lungs. I gasp for air when his lips crash against mine, sucking the air out of my mouth. His tongue forces its way past my lips, clashing against my tongue. When I struggle and try to pull my head away, his fingers dig into my jaw, opening my mouth wider. He kisses me harder. He retreats slowly, biting down on my lips until I taste metal. He pulls away, but not before his tongue swipes away some of the blood dribbling from my lip.

"This wasn't complicated. You are." He jerks my head away from him, releasing my jaw, and I fall to the couch. He scrambles to grab his wallet, phone, and keys off the table and shoves them deep into his pockets. "Fuck you, Elissa," he growls, as he walks down the hallway and slams the apartment door shut.

A soft click echoes through the apartment and a shuffle of feet grows louder.

"E? Is everything okay?"

My focus is in front of me as I stare blankly at the dark television screen, sobbing inside. The cushions of the couch depress, and a soft, warm arm embraces me. A featherlight touch tickles my cheek, wiping away something wet. I realize there are silent tears streaming down my face.

"Oh, honey," Riley whispers. She reaches forward, grabs a tissue from the coffee table, and sits back, cradling me in her arms as I sob. She presses the tissue to my bleeding lip and then presses her lips to my forehead. I bury my face in her chest, inhaling her coconut body wash, as my body grows as cold as the freezing December air outside.

● ● ●

The morning sun pours into my room and warms my face. I crack my eyes open, and the lids drag against my eyeballs. My eyes feel dry and swollen. Puffy little rims obscure some of my vision. I try to roll over onto my other side, and I bump into something. A tiny body shuffles, spinning on her side to face me. A small smile breaks across her sleepy face. I return the smile and wince. My jaw is still sore from last night. Lifting weak fingers to my face, I rub my tender jaw. Sadness, and what seems like pity, scrawls across Riley's face.

"Morning. How'd you sleep?" she asks. A soft, noncommittal groan rumbles in my throat. Riley's small, nimble hand reaches out for my jaw and strokes it. "You're bruising where he grabbed you. Does it hurt?" Tears spring to her eyes.

"Yeah, it hurts a little. It mostly feels fatigued. It's sore when I talk," I say, both of us growing quiet. A few moments later, I speak again. "Think you can help me with makeup today? I have to go into the office." Riley's face tries to smile through the sadness, but her eyes just don't light up and her smile is weak.

"Anything for you, E."

A long sigh escapes me, and it feels like thirty pounds have been lifted off my chest. I tumble out of bed and my feet drag along the hardwood floor toward the washroom. I close the door with a soft click and make my way to the mirror. Tears build in my eyes as I look at my reflection. Twisting my face back and forth, my heart stops as I see the bruises running along my jawline.

Deep plum purples, murky, angry reds, and cold, dark blues in finger outlines mar my face. Embarrassment, shame, and sadness sting my nose and eyes, and I try with all my might to hold back the tears that are fighting to escape. When I can finally no longer look at my depressing reflection, I turn away from the mirror and drag myself over to the shower to get ready for the day.

CHAPTER
TWENTY-EIGHT

ELISSA

I'm perched on a stool at the kitchen island with Riley's ring light beaming into my eyes. She's standing in front of me, shuffling her weight between her feet, looking at my face from all angles. The marble island is scattered with makeup products and lotions. Her teeth are sunk into her tongue, which is poking out from between her lips as her eyes squint in thought. Her hands hover over the mess of makeup as she decides what to start with first.

"I guess the best thing to do first is colour correct the bruises," Riley mutters to herself. She holds up two concealer palettes close to her face, deciding which one will be a closer match. She finally settles on the palette she is going to use, tosses the other onto the counter, and grabs a small fluffy brush. Riley swirls the brush in the creamy tones, blending them together on the back of her hand before applying them to my face. She stipples the brush in light, swift motions, backing off the pressure to ensure she doesn't irritate the bruises.

One hour later and I'm caked in makeup, but Riley did such a great job it'd be hard to tell that I'm covered in bruises. She even made the rest of my makeup more fancy than usual to distract from my jawline. I look in the mirror, and staring back at me is the ghost of someone I once was. Someone who was vibrant, who wore fun, flirty makeup. But that person is no longer here. She vanished last summer and hasn't been seen since. I decide not to stare at myself for too long in fear the mirror or my façade might crack.

Tugging my dresser drawers open, I find some dark-wash American Eagle jeans and the denim scrapes on my skin as I pull them over my muscular, toned legs. I find a soft coral long-sleeved t-shirt and the delicate scent of lavender fabric softener tickles my nose as I slide the shirt on over my head. The top's deep v-neck shows the crests of my cleavage in a tasteful, flirty way. There's a small gap between the hem of my shirt and the waistband of my jeans, revealing a small patch of creamy white skin that's in some serious need of sun. I give myself a quick once-over, check in with Riley to make sure my makeup is still fine, and head out the door to work.

• • •

The fresh winter air bites at my nose as I trudge to work in the sub-zero world. Tiny piles of snow line each side of the sidewalk; my shoes are crunching over the salt as I walk to work. I zip my jacket up further so it's resting against my lips, and I secure my woolly scarf around my neck and tug it up to my nose. Clouds of warm breath worm their way out of the scarf.

The office is only a short twenty-minute walk, but this morning it feels longer. This morning, it feels like agony. My stomach knots and twists, worrying about the makeup on my jaw and if the scarf is rubbing it off. A small puddle of anxiety bubbles inside me. Hopefully, Brandt and I don't need to work too closely today and can maintain a far enough distance away from each other.

I stomp into the lobby, ridding my boots of snow before slipping them off. I set my bag down on the floor and rummage through it to grab the pair of low-top black Converse sneakers I stowed inside. My boots are still slushy, so I give them a good whack on the floor before walking toward the elevator, nodding a hello to the security guard as I pass by. The hum of the elevator fills the empty lobby. While I wait for the elevator to open, my mind drifts to the last moment I was here, in this building, and felt a slice of happiness.

Hundreds of people were crowded into the lobby, mingling, laughing, and dancing under the twinkly lights; I was even one of them for the briefest of moments. A powerful hand supported my lower back while another grasped my hand, leading me around the dance floor. Our chests were close together, we could feel each other's heartbeats. My arm threaded around his neck and my hand slipped up the back of his neck into his hair. An easy smile crept across my face and when his eyes locked onto mine, all he saw was me. All I saw was him. The world melted away in a blur of colours and shapes until we were in a space of our own.

Ding!

The elevator doors grind open, and I'm shaken from my reverie. I step into the elevator and hit the button for the twenty-second level. On the ride up to my office level, as the elevator climbs higher, so do my nerves. My heartbeat quickens and travels up my throat as I near my stop. With everything that transpired last night, I'm not sure if I'm ready to face Brandt. I'm praying like hell that it's not awkward when another ding sounds and the doors slide open.

The corridor is eerily quiet, and the lights are off. The only light comes from the grey sky that shimmers through the windows and a light flooding from under the door in Brandt's office. He beat me here. As I approach his office, I hear a strange, strangled sound. It almost sounds like he's having…*sex?*

My hands fly to my mouth to cover my breathing, my eyes widen and bulge from my skull, and I take careful steps backward to minimize any sound. I hurry to my office, making my legs take me as fast as they can, making no noise, and slip through my door and close it. My body slouches against the door as I try to catch my breath. Pushing myself off the door, I strip out of my scarf, jacket, and toque and stuff them into the arm of my jacket, then hang it up on the coat rack beside my door.

A singular knock raps on my door, and I freeze. My heart stops, and it feels like my air supply is cut off. A deep red flush rushes to my face, burning every inch of skin as it travels along my chest, up my neck, and to the tips of my ears.

"Y-yes?" I try to say in a cool, unfazed tone. A cough rumbles behind the door and my heart throbs as the door handle turns.

"Oh, you are here," Brandt says as the door finally opens. His face seems to be as red as mine. His usually neat golden-brown locks are dishevelled, as though fingers had woven their way through his hair many times. I know it shouldn't matter that he was fucking at work. We used to do it all the time. But hearing him do it with someone else is just…weird. "I, uh, didn't expect you to be here so early."

He fiddles with the tie that's looped around his neck. Even on a Saturday when no one else is here, he's still dressed up. I chuckle to myself.

"Yep, I'm here. Give me a half-hour to an hour to get settled in and we can meet in the conference room," I say, avoiding his eyes and spinning on my heel to saunter to my desk. He mumbles out "Okay" and leaves my office, closing the door as he goes. I brush the hair out of my face, roll my neck, and take a deep breath.

"This is going to be another long, awkward day," I mutter to myself.

CHAPTER
TWENTY-NINE

ELISSA

The next few hours fly by. I avoid talking to Brandt whenever I can after hearing him doing God-knows-what with Lexi. Which is just as well, because after the incident, he started acting cold and strange. He was like an icy pillar, and for now, that is okay with me. I don't want to think about him and Lexi because when I do, a brief pang ripples in my heart.

Since last night, and after calling it quits with Will, I've finally realized that I just might have feelings for Brandt. I'm not sure if those are romantic, gooey, love feelings, or just the kind that simmer in your belly, creating heaps of desire. I'm almost positive it's partly the latter, because the attraction between us is gravity-defying. But I don't know what that means for me. All I know is that I needed to cut Will loose so I could find out what these feelings mean to me. And thank God I did, since Will seems to be maybe more fucked up than me.

Thinking about Will makes the lunch in my stomach curdle. My hand finds its way to my jaw and caresses it as I stare out my office window, looking at the flurries of snow passing by. The sky is a gloomy grey, but the sun is attempting to shine through the wall of clouds. When Riley was doing my makeup this morning, she gently suggested pressing charges, but what for? I'll likely never see Will again, and, knowing my father, he'll just make it disappear, not caring if it's for my benefit. My hand presses a little too hard against a bruise and I wince in pain.

"Are you okay?" Brandt's chilly voice booms. My body goes ramrod-straight, and a small blush creeps onto my face. I twirl around and paste a grateful smile on my face. Brandt's face contorts and hardens.

"Yep, all good. Just accidentally, uh, bit my tongue." Brandt's eyes study me, feigning indifference. I fidget under his judgemental stare, shifting my weight in my chair. I cock my eyebrows at him. "Yes?" I ask in a haughty tone. Brandt's eyes ice over.

"Just wanted to let you know that today is my last day in the office until after Christmas. I need to spend some time at Collins Global before the end of the year, so if you need anything, just have Lori or yourself text or email me." I stand there with my mouth a little agape, a bit shocked at this announcement. For a while there, I totally forgot he was only supposed to be an investor and not work here full-time. I must have really screwed him over when I left because all he does is work at Black & Wells. Well, hell.

"Oh, all right. Well, have a wonderful holiday," I say in a soft, understanding tone. "And tell Lexi I say hi and merry Christmas." I allow a genuine smile to play on my lips, although my heart aches at Lexi's name.

"Uh, yeah. Have a great Christmas as well. And my best to Will." My eyes widen and I have to clamp my mouth shut before I accidentally say anything. He doesn't need to know about Will, especially right before the holidays. It can wait.

"Right. Thanks," I say. His head dips, and the right corner of his mouth isn't as high as it usually is when he smiles. Tingles break out all over my body because every inch of me wants to touch him, wants to feel him, wants to be wrapped in his arms again. Instead of telling him this, I offer a small wave to him, and he disappears from my office. A tiny piece of my heart cracks as he walks away. I bury my head in my hands and stomp my feet under my desk, willing this day to finish.

• • •

A couple of days later, Riley is practically bouncing off the walls, jumping from one spot to another, rushing from my bed to the closet and repacking the things I put in my suitcase.

"Riles, I need you to stop. I would like to finish packing within the next hour so we can leave." Riley's nose wrinkles and her lip curls as she crosses her arms.

"Just because you're staying at my parents' and Lana's over Christmas break doesn't mean you can't look good while doing it. You never know who you'll run into in our hometown."

My shoulders deflate as I realize she's right. Chatham is a small city with about 105,000 people, give or take. It's not like Toronto, where the likelihood of you running into your high school boyfriend is slim. You're bound to see at least one person you know while you're out in Chatham. I groan and spread my arms wide, letting Riley take the lead with my packing.

She rushes back and forth and tosses some super skinny jeans, a few revealing tank tops, some cozies for home, and a few cocktail dresses into my suitcase. I'm not sure what she has planned, but there's a sparkle in her eye that we're going to get into it this week. She's almost finished packing my suitcase when she rushes into the washroom and comes back out a moment later, her arms loaded with bottles and makeup.

The bruises on my jaw still haven't faded yet, so I'll have to apply makeup while I'm away. Truth be told, I was almost too excited to stay in the apartment all week, with nothing on my face and in my pajamas, celebrating Christmas alone. But when Riley heard that, she called up Lana and they ganged up on me to have me stay with their families over the holidays. So, here I am, letting Riley pack for me.

I pull my car around from the underground parking garage and we load up the car with a mountain of gifts and our luggage. I'm sitting down in my seat, about to buckle up, when my phone buzzes. I read the text out to Riley.

Mommy Dearest: *Hello. Thought it would be nice of you to drop by this year and bring your wonderful boyfriend, Will. Your father is looking forward to seeing him again, and I can't wait to meet him.*

Smoke pours from my ears as I read the text message. It takes everything I have not to snap the damn phone in half. Riley's face is full of worry, her eyebrows are pursed together, and her mouth is ajar.

"It's fine. It's fine." I reassure, though I'm not who I'm reassuring — her or me.

Me: *Sorry, can't make it this year. See you in the new year.*

"Ouch, could have said 'Merry Christmas' or something, at least," Riley says. My eyes burn into her face, and she lets out a boisterous giggle. "Just kidding, E. Put this thing in gear and let's peace the fuck out."

CHAPTER
THIRTY

BRANDT

Settling back into my office at Collins Global Collective was strange. My familiar sturdy dark oak cabinetry and desk that I once carefully picked out now feel alien to me. It had been nearly eight months since I'd set foot in my office. I knew going into this deal with Harold was going to take a lot of my time away from my company, but when Elissa fled, I was left with my investment hanging in the balance.

Rhys has stepped up over the last four months, and I couldn't have asked for a better CFO. I know he's been struggling with running the company, but I think he's done a great job. I survey my office and it feels like coming home, but something is missing. The large windows still overlook the Toronto Harbour. My small knickknacks, like pictures of my family, tokens of hard work, and memorabilia, are still proudly displayed and unmoved. Thin coats of dust blanket everything, as if the company cleaners forgot about the CEO's office.

The only thing that has changed is my desk — more specifically, the mountain of paperwork piled on top of it. I groan, wiggle my tie loose, shed my sport coat, and cuff my sleeves to the crook of my elbow. The office chair whirls on the low-pile carpet, and I drop into the chair. It makes a creaking sound, as though it needs to be oiled. I heave a reluctant sigh as I dig into the papers, charts, and files left on my desk.

Trying to focus on the tasks at hand is difficult, though. My mind keeps playing on Elissa's face and her demeanor at our last exchange. I thought it might have been because she almost caught me jerking it in the office, trying to offset the sexual tension between us. But something seemed more off with her, like she was more closed-off than normal. And for her to be all dolled up like that on a Saturday is weird. The way her eyes fell for the briefest of moments when I told her I was leaving for a week to focus on CGC, well… to say it broke something inside me is an understatement.

In that moment, the overwhelming need to reach out and hold her in a crushing embrace was almost too strong to avoid. I had to get out of there. Her being back has only made things more confusing for me, and the other night when we worked late, things felt like they used to. This time around, though, it's dangerous. Dangerous for the progress I've made, or at least, the progress I think I've made. But just one longing look from her, with the sparkle of lust in her eyes, and my resolve comes undone. I almost gave in. I almost tumbled into the abyss that is Elissa's hold on me, and I would have gladly gone tumbling headfirst into the darkness and let her swallow me up whole.

I have a lot of pride, but when it comes to Elissa, it's like all my inhibitions just disappear. The hold that fiery redhead has over me.… *Sigh.* Thankfully, we're both with other people. That's the only thing that stopped me, the thought of Lexi and her being patient with me. But I can't deny what's right in front of me. She'll never be Elissa, and I can't drag this out anymore. It's not fair to her. If it's not going to be Elissa, that's fine. But I have to acknowledge that there's just not much of a spark with Lexi. Sure, she's beautiful, athletic, and nice, but it's just not right.

I grab my phone off my desk and message Lexi.

Me: *Hey Lexi. You busy tonight? Want me to bring over dinner?*
Lexi: *Omg, yessss. It's gonna be a long day at work. I have like five classes back-to-back, so I'll be starved by the time I'm done work. That sounds perf. Sushi?*
Me: *Sure. Sounds good. See you at six?*
Lexi: *Okay! :) *kiss emoji**

I groan, dreading later tonight when I'll have to break things off with her.

I put my phone in my pocket to minimize my distractions and get back to the task at hand so I can hopefully leave here at a decent time. I shuffle through the papers, finding the oldest documents to start reconciling and filing, when I notice Rhys is leaning against my doorframe out of the corner of my eye. A melody of metallic knocks rings through my office. I crease my brows and look up at Rhys through heavy-lidded eyes.

"What's up?"

"So, you're finally back?"

"Well, I'm not a hologram. We haven't perfected that technology yet." My sarcasm falls flat and Rhys doesn't look impressed. "I'm back for the week," I sigh. "After Christmas I need to be back at Black & Wells. Hopefully soon I can relinquish some of my control there and be back here more permanently."

Rhys' face falls, his eyes losing any optimism. "So, you're not coming back yet? Why? Elissa is back. You can leave now. Let her fucking figure it out. I'm drowning here, man." Rhys' face burns red, his eyes full of fury. "I've been doing this alone for four months. Enough is enough. It's because she's back, right? The reason you're staying is because of her. I thought you were with Lexi?" His narrowed eyes pin me down.

A slow, rolling swallow of my Adam's apple is all the confirmation he needs. "You're breaking up with Lexi? For Elissa? You've got to be fucking joking me." His hands cup his face and scrub up and down, then he shakes his head and groans. "So, you and Elissa are getting back together?"

I shift nervously in my chair.

"Not…exactly."

Rhys' hands drop from his blanched face, irritation blooming, seeping across his face.

"What do you mean 'not exactly'?" Rhys' words are heavy with frustration. "I mean, I know you weren't exactly *together*, but you were fucking, exclusively. If that's not exactly what you mean, then what?" He folds his arms, his biceps ready to bust out of the arms of his dress shirt; the veins in his hands are pumping.

"I mean that I'm breaking things off with Lexi tonight because she's not Elissa."

"Well, no fucking shit!" Rhys bellows. He throws his hands into the air. "Isn't that the point — that she's not Elissa?"

"No. The point is because she is not Elissa; I can't continue the relationship. I won't feel anything close to what I feel for Elissa, so it makes little sense to drag this on." Rhys rolls his eyes and scoffs.

"Man, you know I support your decisions, but this is just fucked. I can't believe you're letting the idea of someone you fucked get under your skin and ruin a possibly good relationship." I drown Rhys out while he rants on about my decision. I know part of him is right, but come on. My irritation over him belittling my choice and degrading Elissa bubbles in my gut. A rumbling of sorts slowly builds pressure inside me. "You've gotta move on, man. Seriously. Do you really think you have a real chance with her?" Something inside me suddenly snaps.

I launch to my feet. My chair flies backward and clangs off the window. Rhys flinches and I momentarily worry that I've broken the window. The rage that was bubbling has exploded within me.

"Enough," I growl. I keep my tone level and calm but my eyes narrow, skewering him, waiting for him to say another negative thing. "I am only doing the right thing by Lexi. Instead of giving her false hope of this turning into something more, I'm doing the right thing." I am doing the right thing, right? I may have a lot less experience in relationships than Rhys, but I know this has got to be the right thing to do. No one wants to be strung along.

"Yeah, but the fact that you're doing this for Elissa is ridiculous. She's with someone else. Giving him what she couldn't give you. Yet, here you are, still pining for her when you have a smokin' girl that's totally into you."

"You just don't understand. There was a moment last week…" Rhys stares at me with bored eyes.

"A moment? Are you a fucking chick?"

"Yeah. The night we were working late to finish up the reports. There was a moment — actually, there were a few moments — where I think she would have kissed me, but I was the one who pulled away. I can't explain it, Rhys. But there's just something magnetic between us."

"Yeah — or you just have a problem and need to let this fantasy go."

"I wish I could," I say with a sigh.

• • •

I arrive at my apartment building with the sushi and sweat beads on my brow. Even though it's the dead of winter, I'm sweating buckets. A knot squeezes in my stomach. I'd much rather address this conversation by text message like I did with Selena, but Lexi deserves something more. My jaw clenches and I draw a breath in, steadying my nerves. Chicken shit.

Lexi's apartment is only a few floors down from mine, so it's a shorter elevator ride to her floor. When I get to her door, it swings open, like she was standing there waiting for me to arrive. My heart stutters in my chest, and anxiety roils in my stomach.

"Hey baby," she purrs, looping her arms around my neck and placing a soft kiss on my lips. When her arms release me, her hands trail down my chest, and I step around her and kick off my shoes. I stroll toward her kitchen and place the brown delivery bag on the counter. As I open the cupboard above my head Lexi reaches in front of me, her breasts rubbing against my bicep. She grabs two plates. "Thanks for dinner," she says, her voice low and seductive. Bile travels up my throat and I've suddenly lost my appetite.

"You're welcome," I muster up in reply. Silence falls around us, and only the clinking of dinnerware fills the room. Once we've loaded our plates with food, we both take seats at the island, crack our chopsticks open, and dive in. We eat in awkward silence. It's like she knows what's coming, or maybe I'm just projecting my anxiety.

"How was work?" she asks gently.

"It was good. It's nice to finally be back at Collins Global Collective," I say. Her body and face perk up and her eyes fill with happiness.

"Oh, so you've left Black & Wells?" she asks enthusiastically. Her eyes find mine, searching for the answer she's hoping to hear. Her eyes grow dim when I hesitate, draining the glimmer of happiness she had.

"Not exactly. I'm just spending the last week of the year at CGC catching up on stuff before the new year starts. After that, I've got to be back at Black & Wells for at least a few more weeks."

"Oh," Lexi says in a small voice.

CHAPTER
THIRTY-ONE

BRANDT

Lexi continues to eat in silence. My heartbeat is galloping in my ears, and I suppress the shiver that's threatening to run down my spine. I place my chopsticks aside and turn to face her. Her shoulders slump and her head dips between her shoulders.

"Please," she whispers. "Just let me finish dinner before you dump me." My heart sinks in my chest, and I feel like a fly on a log of shit. A gurgle of guilt bubbles in my stomach, and I squirm on my stool, trying to find a more comfortable position, because it feels like there's a Bunsen burner under my ass.

"How did you know?" I ask. She sighs, picking at her spicy tuna roll with her chopsticks, pushing it around on her plate.

"I could tell from how Elissa looks at you, and how you look at her. When I came for dinner the other night at your work. I just…anyone can see it in how you look at her. I don't know what has happened between you two, but it's clear you want each other."

My mouth opens, but nothing comes out. I'm stunned. Lexi shakes her head, and the hair bundled at the top of her head wobbles. "It's okay. I...I appreciate you being honest with me. It sucks, but I want you to be happy." Her words are shaky and heavy with sadness, and it makes me feel all the more guilty. I wish she'd be mad or throw a fit — something, anything, just more of a reaction to justify the situation. But no, she chooses to be humble. Something must be seriously wrong with my brain if I can't choose her. I wish with everything I have that it could be her.

"I'm sorry, Lexi." I finally gather enough courage to speak. "I didn't mean to hurt you in any way. You're amazing, but Elissa just has this hold on me, and I thought I could let it go."

"Well, I hope you two are happy together, honestly."

I groan, my lips press into a thin line, and I straighten my posture as I turn back to my food, picking up my chopsticks.

"Yeah, I don't think so. She's still with Will." I see Lexi's body tense out of the corner of my eye, and she drops her chopsticks.

"Wait, you're ending this, and you're not even ending up with Elissa?" A hint of bitterness flavours her words. Her face reddens and her eyebrows pinch together, pulling her eyes into a squint. The room feels like it lost ten degrees as goosebumps pebble my skin.

"I know it may not seem to make sense, but I'm trying to be a good guy here. I didn't want to drag this on, letting you think this was going to be something serious when I don't feel that way for you. It's all platonic what I feel for you. Sure, you're beautiful and kind, and maybe we could have had a decent relationship, but there's no passion there for me. I didn't want to waste your time or mine."

Lexi's face turns a darker shade of red, but I think it's from embarrassment or humiliation, rather than anger. Her shoulders slump again, and her eyes brim with tears as she steps down off her stool, making her about a foot shorter. She rests her hand on mine, leans in, and places a delicate, soulful kiss on my lips; her falling tears dotting my cheeks. Our lips part, and her eyes dive into mine to hold my gaze for a moment. A sad smile flickers on her face. She squeezes my hand, spins on her heel, and walks toward her bedroom. When she reaches the threshold, she places a hand on the doorframe and turns her head to look at the doorframe instead of me.

"Goodbye, Brandt. I'll see you around," she says in a hushed tone; so quiet I almost missed what she said. She shuffles her feet into her room and closes the door. Something bumps against the door and a sliding, scratching noise drags down to the bottom of the door. A muffled sob breaks the tension and my heart aches for her. I slide off the stool, my quiet footsteps creaking on the wood underneath as I make my way to the door, grab my shoes, and leave her apartment for the last time.

• • •

Later that week, I lie in bed. The rough and bumpy textures of the drywall mud on my ceiling create these loopy, swirly, swoopy patterns — no doubt a quick way for a contractor to make it look fancier than it is. I study the patterns above me to keep my mind off of Lexi and her small, wavering voice and sodden, red eyes. My fingers thrum against my chest as I lie in bed, staring up at those loops and swirls, wondering if I actually did the right thing. Maybe Rhys and Lexi are right. Did I dump Lexi prematurely for someone who more than likely still doesn't want me? Who may never want me?

I kick the blankets off and a cascade of dark blue satin sheets flutter into the air. I stalk over to my dresser. I rip open one of the sleek black drawers and grab some gym shorts and a sleeveless tee and shove them into my Under Armour gym bag. Grabbing a pair of dark jeans from my hamper, I step into them before grabbing another t-shirt from my dresser and pulling it over my head. I sling the gym bag over my shoulder and make my way to the foyer of my apartment to grab my keys and coat, then head to the gym to work off this uncertainty.

The icy air hits my face as I step outside of the building and into the snow-globe world. Tiny, fluffy flakes flutter and dance around the sky as they fall to the ground. My feet crunch in the snow as I walk. I already regret the choice to walk, but I continue onward as I decide it's better to go out to the gym instead of using my building's facilities. Staying away and avoiding Lexi for the time being is probably the best thing for her right now.

God, I feel like a dick. Is this how every "relationship" feels when it ends, or is it just when you're the dumper? Rhys didn't seem at all phased when he dumped Riley. But then again, this is the first relationship where I've had the dumping responsibilities. I just can't get those sad blue eyes out of my head; they're haunting me.

I finally reach the gym and I'm stomping my feet as I enter the building. It seems a little dead for 11 PM. Usually there's a few more lost souls in the gym this late at night. I make my way to the changeroom, put my stuff away, and get changed. On the way out of the changeroom, I'm digging my headphones into my ears and selecting a playlist when someone bumps into me, and a flurry of copper hair briefly obscures my vision as the other person falls to the ground.

CHAPTER
THIRTY-TWO

ELISSA

It's only been one day back from the holidays and without Brandt at the office, it feels…quiet. Most people are still off for the break between the 27th and New Year's Day, but with everything going on with the new department, me and a few staff are here. I guess it was always the assistants who chatted with him, and his low, gravelly voice that made the office lively. I will admit that it's nice being at the office without all the tension between us. I can never tell just what he's thinking. One minute he's cold and distant, and the next? There's this look in his eyes that seems…I don't know, like longing. I must be crazy, hormonal, or projecting what I'm feeling, because he and Lexi seem solid and happy. Which is…good. Good for him.

Lori's voice crackles through the intercom on my desk.

"Your father is here to see you," her voice squeaks over the line. I press the button down and let her know to let him in.

My father strolls into the room, his hands deep in his pockets. He's wearing a blue Ralph Lauren dress shirt with khaki pants and a matching sport coat. His top few buttons are popped, showing a smatter of salt-and-pepper chest hair, and a small gold chain is wrapped around his neck, glistening under the fluorescent lights. He looks like a wannabe mobster. His medium-length black hair, greying at the temples, is slicked back, but the ends curl near the nape of his neck.

He stands in the centre of the room and twists to look around. A hand slithers out of his pocket and up to his face where it rests, stroking his thick moustache.

"Still in this tiny, dumpy office? Not fitting for the heiress of the company, let alone the department head," he grunts, a twisted smile stretching under his moustache. "When are you moving back to a larger, more respectable office? I can't bear to sit in this drab room and talk to you."

"I'm surprised you're even willing to talk to me, period." I shoot my words back in rapid fire. His eyes roll and then narrow, shrinking me in my chair until I'm about two feet tall.

"Stop with the dramatics, child. I spoke to Will this morning. Apparently, you two split?" I wriggle in my chair, tuck a loose strand of hair behind my ear, and look away from my father. A ghostly throbbing aches in my jaw and I resist the urge to rub it. The bruises are almost healed, like nothing ever happened, and my mind wishes that I could make it so *he* never happened. I sigh.

"I don't see how any of my relationships are your problem."

"That's just it, Elissa. They are my problem when they interfere with the company. You knew Will was going to be one of our newly acquired authors. He called me last night and pulled his manuscript from us because he thought there was going to be a conflict of interest." My father crosses his arms and his stare burns into me, but his arms don't stay crossed for long, as his right hand pops back up and strokes his moustache. I shiver.

"I don't see your point. So he pulled his book? We have other options. Hell, there are many more talented people who have submitted to us. We don't need Will."

My father's teeth crunch as he grinds them, clenching his jaw hard. He drops his arms, and his hands grasp the backrest of one of the plush, rose gold chairs in front of my desk. He squeezes until his knuckles blanch.

"I don't care what it takes. You will get Will back on board. Whether that means falling into bed with him again or falling to your knees begging for forgiveness. I thought Brandt would be good for you, but then you go and fuck that up like a selfish little child —" I cut him off.

"Selfish? You announced to everyone that we were en-gaged — in public — without my consent or Brandt's! I think I had every right to fucking flee and get away from you and your toxic bullshit." Harold sneers and rolls his eyes.

"You act like Brandt was a terrible match, a terrible guy. I didn't see the problem, since you two were fucking any-way," he growls.

"Fucking and marriage are two different things. Two different levels of commitment."

"Like you would know about commitment. You can't stay with anything or anyone longer than a few seconds. I thought Brandt might actually help change you and your slutty ways. He was all for it…" His voice trails off. His nose twitches and his fingers relax, then tense again on the back of the chair.

"W-what? What do you mean? Did he fucking know about the engagement? Or did you put him up to fucking me?"

A smirk sprawls across my father's face. The corner of his mouth twitches, like he's holding back laughter.

"Yes and no. I didn't tell him to fuck you. I may have suggested he seduce you into a relationship, which would lead to marriage. He seemed very enthusiastic about it. Why do you think he was at your graduation? He wanted to meet his prospective bride as part of the contract deal with the merger."

My heart sinks in my chest, cracking and breaking on its way down. So, everything with Brandt was just some big scheme? A fucking contract? My vision clouds red, only to be washed away by the rising tide of tears. I bite back the emotions brewing in me and my gaze snaps to my father's eyes. Laughter bounces behind his stare, mocking me. My nose burns as I hold back my tears, and my cheeks pulse as I clench my teeth together.

I take a deep, steadying breath and say, "Is that all, Father? If so, you may leave now. I will reach out to Will and see what I can do." I lift my trembling hand and wave him out of my office. His face hardens as a vein rises in his forehead and his eyes narrow. He stares at me, challenging me to blink first, but when I don't back down, a creeping smile tugs at his lips. He turns around and heads for the door.

"Make sure that you do. See you in the new year," he says darkly.

When my father is finally out of eyesight, I release a breath I didn't know I was holding. I push myself away from my desk, knocking some papers fluttering to the ground. I walk toward the door and slam it shut. No longer able to hold back the flood of tears, I collapse under the pressure, letting everything I've bottled up over the years out.

Slumping against the door, I slide down to the ground and plop down on my ass. I kick off my heels and pull my knees to my chest, toes pointing inward. I bury my face in my hands and sit and sob for God only knows how long.

• • •

I've finally reined my emotions in and cried literally all the water out of my body and am now dying of thirst. My eyes feel tight and dry, and when I pull myself into an upright position, I look myself in the mirror and see my eyes are puffy, red, and irritated. The redness makes my pretty blue eyes appear to be an even sharper blue because of the contrast. The irritation and puffiness kind of ruins the effect though.

My face is streaked with mascara and my nose is running. My sleeve is damp with snot from using it to wipe my nose. A light knock on my door triggers me to stand up, snort back all my snot and tears, clear my throat, and say, "Yes?"

Lori speaks in dulcet tones through the door.

"I'm heading out for the night, Ms. Black. I'll see you on the seventh." I wipe my eyes with my dry sleeve.

"Thank you, Lori. Have a good holiday. Enjoy the break." A few moments later, I hear the clicking of her heels fade. I look around my dark, lonely office and sigh. I grab my phone off my desk and stare out the window, watching the snow blow across the skyline, Christmas lights twinkling in the night. I scroll through my contacts and click Will's number. With the pounding of my heartbeat thudding in my chest and my ears, I almost miss him saying "Hello" when he answers on the first ring.

"To what do I owe the pleasure?" he says in a snarky, slimy tone. An invisible hand reaches into my throat and grabs hold of my tongue, rendering my voice useless and silent. "I guess your dad must have talked to you."

"Y-yes," I say, my tongue finally loosening. I shake off the nerves and steel myself for the conversation. "You've already signed a contract, Will. You can't withdraw your manuscript now. The deadline has passed, and it is already in production for the cover. I'm sorry, but there's nothing left to discuss on this matter. It seems my father wasn't aware of the status." Soft grinding noises leak through the line.

"I'll lawyer up and say I was coerced by Harold because he found out I was sleeping with you. Either way, I win and get to hurt you and the company."

I sigh as clarity hits me. What the hell did I see in this guy other than a warm body? He's just as slimy and weaselly as my father. I shudder at that thought.

"Fine, go ahead. You won't win, and we will bounce back from any legalities. You're well aware that we own most of the media and printing presses in Canada. There's not much that leaks about our family; my father makes sure of that. So, go ahead. Try to file your lawsuit. It will be fun crushing you in court. And I have photos from the night I dumped you, and Riley as a witness. I'm sure the court would be interested to see those as well." Some unintelligible muttering floats into my ear, followed by a groan.

"Fuck you, Elissa. And fuck your father and his company."

A small smile tugs at my lips.

"Great. I look forward to seeing the first few chapters in my inbox by New Year's Eve. Have a glorious holiday." Will shouts something about that being only days away when I hang up the phone. I tuck my phone into my pocket and drop my head into my hands, scrubbing my face and pulling at my eyes. A quiver in my chest stirs my emotions again, and I feel faint. I pack up my things for the night, flinging my bag over my shoulder and grabbing my gym bag from the armoire in the corner of my office.

On the way to the gym, I pull out my phone, pull my gloves off, and hold them with my teeth as I text Riley.

Me: *Fucking Harold and his fucking games. You'll never believe what happened tonight. Make sure there's a bottle of whiskey for me? Wine isn't going to cut it tonight. Going to the gym.*

I slide my phone back into my pocket with freezing

fingers and shove my hands into the fur-lined leather gloves. I blow my hot breath into my cupped hands to warm them up. As I near the gym, I start pumping myself up, trying to think about all the other priorities I have to accomplish in the next few days before the new year. I quickly sneak into the women's changeroom, get changed, lace my runners up, and strap my phone to my arm. As I place the AirPods in my ears, I make my way to the bank of treadmills.

CHAPTER

THIRTY-THREE

ELISSA

Beads of sweat are rolling down my face, chest, back, and thighs as I walk on wobbly legs to the changeroom. After three hours on the treadmill my legs are fatigued and sore, and my breathing is ragged. My cheeks puff as I try to draw in and breathe out measuredly to regulate my heart rate. I glance down at my phone to see a reply from Riley.

Riley: *I gotchu girl. *thumbs up emoji**

Underneath the text, Riley attached a picture of herself holding a giant bottle of whiskey and kissing it. I chuckle to myself and a warmth spreads over me as I think about how lucky I am to have a best friend like her.

As I near the changeroom, there's a slight charge to the air, but I barely notice the difference until I walk straight into a brick wall and fall to my ass.

"Oh, sorry, I —" A familiar grumbly voice says. Tiny hairs prick up on the back of my neck and goosebumps pebble my flesh. Tears immediately burn in my eyes and my nose wrinkles as I grind my teeth. "Elissa. I didn't see you there." Brandt's smooth, apologetic voice almost gets me.

I flash my eyes up at him, rage boiling in my veins. Clearly my anger is visible, because his face screws up in confusion at my reaction. He reaches out a hand to help me up, but I swat it away. "Don't fucking touch me," I growl at him. His hand drops to his side and he takes a small step back, worry and concern etched on his face.

"Sorry, I didn't mean to knock you over."

"Yeah, yeah. Just leave me alone," I mumble as I clamber to my feet. I brush past him, checking him with my shoulder as I go. An intense burn stings my back as I walk away, and I know that Brandt is watching me. I shudder as tears well up in my eyes, and I swipe at my sweaty face angrily and disappear into the changeroom.

• • •

Attempting to leave the gym took some serious planning. After I finished showering and getting changed, I had to peek my head out of the changeroom a few times to make sure the coast was clear. Finally, Brandt is nowhere to be seen along the path to the exit, so I double-check to make sure I have everything and speed out of there like a dog with his tail tucked between his legs. Just as I'm about to make it to the door, a giant hand clasps my shoulder, whirling me around. Dark green eyes freeze my feet to the floor, not allowing me to move.

Brandt towers over me. He stares down into my eyes, pleading for me to discuss what just happened. His expansive chest rises and falls like he just ran a marathon. My body reacts to his touch, which instantly softens my edges and harsh thoughts. Traitorous body. My eyes flutter closed as they roll back in my head and I take a deep breath, filling my lungs with the smell of sweat and rubber. Not exactly calming and grounding.

When I open my eyes again, Brandt has relaxed his expression. He lets his hand fall from my shoulder, and patiently waits for me to speak. I jiggle my legs and suck in my lower lip, then exhale and relent. "I'm not talking here, and Riley's home."

"My place is close by; we can go there." I bite down on my lip and look around the gym, anywhere but at Brandt. This is such a bad idea.

• • •

I never realized how close Brandt lives to me. He's only three city blocks away. That's practically nothing when it comes to downtown Toronto. In fact, I've never actually been to his place before, a thought that grips into me with sharp claws. We've only ever been alone at the office or my place. A fresh wave of anxiety washes over me, and I focus on my rage to push the anxiety away. You're angry at him; don't go soft on me now, E.

It's a long, silent, and awkward elevator ride up to his apartment. When the doors grind open, he steps off first and holds the doors open for me. I move past him, then let him take the lead again as I carefully take in the surroundings. His apartment complex has sleek black granite floors that are speckled with silver. Gold and black hourglass sconces line the walls every few feet, and the walls are a matte charcoal grey with intricate gold-foiled patterns of roses. Opulence drips down the walls, and it's unlike where I pictured Brandt living.

He throws a glance over his shoulder to make sure I'm still following behind him. I pick up my pace and fall into step with him. He slows as he reaches the end of the hall. I only counted two other units on this floor, so he must have one of the bigger units in the building, but not quite the penthouse. He keys in a code and the door mechanisms grind and slide open. He pushes against the heavy black door and lets me in first. I walk past him with careful footsteps as I enter into his lair.

My stomach sinks. This was a bad, bad idea. There's so much running through my mind. Like how good he looks, and how good he smells, and how infuriated I am with him for agreeing to manipulate me. I kick off my boots, a little harder than expected, and line them neatly against the wall near the door. My eyes wander around his place. It's a large, open-concept floor plan. His kitchen and living room are all one space, and floor-to-ceiling windows line the living space, giving an amazing panoramic view of downtown Toronto. His apartment carries the theme from the hallway: dark, sleek opulence. The cupboards are matte black with gold hardware, and the counters are a black quartz with silver veins.

The island is about eight feet long and wraps around to box in the fridge, which is also matte black. Eight gold stools with black leather cushions are spaced around the edge of the island. I shrug off my jacket and drape it on the cool stone. When Brandt walks past me and heads toward the living room, a gust of wintergreen and tree bark lingers in the air behind him; I catch myself savouring the smell. He stops to turn on the fireplace, then takes a seat on the couch, his arms draped over the back and legs spread open. He tips his head for me to join him.

My socked feet pad over to the living room and I notice a Christmas tree in the corner. It's not very tall, only about my height, and I suppress a smile, thinking about this tall behemoth of a man towering over his Christmas tree. When I reach the sitting area, I don't sit. Brandt gives me a questioning look.

"I don't want to sit. I need to stand if I'm going to yell or be angry." He tilts his head slightly and squints.

"I don't understand. What's there to be angry or yell about?" Brandt leans forward, his arms resting on his knees, making his arm muscles bulge. My teeth bite into my bottom lip as I stare at his bulky arms, so I spin around, facing toward the kitchen and draw a deep breath.

"I know the truth," I mumble.

"I'm sorry, what? I didn't catch that." His husky voice almost melts me to the core, dissolving my anger. I shake my head and amplify my voice a little louder.

"I said, I know the truth."

"The truth about..." he trails off, sounding convincingly confused. Anger seeps through my body, lighting every fuse. How can he play dumb? My breathing increases, forcing air into my lungs in fast gulps. My fingertips tingle and my fingers curl into a fist, my nails biting into my palm.

"The truth about the contract between you and my father!" I yell, spinning around. My eyes meet his and he's as white as the snow outside. His gaze wavers, like he's searching my eyes for something. "Well?" I prod. "What was it like? A buy-in to the company for sleeping with me, and what? Marriage was just a bonus? Or wait, let me guess." My hands fold across my chest, my fingers digging into my forearms, bruising the skin underneath. A dark chuckle falls from my lips as a lightbulb flashes in my head. "You're supposed to be the son he didn't have. The new division was just a distraction for me. Motherfucking Harold."

I glance at Brandt and he's silent, staring off into the void, mouth open. His face is gaining some colour, though that colour is green. His chest is rising and falling rapidly and there's sweat dampening the armpits of his shirt and beads rolling down his forehead. For a moment, I'm worried he might have a stroke or a heart attack. "Brandt?" His eyes flick to me and his consciousness slowly returns.

"It's not what you think," he croaks. My rage grows from a simmer to a boil again, and my lungs are preparing for battle, storing as much oxygen as possible.

"Not. What. I. Think? NotwhatIthink?! I'm pretty sure it's exactly what I think!"

CHAPTER
THIRTY-FOUR

"I know the truth about the contract between you and my father!" Elissa yells. She spins around, seething with rage. But as she continues to speak, the world around me fades. My insides all fail to work, my brain stops functioning, my mouth can't move. My head spins and I'm lightheaded, weak. My thoughts are jumbled. She knows. *She knows? She knows?!* How does she know? I feel the blood drain from my face. A rush of bile travels up my throat. Why isn't your mouth moving? *Say something.*

"It's not what you think," I mutter.

"Not. What. I. Think? NotwhatIthink?! I'm pretty sure it's exactly what I think!" Elissa spits out, her words burying themselves deep into my chest. Hundreds of tiny little needles burrow into my chest and straight into my lungs, making me feel like all my air is leaking out. I gasp for air, trying to get oxygen to my brain to think. I roll my head around my shoulders and curl my fingers into my knees.

"No, I need to explain —"

"Uh, yes. Please do. That's the only fucking reason I'm here, which, by the way, I don't want to be. So, let's hurry this conversation up."

My hands are warm and slick with sweat and my thoughts are still chaotic. I don't even know where to begin explaining things to Elissa.

"Eli, I —" She cuts me off by holding her hand up, a grimace on her face.

"Don't call me that. Don't call me Eli. My name is Elissa; you don't have that privilege anymore." My heart plummets. I try to talk several times, each time tripping over what to call her. The fireplace crackles in the background, breaking the momentary hush in the room.

"I needed a business to invest in and the board chose a media company — your father's media company." My lips start moving and I hear half-truths pouring out of my mouth. "Your father wanted a more sizeable investment from me for the new division, but I didn't think it was worth what he was asking. So, instead of fiscal remuneration, he added a stipulation that if I was interested, I could marry you. He wanted a *son*, he said, 'to rightfully take his place' for when he retires or dies. I would get full control of the company."

Her face is unphased; she predicted the truth pretty much down to the exact detail.

"So, you accepted and lied to me this entire time?" Heat spreads through my veins, burning my skin.

"Yes…but it wasn't all a lie. Regardless of the stipulations of the contract, I wanted to be with you either way once things started between us." Elissa scoffs at my comment and rolls her eyes.

"You're just like him. Harold. Just as sneaky and manipulative as him. I was only ever honest with you, and you lied to me just to take over my father's company." Elissa's words are broken and weak. I jump up off the couch and close the space between us, a burst of anger sparking in my chest.

"I am *nothing* like your father. Do not compare me to him." Her chin tilts as she looks up at me. Her eyes are defiant and blazing with anger, but also brimming with sadness. It takes all my strength not to reach out and smother her in a crushing embrace, to kiss away the anger and sadness. My hands twitch as I keep them at my sides, forbidding them to reach out and capture her.

"You're just like him," she says again, her hardened words pummelling me in the chest, knocking the air out of me. "You played me like a pawn, just like Harold does. Dangling love, attention, and acceptance for me to —"

My mouth crashes against hers as my arms coil around her waist, pulling her in tight. She struggles for a moment, trying to push against my chest, and just as I'm about to pull away, her hands slink around my neck, locking on tight. Elissa's eyes soften as they flutter closed. Her mouth widens, opening to deepen the kiss. Her tongue flicks against my lips, coaxing them open. Our tongues touch and a rush of excitement shivers through me. Goosebumps chase the heat swirling in my abdomen to my groin, tightening against my pants.

My hand leaves her waist and travels up to her face, cupping her soft, creamy skin. When my hand is resting against her rosy cheek, she jerks her head away. Her eyes screw up; scrunching closed before her lids shoot open to glare at me. Elissa tugs her head away, breaking our kiss, and pushes against me. Planting a hand on each pec, she launches herself out of my arms.

She staggers back, shaking her head as her fingers brush against her lips.

"No, no, no," she whispers. Her eyes clamp shut again, and she shakes her head in disbelief. Her eyes dart open, finding mine in an instant. "No. This isn't right. You can't just kiss me and make everything better; that's not how it works."

"Elissa —"

"Stop, Brandt. Not only can you no longer manipulate me, but you can't do that to Lexi. I may be loose and sleep around, but I draw the line at cheating."

I'm at a loss for words. My mouth opens and closes several times as I try to think of something to say. My heart bangs against my ribs and blood rushes to my brain.

"I never meant to manipulate you. I'm sorry. I really, truly am. It's just, once I met you, I wanted there to be something either way. Contract or not. I dislike your father as much as you do. Please believe that. But once we got together, I didn't even think of it as a contractual thing. And there is no Lexi. I broke up with her because she wasn't *you*. And I know you're still with Will, but I'll wait. I'll wait for as long as it takes. I know you don't —"

"There's no Will," she mutters. My heart skips a beat and I shake my head, wondering if I heard her correctly.

"Sorry? There's no…"

"Will. There's no Will. I ended things a while ago," she says, a little more clearly. She wraps her arms around her waist and squeezes. The beating in my chest restarts and is suddenly going a thousand kilometres an hour. My brain stops functioning. Relief floods through my system and ignites a flicker of hope. *We're both free.*

"Elissa. Please. Can we start over? I meant everything I said and did. I regret ever agreeing to your father's stupid clauses, but that's how badly I wanted you after I met you. I couldn't say no."

Her glassy eyes find mine. They soften at the corners as she nibbles her bottom lip, her resolve clearly wavering. I take a careful step forward, and she matches my step, only moving backward. My eyes plead with her. What I'd give to have her press her lithe body against mine, her breasts rubbing against my chest, her hands in my hair, my hands on her ass. Lips touching, kissing, sucking.

"Please, Elissa." I'm begging now, ready to drop to my knees. She twists her head around as if she's looking for the exit. Her eyes refocus on me, and I can see her walls crumbling. I take half a step forward and she doesn't move. So, I take another. And then another. Until I'm towering over her again, looking down into those beautiful ocean-blue eyes that drown me. Tears rim her eyes, and as she closes them, one escapes to roll down her cheek. I cup her face and my hand looks gigantic resting against her cheek. I swipe away the tear that's fallen with my thumb.

Her head nuzzles into my hand and she brushes her lip against my thumb. Her lip pulls back, exposing her teeth. She nods her head in a gentle, quick motion, and my heart swells. My hand moves to under her chin, tilting her face up, and our eyes lock. Lingering on this moment, savouring it for later, I take my time as I move my head toward her. In slow increments, our faces near each other as Elissa parts her lips and her eyes blink closed.

CHAPTER
THIRTY-FIVE

My pulse races as my heart throbs, making a racket in my chest. My eyes slowly drift closed as my lips part, waiting for Brandt's lips to press against mine again. The anticipation and urgency grow the longer he takes to place his lips on mine. The humming in my body intensifies, vibrating the cells in my body at an alarming rate.

"Elissa?" His deep, smooth voice spikes the adrenaline coursing through me.

"Mmm?" My eyes are still shut, and I'm breathing in his wintery scent. It becomes stronger and mixes with a minty coffee smell as his lips brush against mine. A light, dry kiss touches my lips, his lips briefly sticking to mine as he pulls them away. Then his hungry mouth collides with mine, devouring every part of my mouth like he's been starved for too long. Our teeth clash together, parrying each other's advances, fighting for dominance. A hot tongue makes its way into my mouth, licking every corner and tangling with my tongue.

His hands dive into my hair. He twirls my copper ponytail around one hand and tugs gently, tilting my face to give himself better access. The other hand grips the back of my neck, pulling my face closer to his. I lace an arm around his neck as I lift myself onto my toes, leaning into his hard, pumping chest. My free hand cups his face, my fingers settling behind his ear as my thumb strokes his sharp cheekbone.

He tugs on my ponytail, which jerks my head to the side, and kisses cascade down my neck. Golden-brown hair tickles my chin as he's sucking and tugging on my neck; a sweaty gel scent lingers every time he moves his head.

"Brandt..." I whisper. "We really shouldn't do this." His lips break from my neck, his dark, intense eyes finding mine.

"Is that a no? Do you want me to stop?" Desire burns like a thousand suns in his eyes. His thoughtfulness and willingness to stop tug at my heartstrings. I wrestle with the momentary choice. *What does this mean if we continue?* The bottom of my lip rolls in and I bite down on it. A growl rumbles in Brandt's throat. "If you keep biting, I won't be able to stop." My lip pops from my mouth as a blush blooms across my face. And I make my decision. I tumble into the pleasure of the moment, headfirst, consequences be damned.

I move my head a millimetre toward Brandt, and he takes it as my "yes." He plasters his face to mine, a groan gurgling in his throat. His hands reach for my ass and he cups it, lifting me up and squeezing as I wrap my legs around his waist. "Yes?" he asks in a murmur. I nod, answering him with a breathy "Yes."

He carries me, wrapped around his body, to a door off the living room. He nudges it open with his foot, just wide enough for us to fit through, but then catches it with his ankle and slams it shut behind him.

His room is just as dark and sleek as the rest of the apartment and building. I wonder hazily if he hired the same decorator as the building. He tosses me onto the dark satin sheets and crosses his arms around his waist, grabbing the hem of his shirt and lifting it over his head. As he steps out of his running shorts, I sit up and pull my soft cashmere sweater off, revealing a black see-through lacy bra. The black boxer briefs Brandt's wearing pulse from his erection. My tongue slides slowly along my lower lip, and I bite down into it. It's been so long since I've seen his beautiful cock.

He tugs his boxers down and his cock flies free, all nine glorious inches standing at attention. His thick girth is corded with throbbing veins wrapping around his length to the base, where a sculpted pubic area awaits my eyes. The tip of his cock stares me down, waiting patiently for me to reach out and touch it.

I crawl along the silky sheets and meet Brandt's imposing eyes as I stack my hands around his cock, slipping the tip into my mouth. I quickly swirl my tongue over the tip before I slowly take him into my mouth, inch by inch. His body shudders and his head dips back, his chest rising and falling in deep, fast breaths. I take one of my stacked hands and steady myself by grasping onto his thigh. The thick muscles flex under my touch.

With one hand wrapped around him, I move it opposite to the way my mouth is bobbing, creating two different stroking sensations. A growl rumbles from his mouth and his dick leaks salty precum into my mouth. With each dip of my head, I slide my lips along another inch of his thick, pulsating cock until he's hitting the back of my throat. His rod jams into the back of my mouth, making me gag, and tears burn my eyes. I stare up at him through heavy lashes, pride swelling in my body that I can make this strong, powerful man come undone with my touch. Warmth pools below, my panties growing slick with moisture.

I cup his balls and roll them around in my hand as his dick continues to thrash against my uvula. I shuffle my knees closer together as my throbbing clit begs for attention when his moans get louder. "F-fuck, Elissa." That's the only encouragement I need to pick up the pace. My tongue flattens along his shaft, and I bob my head faster and faster, adding a little squeeze to his balls. His rock-hard thighs clench and I feel his balls tighten as he gets ready to release.

I deepen the suction my mouth has around his cock as saliva drips down my chin and neck. My other hand grips onto him, pulling him deeper into my mouth. His dick slides down the back of my throat, almost choking me. "A-a-hh! E-E-Eli," he says on a stuttering moan. A second later, he is rocking and thrusting his hips into my face, pumping coils of hot semen into my mouth. I swallow it as it flows.

When he's finished, I clean his shaft with my tongue, sliding it along the ridges of veins. His large hand pushes me down and lifts my legs, tugging my pants off without undoing the button. His arm wraps around my waist, pulling me up on the bed and laying my head on the pillow. He rolls onto his side and pushes a hand into my underwear, splitting my lips and using a thick finger to stroke into me.

"You're already so wet," he mumbles, closing his lips over mine. His feverish kisses grow faster, and so does the pace of his finger stroking me. He hooks a finger and pulls down my panties, flinging them across the room. Without breaking the kiss, Brandt reaches behind him and extracts a silver packet from his nightstand. He maneuvers his body and kneels in front of me, then nudges my legs open. He rips the packet open with his teeth and rolls the latex down his length.

He leans on his forearm, hovering over me, and wraps a hand around the crook of my knee, pulling me down on the bed. I lock my legs around him as he leans forward and captures my lips again. Our hot tongues collide frantically, my hips gyrating into his hard abdomen, begging for him to fill me. He circles his hips, points the tip at my entrance, and without warning, plunges deep inside me.

Brandt is only still for a moment, not letting my body adjust to his thickness before he rocks inside me, bringing his cock out to the tip before slamming it inside me again. I roll my hips and ride his cock from below, slipping my hand between us to rub my clit. My pussy flutters around his cock, a preamble to the big finish. He picks up the pace, fucking me harder.

"Ahhh," he moans, his biceps thick and flexing as he holds his weight on top of me, careful not to crush me under his two hundred pounds of muscle. Our bodies are dripping with sweat as we hurtle to the edge. I open my eyes and find dark desire staring back at me, locking me into place. I can't look away; it's like I'm hypnotized. His arm cradles around my head as he pumps into me. "Come for me, Eli," he demands. My insides clench and squeeze at his girth. My mouth falls open and my toes curl as a bright light flashes behind my eyes. Seconds later, he follows me over the edge, making a final thrust inside me and depositing into the latex.

Our chests heave in unison as he rolls over, collapsing on his back beside me. He tugs the sheets out from underneath us and covers our naked, sweaty bodies. Neither of us dares to speak in the post-orgasmic high. Brandt eventually makes the first move, burying his hands into the blankets, mussing around, and pulling the condom off. He ties it up and tosses it into the trashcan beside his bed, then stretches his arms wide before folding them under his head and turning to look at me.

"So," I whisper, then chuckle awkwardly.

"So," he repeats slowly. Suddenly, he grabs me by the waist and rolls me to straddle his body. He grabs another condom from the nightstand and rolls it on his cock, staring at me with dark eyes. "We go again."

•••

After another two rounds, we have completely exhausted ourselves. Brandt slides out of the bed and makes his way to the washroom. I bunch up the surrounding sheets to hide my nakedness, looking for my clothes. I'm wondering how late it is as I peer over at the alarm clock on the dresser. It's almost 2 AM, and I bet Riley is going to be worried. I hear the squeak of the shower turn on and a rush of water hitting tile. With the sheet wrapped around my body, I go out into the living room to find my phone in my coat pocket.

Riley: *Girl, where you at?*
Riley: *??*
Riley: *Please respond so I know you're alive. If I don't hear back in 15 mins, I'm calling your father's PI.*

Her last message was sent a few minutes ago. I scoff at her audacity at leveraging my father's service to find out where I am. I type a quick message back.

Me: *Uh, long story. With Brandt. Talk later.*

"Elissa?" Brandt's voice carries out into the kitchen and living area. I turn around to answer him and he's standing in the doorway, water dripping down his hard, chiselled body and soaking the towel he's holding around his tapered waist. *Lord help me.*

"Sorry, I was just messaging Riley to let her know not to send out the search dogs," I awkwardly joke. The corner of his mouth twitches before settling in a thin line.

"Did you tell her where you were?"

"Not exactly," I say, tucking some of my tousled hair behind my ear. "I did mention I was with you, just not in what state…" He gives me a slow nod, his expression unreadable. We're trapped in an awkward silence for a few moments, staring, each of us daring the other one to speak first. I break eye contact first, biting into my lip and looking around his apartment.

"This place is nice. I didn't expect you to live in such a modern-gothic looking place." I try to lighten the dark, tense mood that has fallen over the room. The sheet wrapped around me loosens with my shifting weight, making me gather it again to cinch it tighter. "Do you mind if I get dressed?"

"What is this, Elissa?" he says, his voice breaking slightly. My uncertain eyes flicker to his as I remain quiet.

"I…I don't know. What do you think this is?" He stalks toward me, closing the gap between us in a few strides. His eyes level with mine and a small but serious smile tugs at his lips.

"It doesn't matter what I think it is, it matters what I want. I want you. I want a relationship, a partner. I want that with you. I want to go on dates, be seen in public, hold hands, and fucking snuggle." I feel the burn spread across my chest and face as he talks, my heart stuttering inside my chest. My breathing speeds up, and tiny black and white dots obscure my vision. I grip the sheet that's wrapped around my chest as he continues "But I want that stuff with you. And I know you may not be ready for that kind of commitment, but if this is gonna keep happening, I need to know that you'll consider it. Because you are not just a contract or a pawn to me."

CHAPTER
THIRTY-SIX

ELISSA

I didn't realize how badly I needed to hear those words until Brandt said them out loud. *You are not just a contract or a pawn to me.* A swelling in my heart takes over as my quivering eyes stare at him. And the crazy thing is, I believe him. It may have started like a business deal to him, but no one can fake that kind of chemistry. There's been too many times that we've been in the same room, not even touching, and it's been electric. Strike a match and there'd be an explosion from all the tension hanging thickly in the air.

"I don't know, Brandt. I don't know if I can give you what you want."

"All I want is the possibility of it growing into something more. I want you to be open-minded. You can give me what I want, because I want you, however I can get you, as long as you promise to be open to something more. Give us — give yourself — a chance."

My skin hums and anxiety prickles at my consciousness, making me fully aware that I am still naked and vulnerable in front of him. He saw me cry, lose my temper, and give in to desire, all within a brief span of time. He's still here, wanting me. The grey hardwood floor creaks as he steps toward me, reaching out for me and enveloping my hands in his warm, gentle ones.

"I know it's hard for you. But say yes, try something new. We can take it one step at a time." Sturdy fingers brush the chaotic mess of hair out of my face as he tugs the other hand he's holding, pulling me closer to him as he anchors his hand at the small of my back. I'm staring up into his warm, caring eyes, and my body and heart are screaming, *Do it. Be with him!* But my obnoxious brain is telling me, *This won't end well.* Brandt's eyes glimmer with hope and possibilities, and I don't want to let this gorgeous, kind man go again. I don't want to see him with anyone else. Seeing him with Lexi withered away part of my heart.

My inner voices wrestle for an answer as Brandt waits patiently. I turn my head to look out the window into the middle of the night (morning?) sky. The obsidian horizon is speckled with tiny glowing dots. Snow has finally stopped falling, and the sky is clear. The skyscrapers across the way are decorated with twinkly lights on the balconies, ringing in the last few days of the year. As I look out at the dark night skyline, a shiver passes through me, as if the cold is seeping through the windows, chilling me to the bone.

Little speckled bumps raise the hair on my arms as the shiver rolls through me. Maybe it's because I'm naked, or because there's a surge of good anxiousness that's waiting for me on the other side of this conversation.

BRANDT

Elissa looks petrified of what I'm asking of her. Her face is pale, solemn, and her eyes are wary as they dart around the room. Her hand has a slight tremble as I enclose her hands in mine. I notice the hairs on her arms are raised, with tiny bumps travelling across her skin. The thin, silky sheet wrapped around her body does little to keep her warm, even though the fireplace crackles in the background.

She's looking at me expectantly now, and I can't tell if she's waiting for me to tell her it's all a joke, relieving her of the pressure of choosing. I lift her hand to my mouth, placing soft kisses on her cold knuckles, the back of her hand, and the inside of her wrist. She shivers again and closes her eyes softly, like she's savouring the feeling.

"Please say yes, Eli," I whisper against the sensitive skin on her wrist. I place another soft kiss on the inside of her wrist before tugging her in close and wrapping my arms around her tightly. She relaxes into my embrace; her shoulders release their tension, and she rests her forehead against my collarbone. Her head wiggles back and forth and my heart aches as a heaviness presses down on my chest.

"Brandt…" she whispers into my chest. One of her fingers finds the smattering of golden locks running down my chest and she twirls a finger in the soft curls. Her shoulders rise as she heaves a heavy, deep sigh. I feel soft, cushy lips moving against my chest, but I don't hear what she's saying.

"What was that?" I ask. Again, her lips mumble something into my skin, leaving traces of unspoken hopes and fantasies.

"I'll try," she mumbles, an octave louder. The world shifts from underneath my feet and I feel like I'm weightless, floating. My pulse strums along to one of the most romantic classic songs, and joy pumps through my entire body. *Did she just say yes? No, idiot, she said she'd try. Close enough.*

My crushing embrace lifts her off her toes, and I kiss her as her body slides down mine. When she's at eye level with me, I claim her lips with urgency and lust. My tongue presses against the entrance of her mouth, asking permission to come in and take refuge in the warmth. My fingers thread through her dishevelled hair, revelling in the notion that it looks that way because of me.

With my arms secured around her, I take a step back, and then another one, leading us toward my bedroom one soft movement at a time. Our steps are timed and fluid like a waltz. When we reach the door, I spin us around so she's taking backward steps as I guide us into the room until there's nowhere else to go but down onto the bed.

Our bodies crash onto the buttery sheets and I tear at the one wrapped around her narrow frame and toss it aside. Our lips dance across our bodies, our breaths tickle against sensitive skin, and our hands roam over our contours and valleys. Purposeful kisses ignite wicks of passion that set our skin on fire and heartbeats run rampant, boiling our blood until beads of sweat are rolling down every inch of our bodies.

My dick is so hard I don't know if it'll ever go down. I'm so overwhelmed by this insane feeling; I can't believe she agreed. *I can't fuck this up again.* To think I finally have Elissa, again, and she's willing to try. I don't know what this means for my deal with Harold, if she's going with it, or what. But I can't ask her now. For now, I will let things go, and give her some time to come to terms with things.

Deep breaths echo through my quiet, dark bedroom. I look over and Elissa is asleep on her side, facing the windows looking out at the glittering Toronto skyline and the lake beyond. Her measured breaths rise and fall, softly and gently. I lift the blanket, and with careful movements I get closer to her, wrapping a heavy arm around her waist and snuggling our bodies together. She stirs, but doesn't wake, and relaxes her back into my chest. I inch closer until my face is buried in her cloud of copper hair. I listen to the sounds of her breathing, in and out, lulling me to sleep.

• • •

A soft, pleasant warmth radiates against my face, waking me from my sleep. I reach over to hold Elissa, but my hand falls on an empty mattress. Panic sets in as I realize she's left sometime in the early hours. An aching in my chest tells me it was too good to be true. That I should have known better, that people rarely change. Amid the strangling panic that's setting into my heart, I hear the toilet flush, and the bathroom door creaks open.

Elissa tiptoes out in one of my black Calvin Klein dress shirts. It's barely long enough to cover her cheeky ass. And God damn if she doesn't look like a ruined, beautiful goddess. When she looks over at me, she halts, and a crimson flush floods her face. Her perfect, supple lips part, and a weak, shy voice spills from her lips.

"Oh, you're awake." She glances down to where my eyes are glued. "I hope you don't mind. I grabbed one of your shirts out of your closet." Her hands fumble with the cuffs of the shirt, her knees pinched together and her toes wriggling. She looks like a nervous puppy, waiting for her owner to praise her and give her cuddles. A laugh tugs at my mouth, but I swallow it down. I push myself into a sitting position and shrug, letting her know I don't mind. She strolls over to the right side of the bed and plops down, shimmying under the covers and hiding her face beneath the sheets.

CHAPTER
THIRTY-SEVEN

We spent the next two days lying in bed at Brandt's place, eating and fucking. I only returned to the real world once in that time to message Riley again, so she knew I hadn't been kidnapped or something.

Riley: *So, what? Are you guys back together?*
Me: *Uh, kind of. I think so. Yeah…*
Riley: *??? I NEED DEETS.*
Me: *Soon. Xx*

I shove my phone back into my coat pocket and return to Brandt's large, dark bedroom. The steam from the shower curls out under the bathroom door; the water is still beating down onto the tile. I place a light hand on the reflective glass of his ceiling-height closet wall, and a light turns on inside. It takes me by surprise as I hop back. The glass door is actually a window that illuminates from inside the closet, and a rough outline of his clothing and shelves can be seen. I walk along the closet windows, barely brushing my hand against the glass as the lights pop on one section at a time.

Astonishment descends on me as I stare out of the massive window in his room. The Toronto harbour skyline is even prettier during the day, all dusted in snow. As I'm taking in the beauty of Brandt's view (which is much better than mine), still wearing the same dress shirt of his, two corded arms wrap around me. One slides around my waist and the other sneaks into the open, unbuttoned part of the shirt and a large hand palms my tit. Brandt's scruffy face scratches against my neck as he places light, playful kisses on my sensitive skin. Delicious shivers pulse down my spine.

"What do you think of going out today?" he says between kisses. Tension grips my body at his suggestion. He must have noticed, because he continues gently. "We can go somewhere low-key, like the Nathan Phillips Square rink." He trails the kisses up my neck to behind my ear.

"Hmm? Something laid-back, no pressure, in public. I promise there will be no public displays of affection," he whispers in my ear. My tummy flips as a rush of adrenaline bursts through me. I'm nervous, anxious, and a little excited, all at once.

"Sure," I say. My tone is soft and breathier than I want. "But I need to go home first, to get changed and get my stuff to go skating."

"I'll meet you at your place in an hour to get you," Brandt grumbles in my ear. I move to collect my various clothing items from where they've been thrown around his room and quickly get dressed. As I'm untucking the copper twists of my hair from the collar of my shirt, a giant hand smacks my ass. "Hurry up, or I'll change my mind and we'll just stay here all day again."

I bat my lashes and look up at him.

"Don't give me any ideas," I say seductively. He swaggers over to me, naked, and tugs on the back of my head, bringing my face to bump against his. His lips cover mine passionately, giving me one last sloppy kiss before I leave and making my legs melt into gelatin.

Riley practically pounces on me the minute I enter the apartment, drooling like a dog waiting for a treat. Without letting me even take off my jacket and only allowing enough time for me to kick off my boots, she tugs me down the hallway. When we reach the living room, she pushes me onto the couch.

"So?" she pants, bouncing from one foot to the other. "C'mon! Tell me. I need to know. It's been two days. I'm dying to know what happened."

"What. The. Fuck." Riley is shocked. "Harold arranged the whole fucking thing between you two?" Her mouth drops open and her eyes look like they might pop out of her head. "And Brandt just went with the deal, like you're some kind of prize?"

I had little more to say after telling her everything that had happened. My father showing up at the office and letting the "contract negotiations" slip, me bumping into

Brandt at the gym, our fight, and then getting back together with him.

"And you just took him back?" I think this is the part that shocks her the most. "Elissa, I don't know if you realize what you agreed to. This means you're in an actual relationship. You're going on a date, for goodness' sakes!" A pink flush spreads across my cheeks, warming me up at the thought of an actual date. Something flutters in my chest, making me feel as though I'm floating. *What is this?* "Earth to Elissa…" Riley waves a hand in front of my face, breaking me from my inner thoughts.

"Will you just help me get ready?" I ask her, giving her my best puppy dog eyes and pouty lips. She grumbles and groans and rolls her eyes, but eventually tugs me to my feet and pushes me toward my room.

"Yes, I will help you. But later, we're going to re-examine this whole situation and figure out what it all means. You can't just forgive someone just like that for deceiving you for so long."

"Normally I wouldn't, but with Brandt, it's different. I can't explain it. It's like I'm stuck in a room and all the air has been sucked out of it and I can't breathe. He suffocates me. But, at the same time, he's the only one who can supply me with oxygen. I know he's near me before I can even see him. It's like I have a superpower that tingles when he's within a certain proximity."

"Girl, it sounds like you're in love."

I scoff, waving her off.

"No. No. *No.* I am not in love. Sure, there are some feelings there. I certainly don't hate him. He's good-looking, caring, and great in bed. But *love*? Ugh. No…no?" A fluttering in my chest makes me heat up, and I start sweating in my bedroom as I stand in my bra and panties, mid-change. I wave my hands in front of my face, fanning myself to cool down. "I-I-I'm not in l-love." My breathing becomes rapid; short, shallow breaths ricochet inside my lungs and my head becomes fuzzy.

"Breathe," a soft voice coos. Riley's gentle hand rubs my back and she simulates breathing techniques. I shrug her hand off me.

"I'm fine now. I swear." My words have little effect on her as she rolls her eyes.

"So, what are you going to do about tonight? It's New Year's Eve." I cock my head at her question.

"What do you mean?"

"Well, I assumed it'd be us going to a club tonight, but now that you're seeing Brandt again, I guess you'll be with him." *Is it New Year's Eve already? I guess Brandt and I spent too many days locked away in his apartment, wrapped up in orgasmic bliss.* My shoulders sag as I sigh, and Riley turns her face away from me.

"I didn't realize what day it was. When I meet up with Brandt for skating, I'll tell him that I'm hanging with you tonight. Promise."

Riley's face perks up, her eyes reflecting the midday December sun that's shining through my window. She stretches her body like a marionette being pulled from above and clasps her hands together, giving me a rather brilliant look.

"Deal. Now let's get you ready for your first date."

•••

The nerves in my body hum along with the elevator as I ride it down to meet Brandt in the lobby. I catch a glimpse of my reflection in the doors of the elevator, and I have to say, Riley killed it. She paired my soft black Lululemon leggings with a teal long-sleeved tee underneath my burgundy Wunder Puff Lululemon jacket. My Roots cabin socks were pulled up and poking over the top of my roll-top Timberland boots, with the socks' signature red band running around the top of the thick grey knit. My copper curls hung free, with some cascading over my shoulders underneath my black toque. Riley went light-handed on the makeup to make it look natural; "makeup that doesn't know it's makeup," as she would say.

As the elevator car slows down, so does my heart, or maybe it's time altogether. But as the doors inch apart, little by little, I catch a glimpse of the beautiful man standing in the lobby looking at his phone. His gorgeous golden-brown hair pokes out in wisps around the edge of his beanie. He looks up from his phone for a moment, then back down, and then his eyes fly up to meet mine as a crooked smile spreads across his face. His beat-up black hockey skates are tied together by the laces and hanging over his shoulder.

When I reach him he smiles a little wider, revealing a sliver of shiny white teeth, and his eyes crinkle at the corners. He takes my pink duffle bag with my skates off my shoulder and leads us outside, where he has a car waiting to take us to the outdoor rink.

I slide in first, stomping my feet to rid my boots of the snow before getting in. A light snowfall starts, and I'm mesmerized as I stare through the car window up at the glass and metal and brick buildings that seem to stretch on forever down here at ground level. The diffused sunlight glares off the sides of the building, competing with the grey clouds for dominance.

When Brandt gets in beside me, he places the skates on the floor between his feet and unzips his jacket a little bit. He turns to face me and catches my eyes and smiles. My heart melts. I return his smile and he takes the opportunity to slide his gloved hand into mine, locking our fingers together. My pulse quickens as I stare down at our point of connection, my heart pumping heat throughout my body. It amazes me how a simple gesture feels insanely intense when it's with Brandt.

CHAPTER THIRTY-EIGHT

ELISSA

The easy melodies of the most popular pop songs of the day dance in the air as we pick a bench at the side of the rink to sit down and put our skates on. Brandt sets my bag down and crouches, waiting for me to sit and take off my boots. Unzipping the duffle bag, he extracts narrow, white figure skates. I kick my boots off one at a time and tug up my socks, which have slipped down. Heat radiates through his gloved hand as he picks up my ankle and slips the skate over my foot.

His fingers move swiftly, lacing up the skates and tugging on the cords until the skate is snug against my ankle. He repeats the same motions with the other foot, and I feel a little silly that he's doing this for me. Like when Prince Charming is putting on Cinderella's glass slipper. Brandt's lips are curved into his sharp cheekbones, and his jaw is speckled with golden stubble, much longer than he typically keeps it. I reach my hand out and ruffle his growing beard. A blush stings at my cheeks and I'm instantly grateful we're outside, so the cold can cover up all evidence.

Once he's done securing my skates on my feet, I stomp my feet on the rubber mat that covers the cement sidewalk as he sits and puts on his skates. He's bent over, propping up his forefoot, and I watch his deft hands work the laces, getting lost in a trance. I blink away the fog and sit up straight.

"So," I say. "What are you doing tonight for New Year's Eve? I was planning on hanging out with Riley tonight, if that's okay with you. I'm not sure how this thing works with us now." My knees wobble as I step onto the ice pad, holding Brandt's hand to steady me. I sway as a foot skids underneath me by a few millimetres. He chuckles at my fumble.

"That's fine. We did just spend two days together locked in my bedroom," he says beside my ear. The low grumble of his voice tickles down my spine. His firm grip crushes my hand as he takes his first stride, his thighs clenching as he pushes off, dragging me along with him.

"I'll message Riley when we're done and see if you can join us tonight. We were just going to go to one of the clubs nearby and go dancing." Brandt's body tenses as his hand grips a little harder, and his jaw ticks. A gust of cold wind rips by us, and his shoulders relax; his hand loosens its grip. He clears his throat and nods his head.

• • •

The afternoon sun is warm, though the wind is cold. Our cores are sweating while our extremities are freezing and numb — especially my pinky toes. Brandt speeds up, spins around and skates past me, then comes up behind me and wraps his arms around my waist, tucking his head between my shoulder and ear. His lips graze against the earlobe that's sticking out of my toque. He takes out his phone and holds it up with the front camera facing us, clicks the little white dot, and takes a photo.

My phone buzzes in my pocket. I dig it out of my jacket and see my father's caller ID on the screen. I groan and reluctantly answer it. "Yes, Father?" I shuffle my feet over to the edge of the rink and hop off as I near the curb back by our bench. "To what do I owe this displeasure?"

"You can stop with the childish antics. I need you in the office within the next hour. There's going to be an emergency meeting and it's your fault. Will is being an asshole. Get your ass down here, now." The line goes dead, and my phone's screen goes dark. Brandt's eyes wrinkle in concern, but I wave him off.

"We've got to go. And I suspect you'll —"

Brandt's phone starts to ring, and he turns the screen toward me to show Harold's name pop up. Just as expected. I sit down on the bench and start unlacing my skates as I chew on the inside of my cheek. What does Will think he's going to achieve? Brandt skates over to the edge of the rink as the wind whips around him. His phone is tucked neatly between his hand and his ear as he chats away with my father. His eyes are dark when he looks at me, and a slow swallow rolls down my throat.

"Let's go," he says as he sits down to take off his skates. He rips through undoing the laces, then stands and tosses the skates over his shoulder. He grabs my hand, and his giant legs take giant strides toward Queen Street West to hail us a cab. My legs are struggling to keep up with his pace, and I'm practically running behind him.

"Brandt, please slow down," I call out to him, my feet almost dragging along the sidewalk as he pulls me. He keeps his pace steady and barrels forward, people splitting around him like the Red Sea. His head flicks over his shoulder to see me jogging to keep up with him, and his angry expression becomes one of concern. He slows his pace, but it hardly matters, as we've reached the sidewalk. His arm flies into the air as he flags down a car, opens the door, and, with splayed hands, ducks my head inside like he's a cop.

We head directly for the Black & Wells Publishing and Press building, without stopping to change or drop our skates off. We ride the elevator up in tense silence. I glance at Brandt, trying to read him. His cold eyes stare ahead, and he's silent and unresponsive. He'd been like this for the whole five-minute drive. I fold his hand into mine and give it a squeeze, trying to get him to focus on me and tell me what's wrong. He doesn't flinch or make any attempt to look over.

I drop his hand when the doors slide open. I exit first and make my way down the hallway, my bag swooshing behind my back. I jerk open the door to the conference room, dump my bag in the corner of the windowed wall, drag a chair out from underneath the table, and plop down into it, the compressed feeling in me releasing a bit.

Brandt enters the room a moment later and places his skates neatly beside my bag. He unzips his jacket and tosses it over the back of a chair across from me, then takes a seat, the wheels squeaking as he settles in. Harold and about five other middle-aged men my father's age sit around the table. My father's eyebrows are raised, and he's stroking his moustache. His lips are crooked at one corner. The fingers of his free hand thrum on the table as he waits for us to get settled.

Mr. Secord, the company's head (and oldest) lawyer, heaves a dry cough while his hand runs over the sparse, slicked-back grey hair on his head. With his glasses perched on his nose like Mother Goose, he looks over the rims of them and his stare narrows at me. I swivel my chair and chew on the inside of my cheek, fighting the heat that's simmering below.

"Ms. Black, I am sure you are aware of the ploys Will Burke is insinuating in order for him to be free of his contract with his book here. He is claiming coercion and pressure due to sleeping with the CEO's daughter. While we know about your…liaisons with Mr. Burke, we need to make sure that we have a strong defence and a strong countersuit. Please start by giving us a timeline of your history," Mr. Secord says, his voice wobbling as he talks. I glance over at Brandt, feeling a pit open up in my stomach.

"Uh. Okay," I mumble. I wiggle in my seat, correcting my posture, and pull the toque off my head. I fluff my hair and toss it over my shoulders, my bronze curls cascading down my back. I fold my hands in front of me and rest them on the glossy cherry wood table.

"So, when I was working at Wellington Drive Publishing as a junior editor, I was in charge of editing Mr. Burke's manuscript. One night, after going over some revisions, one thing lead to another, and we ended up sleeping together in the office…" I try to catch a surreptitious glimpse of Brandt as my cheeks burn. "Since then, until recently, we've been together. I broke it off about three weeks ago."

"Okay…why did you end things with him?" Mr. Secord asks, his pen scratching across his yellow legal pad. My stomach flops, and a chill breaks out over my body. Panic starts to set in as I recall that night. The pressure of his hand on my jaw, forcing my mouth open. His hot, musty breath tinged with beer. The slick, darting tongue that pushed its way into my mouth…I shudder. I take a deep breath and force the saliva pooling in my mouth down my throat.

"May we speak in…private?" I ask Mr. Secord. Over half a dozen eyes rest upon me, curiosity filling their prying stares.

"I can assure you that all of us here will take what you say with the strictest of confidence, Ms. Black. Mr. Gorges, Mr. Rawlins, Mr. Blakely, Mrs. Valente, and I are all lawyers, and will not break client confidentiality." I chew the corner of my mouth, wavering on my resolve to tell them everything. I look at my father and he seems unperturbed and uninterested, and I don't even try to see what Brandt's face looks like. I can feel his eyes burning into my skin, I can hear the wheels turning in his mind as to what the hell happened. I clear my throat.

"Very well, Mr. Secord. But I please ask that Harold and Mr. Collins are removed for this portion of the statement process."

Mr. Secord nods his head and gestures for both of them to leave. My father huffs and pushes away from the table. The chair clangs off the back of the cabinet behind him, and he stalks out of the room. Brandt silently looks at me, but I stare straight ahead, not wanting to look him in the eyes. I know that if I do, I might just break, and now is not the time to show weakness.

Once Brandt leaves, I suck in a deep breath. My knee bounces underneath the table as I pull out my phone and bring up the pictures of my jaw. "There's another person you're going to need to talk to as well," I say. "Riley Jaimeson."

CHAPTER THIRTY-NINE

RILEY

My stomach gurgles as I wait for Elissa to get home. She messaged me about an hour ago, saying her date got interrupted by a call from her father about something business-related. I stretch, reaching both arms above my head until my tee lifts to expose a small section of my midriff. I tug my shirt back down and heave myself off the couch, then pad my way to the fridge to grab something to eat.

I'm rinsing off my plate from the leftover Chinese when the front door beeps open and I hear grumbling down the hall. "'Lissa, I'm in the kitchen," I singsong. I take a swig of my diet ginger ale and a burp bubbles up my throat.

"Nice," Elissa says sarcastically. She drops her jacket on the back of the couch and kicks off her boots, then walks back down the hallway to turn them upside down over the heater vent. When she comes back into the kitchen, she's grumbling to herself.

"Everything okay?" I tuck some glossy black hair behind my ear, leaning back against the counter and folding my arms. Elissa's eyebrows crease as her eyes flicker with flames. *Whoa.* "What happened at the meeting?" Elissa sighs, her shoulders drop, and she buries her face in her hands as she plops onto a stool at the island.

"Will happened. He's trying to sue us for breach of contract, on the count of coercion or something, because we were sleeping together at one point." My mouth drops open. She nods her head, and her eyes droop along with the rest of her body. She inhales deep and controls her exhale. "I just didn't know what to do. So, I had no choice but to tell them everything that happened between Will and me. Which means you'll be getting called on soon to go in and give a statement about…you know." I did know. I give her a weak, reassuring smile. I pad over to her and cradle her head into my chest, stroking her unruly curls.

Suddenly, my gut twists and gurgles so loudly that Elissa pulls her head away from me and looks concerned. Saliva pours into my mouth, and a sour taste is puckering at the back of my throat. I take a deep breath and swallow, cleansing myself of the wave of sickness. *It's probably the pop mixing with the old Chinese food*, I try to tell myself. Bubbles percolate in my stomach, forcing them to rise up my throat. My cheeks puff with air as gasses are released from my throat. I run to the washroom, slam open the toilet seat cover and spew into the toilet, violently.

A loud knocking on the bathroom door shakes me. "Riles? Are you okay?" Elissa's voice is strained and laced with worry. "Open this door, and do *not* puke anymore. I'm getting your therapist on the phone right now."

"No, I didn't force myself to puke. Wait, Elissa!" I croak out as I rush to my feet and swing the door open, wiping my mouth on the back of my hand. "I didn't mean to puke. I think it was the pop and old Chinese food I ate. I swear." Her eyes burrow into me, full of concern and distrust. She hesitates, her thumb hovering over the round green button on her screen. "Really. I'm fine now. I feel better." Her eyebrows crease and then she lets go of a sigh.

"Okay, but I'm keeping a close eye on you." I raise my hands in defeat, turn around, and unscrew the cap of the mouthwash. I swish it around, letting the burn cleanse my mouth.

Later, Elissa and I are getting ready for the evening when I grab a pair of my skinny jeans out of my dresser. I slide them on and they're…snug. Tighter than they were the last time I wore them. My mind goes back to how many calories I've been consuming lately, and anxiety blankets my body. *Have I gained that much weight so quickly?* I'm sure my doctor and therapist will say it's a good thing and that I'm still healthy, but these jeans were already a size one.

I finally get the jeans past my thunderous thighs and try to button them up. The pieces of denim with the brass buttons on them are stretched to their limits as I try to pull them together. Holding my breath, I grow lightheaded as I heave and pull. I give up.

"'Liss? Do you have some jeans I can borrow. Mine are…too small?" I say, confusion rippling through me.

She walks into my bedroom, her heels clicking on the floor, and her legs look deliciously long and toned in the jeans she's wearing. They curve around her hips and ass, making the perfect silhouette. She tosses me a couple pairs of her jeans as the front door buzzer goes off in the background. She turns and walks down the hall to answer at the speaker, then appears in my doorway again, a sheepish smile on her face. "What?" I ask.

"Well, you see…um…" Elissa stammers, biting her lip a few times in between. "I invited Brandt to join us tonight. That's him with the pizza now."

"What? I thought you said it was going to be just us?"

"Well, I did. But I felt so bad that I had Brandt kicked out of the conference room and he was all moody, so I suggested he come out tonight with us. I told him not to invite Rhys."

I groan, rolling my eyes as I stretch my legs through a pair of her black denim capris. I'm so petite that her regular jeans would be way too long on me, so her giving me capris is as genius as it is insulting. Smart ass. Her size four jeans are a smidge too big around my hips, but nothing a belt can't solve. *Huh. A size one to a size four in two months? That's quite a difference, no?*

I lift my shirt and twist my body in the mirror. I try not to spend too much time focusing on my body and what it looks like naked, as it can be triggering. But today,

I need to. My small frame is still small. There's a bit more of a puffy skin roll on my midsection, and my small, perky boobs seem to have swelled a bit too. Panic grips at my throat as I start to spiral, thinking of all the things I've been eating lately that I normally wouldn't.

My breathing quickens and grows shallow as I press a hand to my chest. Elissa yells, "Come in," but I barely hear her. My thoughts are running through my mind like a hamster on a wheel; how much I ate, what I ate, when I ate, and so on. *That's 100 calories here, maybe another 10 there, oh, there was that Big Mac I had…300, 400, 900 calories. Shit, shit, shit.* Not again. Stop this, Riley.

Elissa passes by my room but then reappears in front of my door. "Are you okay, Riles?"

Muttering numbers under my breath, I can feel Elissa's eyes on me. Soft footsteps click into my room. "Riley?"

"How many yesterday?" I mumble to myself. My hands appear in front of my face, fingers popping up as I count. I rush over to the top drawer in my dresser and yank. It grinds open and I grab my journal, flipping through the pages, back and forth, and back and forth. Then an aroma floats into the air, warm and doughy and…meaty.

My tummy turns, flips, flops. It gurgles and bubbles. Scorching, acidic bile travels up my esophagus, burning my throat. I push past a wide-eyed Elissa, knocking her into the doorframe, and catch a whiff of the steaming pizza Brandt has in his hands. I clasp my hands over my mouth, which is bursting at the seams. I slam the door shut with my foot and curl my heaving body over the sink, not even able to make it to the toilet.

The door creaks open and Elissa's face appears, her alarmed expression morphing into sadness and concern. "Hun?" she whispers. I look at her, my eyes pleading and wavering. "Go get some comfy clothes on. I'll be right back." She turns and disappears, and a moment later I hear the front door click closed.

I shuffle out of the washroom after cleaning myself up and look around. There's no sign of Brandt, or the pizza. I go back to my room, my stomach trying to settle, and I change into some sweatpants and a sweater, pull on some long, fuzzy socks, and head to the living room to collapse on the couch.

• • •

A half-hour later, the apartment door opens, and the stomping of feet distracts me from the television. I look over from the couch and see Elissa dusted in snow, shrugging off her jacket and toeing off her boots. Her hands clutch a brown paper bag. She saunters over, perches on the edge of the couch, and passes me the brown bag. I stretch my hand out, taking it cautiously. I open the bag to peer inside, and my nerves start to vibrate.

My body buzzes, and I'm flooded with numbness and chills as I walk to the washroom, the length of the hallway stretching out abnormally long in front of me. Goosebumps pebble over my skin, tiny hairs rise up all over my body, and my heart is pounding in my ears. I feel around the wall for the light switch in the washroom and enter, padding over to the toilet.

I sit down on the cold plastic seat of the toilet, my ears still throbbing as my blood pounds. I open the rectangular, baby blue box and dump out the contents. A little stick clatters onto the marble countertop. I swallow hard, and the stick clicks when I uncap it. My leg bounces repeatedly, and my hands dampen and tremble. I lean forward and hold the stick underneath me.

CHAPTER
FORTY

ELISSA

Two minutes pass. I'm rooted to my spot on the couch, terrified to move. The door opens and I twist my body to look at her. She walks out, her arms rigid at her sides. Her head is dipped, and her face is blanched. Tears are streaming down her face, and I get up and run to her. She falls to the ground, the pregnancy test clatters to the floor, and her hands hide her face as her breathing grows ragged. I drop to my knees and pull her in close, wrapping my arms around her lithe body and rubbing her back.

I rock her, like a small baby in my arms. Shushing her, soothing her.

"It's going to be okay," I murmur. "I'm here for you. We'll figure it out together, I promise." Her sobs are coming out broken and hard; she struggles for air as her shoulders and chest cave in. "Shhh. Riley, everything will be okay."

· · ·

What a way to ring in the new year. We sat on the couch and Riley cried all night until she finally fell asleep. I grab the fuzzy pink blanket off the back of the couch and drape it over her fragile, sleeping body. She wriggles a bit, seeking a more comfortable position, and falls back into a deep sleep. I press a kiss into her hairline and tiptoe to my bedroom, closing the door with a soft click.

I pull my phone out of the back pocket of my jeans and the time shines on the screen — it's 1 AM. I have twenty-four notifications. I scroll through them quickly and see some generic "Happy New Year" messages from some of the friendly faces I miss from Kingston like Teddy, Liza, and Becca. There's a gushy message from Lana, and a couple of other people I know. But I find two from Brandt.

Brandt: *How's Riley doing?*
Brandt: *Happy New Year. Text me when you can.*

I start typing a response on my phone but delete it. Instead, I buck up the courage to give him a call, hoping he's still awake. I pop open my door a crack to check on Riley, who is still sound asleep on the couch. Pushing my door closed, I click Brandt's name on my call list. It rings about three times before he answers in a deep, scratchy, sexy voice that makes my clit throb.

"Hey, sorry. Did I wake you?"

"Mm. I was just dozing, waiting for you to message me back." Butterflies flap and swoop in my tummy as he breathes heavily over the phone.

"Okay, so I have to tell you something, but you *cannot* tell anyone. I mean it, Brandt. *Especially* no telling Rhys." He groans, and I hear sounds of ruffling and shifting; I assume he's sitting up. I wedge my phone between my ear and shoulder and pick at my nails. Brandt doesn't say anything, so I press. "Please promise me you won't say anything." His silence worries me, and my insides flip and flop as I wait to hear him promise. When he finally agrees, relief floods through me.

"Riley is…pregnant." Silence settles in the air again. There's no sound except for Brandt's breathing crackling through the phone. "Brandt?"

"Whose is it? Is it Rhys'?" he asks in a frosty tone.

"I…I don't know," I stammer. "She wasn't really in the mood for talking, but the baby is most likely his." More silence, except for the beating of my heart in my throat.

"I have to tell him, Eli," he finally says dejectedly. The beating of my heart quickens, and I start to feel faint.

"You can't. It's not your business. Riley will tell him when she's ready. You promised."

"But this isn't a simple promise. This isn't me keeping from him that she's hurt something, or overspent on her trust fund. This affects someone else — my best friend. I know she's yours, but I need to think about mine, too." I grind my teeth together as my jaw hardens. I clench my fists and relax them.

"Yes, I get that, I do. But we need to take it one step at a time. Let Riley come to terms with it. Give her a few days and then we'll have her tell Rhys. Please?" A long, heavy sigh tickles my ear.

"Fine," he growls. "So, I take it you're not coming over today?" I bite my lip and shake my head, then realize he can't see me, so I mumble "No." There's a little more silence before he says good night and hangs up the phone. I fall backward onto my bed and throw my arms wide open, my phone bouncing on my bed.

A few days later, I make plans to go over to Brandt's house after work, so when I go into the kitchen, I plan to tell Riley just that. I find her sitting at the island, moping over a bowl of Captain Crunch. My shoulders slouch and I curl my arms around her shoulders.

"It's going to be okay, Riles. I promise." She sighs.

"I know…I just need to tell my parents."

"And Rhys," I say. She tenses, freezing on the spot. Her spoon slips out of her hand and clatters into the bowl, splashing milk and cereal on the counter.

"What do you mean I need to tell Rhys?" she says icily, her words like daggers. I slump my body and give her an "are you joking?" face. "I don't even know if it's his."

I cock my head. "What do you mean?" Riley sighs again, bigger this time.

"Well, I kind of hooked up with this hot bartender before Christmas. You know, the one at Mode Hotel, where I decorated for a holiday party? Well, I met him there, but we used a condom. So, it's most likely Rhys'…we didn't use a condom once, but I'm on birth control!" The words tumble out of her, tinged with anger and confusion.

"Honey, but you were just putting your body through a hell of a relapse. Your body could have been so fucked up and the birth control didn't do its job," I say delicately. Her eyes brim with tears and I squeeze her shoulders a little harder. "I've got to go now, and I'm going to Brandt's after work. If you need me, just call, okay?" She shrugs and nods, then switches back to moping over her cereal.

At the office, when I first step into the lobby, I wave to the security guard as I stomp off my boots. Gentle music lingers in the air and as I approach the security desk a shadow appears beside me. I smell a metallic, musty, oaky scent. *My father.*

"Elissa, my office, please." His curt, cold tone freezes me down to the core. He doesn't even wait for a response as he strolls toward the elevator, hands in his pockets and his jacket bunching at the sides.

When I arrive in his office, Brandt is also there, sitting opposite to my father in one of the chairs. I sit in slow motion, confused as hell as to why we're both here, when my father clears his throat and speaks.

"So, it appears that Elissa has found out the arrangement between us, Brandt, but it doesn't matter, does it? Seeing as you two are…back together?" He says the last part cautiously. I roll my eyes.

"It's just like you to get into the middle of this. It's none of your business —" My father cuts me off.

"Shut up, I beg you." My face burns. "I called you both here to discuss your nuptials. Now that you are together, it's time we closed this deal, Brandt." Harold sits there and talks to Brandt, not sparing me a glance or a say in my future. I shouldn't be so surprised by now, but I'm floored. Marriage?

"Father, we've only just gotten together. Please, for fuck's sake, back off." His head swivels and his burning eyes focus on me.

"You'll do as I say, Elissa. It's time to put away this petulant child act and do what is right. No more rebelling, no more partying, no more sleeping around, and no more embarrassing me and the company." His jaw ticks and his hand is glued to his moustache, stroking it. "To have such a useless and ungrateful daughter is beyond me. You should have been born a boy, then I'd have something to show for all my hard work. You're too immature and emotional to take over this company. Now shut up, get married to Brandt, do whatever the hell you want behind closed doors, and finally be worthy of the Black name."

Jagged cracks and chips rip across my heart and I feel all my defences weakening. I feel the fight and the drive slowly drain out of me. I knew this would happen. I knew I'd never be good enough for him, or my mother, the way I am. The way I need to be. Useless. They need a son, a respectable son; he needs Brandt, not me. Never Elissa.

I grip the chair arms and push myself to stand. My head is bowed, and I clasp my hands in front of me, wringing my thumbs. "As you wish, Father," I mumble. I turn on my heel and walk out of his office, not looking back, although I know Brandt's eyes are following me.

I stop by my office for a brief moment, collect my things, and head out. I tell Lori on my way that I'm taking the day off because of an emergency and leave the office. I'm numb as I take the elevator down to the lobby. I'm numb as I'm outside in the frigid air walking home. I'm numb as I walk into my apartment and hear the sobs of my broken roommate. I shut the door behind me and slump against it, letting my purse fall to the floor.

My phone buzzes in my pocket, I check my watch to see who it is, and it's Brandt. I tap my hand over the watch to silence the call, take my boots off, and shuffle to my room, where I slam the door shut. I peel off my clothes, dropping them on the floor in my wake, and crawl into my bed to hide under the covers. The smooth, buttery fabric falls slowly around my body, and for the second time in my life, I allow myself to cry.

I wake up a few hours later to a few text messages from Brandt.

Brandt: *Please answer your phone.*

Brandt: *Harold's an ass. We don't have to get married right away; we can push it.*

Brandt: *Please Eli, don't shut me out.*

I sigh. I pick up my phone and message him back.

Me: *I just need some time to digest this info. There's no real way of fighting or getting out of this, so I'm done trying. I just need some time. Please.*

Brandt: *Promise me you'll talk to me before you think about disappearing this time. Please?*

A small smirk tugs at my lips and a chuckle wriggles out of me. Yes, I type back. I slide my phone under my pillow and drift back to sleep.

It's several hours later when I wake up, and I have a handful of missed calls from my father. I ignore the calls, slide out of my bed, and rummage through my dressers to find some track pants and a top to put on. I shimmy into my grey Roots sweats and a lavender t-shirt. Scraping my chaotic mess of hair off my back and shoulders, I tie it into a knot on the top of my head and head to the living room.

Riley is still wearing the same clothes from three days ago, when she found out she was pregnant. Her hair is slick with grease, her face is sullen and sallow, her eyes are rimmed with dark circles, and her once plush lips are chapped and raw.

My heart breaks seeing her like this. She looks just as bad as she probably feels on the inside. I walk over to her, tug her to her feet, and push her toward the washroom. I follow her in, help her shed her clothes, and turn on the hot water until steam is curling through the air. The humidity plays with my curls, making them buoyant and full of moisture; my hair feels damp from standing in this steamy room.

I push Riley into the shower and clap my hands in front of her face.

"Time to wake up, Riley. Get fucking showered, you stink." The wheels of the glass shower door clang as I roll the door shut. I gather her dirty, stinky clothes and toss them into the hamper, then head to her room in search of new clothes. When I return, she's finally out of the shower, wrapping a towel around her thin body. "While you were in the shower, I booked you a doctor's appointment for this afternoon," I say, passing her the stack of clothes I picked out for her.

She nods her head solemnly and towels off, bending to the side and shaking out her hair into an extra peach towel. I place the clothes on the counter and back out of the room, closing the door to give her some privacy. She emerges from the washroom a few moments later, steam spilling out of the doorway. She looks refreshed, and a bit more alive.

"Ready to talk and get some things organized?"

CHAPTER
FORTY-ONE

ELISSA

Over the next few days, I ignore my father's calls and only message Brandt here and there. I focus on Riley and figuring out what she's going to do about the baby. Once she settled on keeping the baby, we had other things to talk about. Like telling her parents, like telling Rhys.

"But what if he doesn't believe me?" she whines.

"Well, if he doesn't, then we'll just have to do a paternity test and prove it." Riley groans at my answer.

"Let's just focus on telling my parents first. Then I'll deal with Rhys," she says, flipping through a baby catalogue. "First, I need to figure out where I'm going to live. I can't ask you to take in a baby as well."

"I can always find another place and you can have this one, hun. No sense in uprooting your entire life for a baby." Her mouth drops and she shakes her head vigorously.

"I can't ask you to do that. This," she says, pointing to her stomach, "is not your problem. I need to figure some things out, but I can't stay here, with or without you." I wave my hand in the air, squint my eyes, and press my lips together.

"Of course, you can, I'm offering. And this place is already paid for, so one less bill for you to worry about. Really, it's no big deal. Besides, I'm getting *married* soon, so I suspect I'll be finding a new place with Brandt." I roll my eyes as Riley suppresses a smile.

"Oh yeah, so how's that going?" I cringe, wondering how in the hell this is going to work, and how the hell I'm going to answer her question.

"It's not, really. I'm avoiding all calls from my father. I told Brandt I need space to digest this, but I'm keeping him in the loop. You know, touching base and texting him every now and then."

Riley grimaces.

"I don't know, 'Lissa. I think this could be a good thing for you. You seem to really love him." My stomach sinks and the blood drains from my face.

"No, nope. Not love. I can handle feelings, but it's not love. Even if it is, it's just feelings. Okay?" Riley shakes her head and rolls her eyes at me, adding a little giggle. "Now, let's get back to talking about you. Rhys, you need to tell him. Sooner rather than later. You're already more than halfway through your first trimester. You'll be showing soon."

"Ughhh, I know, I know," she grumbles. Her page flipping turns more aggressive.

"I think you should get dressed and go over to his place and talk to him. Just do it. Like right now, don't give yourself time to think about it. We'll grab a car and I'll come with you and drop you off and I'll go to Brandt's."

Riley chews the inside of her cheek, flipping absentmindedly through the magazine. Her answer mixes with her exhale.

"Fine…"

The cab pulls up in front of Rhys' apartment building and Riley stares out the window. I jostle her shoulder, and her head bobs with the motion. "C'mon Riles. You can do this." I grab her hand and squeeze her tiny, frozen fingers in mine. She looks pale, but also like she's going to throw up. Her leg jiggles up and down as she works up the nerve. I reach over, stretching across her body, supporting myself on her thigh, and push open the door for her.

"Is your friend gettin' out?" the cab driver asks.

"Yes," I say, directing my next words at Riley. "She's going *now*. I'll see you later. Call me after you guys talk." Her big, glistening, chocolatey eyes find mine. I give her hand another squeeze and shove her out of the car, the door clunking closed behind her. She stares at me a beat longer, then turns and walks into the entrance of Rhys' building. I tell the driver the address of Brandt's place and we head off.

Brandt buzzes me up, and when I enter the lobby, a familiar mess of blonde hair blows by me. I stop and turn around, and so does she. A gentle smile is painted on Lexi's face, and I return the gesture.

"So, looks like you guys got together after all," she says in a hushed, sad tone. "Well, good for you. Don't fuck it up, he's a great guy." I widen my smile and nod my head. Lexi turns around to leave. Her bright, tie-dyed leggings clash with the buffalo striped jacket she's wearing, and her hair is pulled back in a sleek ponytail that swishes as she walks away. I reach for the button to the elevator, feeling a little warmth spread through me as I step into the car.

Brandt greets me at the door, tugging me into his arms and placing light kisses on my forehead. He smiles wide and looks like a puppy dog with his tail wagging behind him, happy to have me back at his place. My heart swells with happiness too. After I remove my shoes and jacket, he folds my hand into his and leads us further into his apartment, his thumb rubbing across the surface of my hand.

We settle in his kitchen, and he reaches to the cupboard to pull down a bottle of merlot and two wine glasses, placing them on the counter. He unscrews the cork and the red liquid sloshes into the glass, curling along the curve of the glass. The undertones of oak and fruit tickle my nose. Brandt swaggers over, his tall frame moving swiftly as he closes the distance with two steps. He towers over me as he passes me a glass and holds his up, waiting for me to clink my glass against his.

We both take a pull of the wine, letting the flavours dance across our tastebuds before swallowing it down. His lips curve salaciously up to his cheekbones as his eyes darken and grow hazy, full of lust. Brandt's hands wrap around my waist, lifting my feet off the ground and sliding my ass onto the island counter. He nudges my legs open and steps in between them, his hands wandering to the curve of my ass. His head dips as he places wet, wine-soaked kisses on the crest of cleavage peeking out of my shirt.

His kisses make their way up my throat and to the ticklish spot behind my ear, the spot that sets my skin on fire. "Mmm," I moan. My arms wrap around his neck and his hands travel up my back as his tongue caresses my skin. My phone buzzes. I pull it out of my butt pocket and check who it is. *Mother Dearest.* She can wait; I was worried that it would be Riley.

"Put your phone away," he grumbles, his gravelly, rough voice biting into my ear. I flip it over on the counter and cup his face to bring his lips to meet mine. A soft, chaste touch of our lips is all that happens at first. Our lips brushing against each other, I slip my tongue between my parted lips and run it along his bottom lip, so lightly that it barely leaves a wet trail. Brandt growls at me and fists the back of my head, crushing our heads and lips together. His chest rises and falls, fast and furious.

I feel his hardness pressing against my thigh. My hands unlink and slide down his honed chest. I lift his shirt up, dragging it out and making the rough kiss last. When the shirt has nowhere else to go other than up and over his head, the kiss breaks with a pop and I rip the shirt the rest of the way off.

My phone buzzes across the counter and I slump, giving Brandt an apologetic face. I flip my iPhone over quickly to see that it's my mother, *again.* I double-click the power button and send the call directly to voice mail. My hands wrap around my wine glass and I down the rest of it in one swift gulp. Brandt cocks his eyebrow at me, and I lace my fingers through his soft, golden-brown hair and pull him toward me. My tongue darts out and presses against his lips, he opens. Our tongues collide in a heated frenzy. His giant hands rip my blouse open, the buttons popping off and clinking against the counter and wine glass.

My phone buzzes again, this time a short one. I sigh, break the kiss, and pick up my phone.

Mother Dearest: *Please call me. Emergency.*

I groan. If mother called twice and sent a text, it must really be an emergency. I turn the screen to face Brandt and he gives a solemn nod. I hop off the counter, my feet splaying against the floor, and dial her back, pressing the phone to my ear. My nerves are like live wires. What could possibly be this urgent for her to call me?

"Elissa, finally," my mother drawls. "It's your father, he's in the hospital. He had a heart attack," she says, her misty voice breaking. She actually sounds sad. "Please come meet me at Mount Sinai." Her voice is earnest and I'm slightly worried for her mental state, but then, at the back of my mind, it could be a ploy, if the media has already been alerted to the situation and she's putting on an act. I sigh, grumbling under my breath.

"Yes, Mother. I will meet you there."

• • •

The car pulls up to the hospital, dropping us off under the beige marble tile overhang. Brandt's hand finds mine and he wraps his fingers around mine, bracing me. Bracing me for what, I don't know. Out of the corner of my eye I see security guards holding back a handful of people and realize it's the press. *This is why my mother called me down here.* I step toward the large, gold-framed doors as reporters start shouting out rapid-fire questions.

"Elissa, do you know the condition of your dad? Will Harold be alright? What does this mean for Black & Wells Publishing? Are you worried for your dad? Why is Brandt Collins here with you, holding your hand?" Brandt drops my hand, then he wraps an arm around my shoulder and hurries us indoors, away from the cameras, flashes, and questions.

We rush inside and are immediately surrounded by people bustling about, coughing, hobbling, and moaning. The lobby of the hospital is one of the busier places, other than the emergency room and cafeteria. There are old people wearing hospital gowns being wheeled in chairs, people walking around with casts or bandaged up, and parents shepherding their children around, trying to navigate the hospital.

We approach the information desk and Brandt takes over, pasting a smile on his face for the receptionist sitting at the desk and schmoozing her into telling us where Harold's room is, even though it's after visiting hours. The glossy, raven-haired woman flushes when Brandt leans into the desk, hovering closer to her. She fumbles with the pen in her hand, dropping it as it clatters to the ground.

Brandt bends down, grabs the pen for her, and squats in front of her, holding the pen out. A shy hand reaches out and grabs the pen. I roll my eyes and fold my arms, wishing this pathetic attempt at flirting would end. It's something right out of a movie, but this woman is falling for it. Hook, line, and sinker. She scribbles something down on a sticky note and brings it close to her chest before handing it over. No doubt it has loopy, flirty writing on it with her name and number. Brandt winks at her, turns to me, and holds out a hand.

I walk past him and make my way to the elevators. When he approaches me, I take the sticky note out of his hand, and sure enough, her number is on it, along with my father's floor and room number. Brandt smiles crookedly as he rests his hand on the small of my back. I press the floor button for the cardiac wing and the doors slide closed with ease.

When they reopen, we're greeted with the shrill cries of a woman and my heart stops. It sounds like my mother. The world slows down as I step off the elevator and Brandt's arm wraps around my shoulder. My head bobs in slow motion as I walk, the clicking of my heels ringing in my ears, along with the beeping of machines and crackling of the intercom. Nurses rush past me in a blur, but I feel like I'm walking underwater. My mom is sitting down on a plastic, cushioned waiting room chair, doubled over, bawling. Her sobs echo throughout the corridor.

The world seems to snap back into normal motion as I approach my mother. She tilts her head up to face me. Her face is swollen, her eyes are puffy from crying, and her nose is dripping. My breathing grows shallow and my heartbeat slows as I realize my mother might actually be upset, that she's not faking. Her shoulders collapse on a sob, and she stands and pulls me into an embrace, which sends goosebumps rising all over my body.

"He…he…he didn't make it," Collette sobs into my shoulder.

ACKNOWLEDGEMENTS

First off, I have to thank my wonderful readers. This couldn't
be possible without you. Getting to take you along on this
journey with me means the world to me. It's been such a joy
to see all the excitement from my first book, which leads us
to this one. A special thanks goes to my team of ARC readers. Your level of enthusiasm toward my work is indescrib-
able. Thank you for being part of my team of people.

Secondly, I need to thank my wonderful editor Lesley-
Anne Longo, without whom this book would never exist,
and for making me a better writer. Thank you for always
being there and answering my emails and working with my
chaotic deadlines. You're a true gem.

I also need to send a big thank you to my designer,
Laura Boyle, who is always so patient with me and my

unorganized, undereducated ways in this industry as I navigate it. Your artwork is always on point and beautiful. Thank you for continuing this journey with me.

And, as always, the biggest thanks go to the ones in my life who are my biggest cheerleaders. My mom, sister, nana, husband, and best friends J, M, and L: Thank you for all your support, feedback, and the extra push when I needed it. But mostly, thank you for being in my life. Thank you for sticking by me. I love you all.

ABOUT THE AUTHOR

Kate Smoak lives with her husband, daughter, and fur babies in a small town in Ontario, Canada. When she's not writing, she can be found curling up with a good book, playing video games, or camping at the trailer with her family.

Instagram: @katesmoakwrites
Twitter: @katesmoakwrites
Website: www.katesmoak.ca

If you enjoyed this book, it would mean
the world to me if you would leave a review.
Reviews are like tips for authors.

For more goodies and exclusive content,
please sign up for my newsletter!

A *brilliant* SPRING

Sample Chapters

KATE SMOAK

CHAPTER ONE

ELISSA

My mother's copper hair, once sculpted perfectly, is now frizzy and pieces are sticking out of the bun up-do. Her Chanel No. 5 assaults my senses as she sobs into my jacket, her shoulders trembling. The hairs on the back of my neck stand, and a cold sweat breaks out over my body at the oddly intimate gesture between us.

"He… he… he didn't make it."

My world halts. Harold didn't make it. What does that…

"They had to take him to surgery… to clear a block-age… and he had another attack on the table and…" My mother's cries ring out throughout the cardiac wing. "What am I going to do?" she cries. The busy hospital pro-fessionals' shoes squeak around us as they constantly move between rooms and the nurse's station. Beeps, whirrs, and voices surround us as I stand frozen, rigid with my mother's arms crushing around me.

"Uh, Mrs. Black?" A tall, handsome nurse wearing light-green scrubs appears behind my mother. She straightens her back, pushes the tears off the side of her face, and turns around, trying to be composed. "Would you like to see him now?" My mother gives the handsome nurse a curt nod and follows him down the hallway. After a few feet, she stops and turns to look at me.

"Elissa," she hisses. "Aren't you coming to say your goodbyes to your father?" Her eyes narrow at me, but her sniffling breaks the stern look.

"Uh, maybe in a second. I need a minute." Isn't that what the funerals are for? The goodbyes? A warm hand rests on my shoulder, giving it a small squeeze as another nurse bustles by us, tugging her stethoscope off her neck and hooking the earpieces into her ears. I turn to Brandt, and his eyes are shadowed with uncertainty. "I'm fine," I whisper to him.

"Are you sure? It's okay to be sad, or you know, not okay." His eyes waver between mine, looking for any signs of sadness or morose, but I'm fine. A little numb, maybe. A little angry over the fact that I'll never get my father's respect like I deserve. But who am I kidding? That was never going to happen anyway. I pull out my phone from the purse that's slung over the crook of my arm, and message Riley.

Me: *Harold's gone. Had two massive heart attacks. One during surgery and croaked.*

"Wow, a little insensitive," Brandt says with a hint of judgement in his voice. I shrug off his comment.

"Riley knows me. I don't have to pretend with her." A second later my phone bleeps.

Riley: *Do you need me to come down there? U okay?*

I smile at my bestie's unwavering support. I message her back saying I'll be home soon, grab Brandt's hand, and follow the path my mother took down the hallway of gloom to see my dead father.

He looks swollen. The person lying in front of me looks so unlike my father. The man before me is calm, relaxed, and peaceful. But… swollen. The doctor said that it's a side effect of the surgery. Collette is leaning over the bed, arms stretched out with hands wrapped around my father's hands, sobbing uncontrollably, and it's unbearable. I don't think I've ever seen her shed a tear my entire life, so to say it's uncomfortable is an understatement.

It's strange how it hits me that these two people in front of me right now are people I don't even recognize. My mother has actual feelings, which I assume she's having because she now doesn't have a husband to rely on and not because she loves him. She loves the money. And her pool boys.

But the biggest stranger is my father; he always has been. And now, that's all he'll ever be. A stranger. It's weird that I feel nothing. Well, that's not entirely true. I'm angry, sure. But only because I'll never have that moment. The one in the movies of the father finally saying, *I'm proud of you*. I'll never have that.

I tear my eyes away from my mother and father and look around the bleak room. It's painted a dull, murky blueish grey that just reeks death. That's all I smell, death. And maybe that's all in my mind, but it's what I smell. Well, death and that weird clean-but-doesn't-feel-clean smell of hospitals. A greyish curtain is piled against the wall, resting beside an end table that has a vase of fake sunflowers, as if it brightens up the morbid room.

I shuffle my feet in my spot, trying to find anything other than this to do. Brandt's shoulder nudges me from behind, and I lurch forward, his action catching me off guard. I catch myself a step closer to my mother, and she looks up at me, tears brimming her eyes, the blue looking more turquoise because of the redness.

Her hand falls away from my father, Kleenex wedged and sopping in her palm, and stretches to reach for mine. I'm frozen, not sure what to do or how to comfort her. Brandt's large hand rests on my shoulder blade and nudges me forward again until I'm in my mother's reach.

Her long, slim fingers weave around my hand and squeeze, and the moisture from her tears and snot collide with my hand. I resist the urge to gag. Her eyes lock onto mine and quiver as a small, warm, genuine smile stretches across her face.

"Thank you for being here," she whispers. My heart does this flip and I'm not sure why. I gently squeeze my mother's hand before slipping out of her grip.

"We're going to head out now," I say. "Do you need a ride home?" Collette shakes her head, her bangs swishing across her forehead.

"No, thank you. I have the driver downstairs waiting. Have a good night, you two." My mother stands up, brushes the wrinkles out of her skirt, and her heels click as she steps into me, wrapping her arms around my stiff body. Frozen in place, with my arms rigid at my side, my mother's embrace stifles me. My breathing quickens and shallows, my heart rate spikes. She lets go of me, arms dropping, and her hands slide down my arms with a tight smile on her face.

I step out of her reach, backing away until I bump into Brandt's hard chest. His arm snakes around my waist, and I offer my mother a silent nod before we turn and leave the room. I can feel Brandt's heavy gaze lingering on me as we walk towards the elevator. I sigh.

"I'm fine. I promise." But my words seem to do nothing to assuage his concern. His arm tightens around my waist, tugging me closer to him. We step into the elevator, surrounded by nurses, patients, and doctors. I lean in a little closer to Brandt and rest my head on his shoulder.

We step off the elevator, this time in my building, and head for my apartment. Before I have a chance to key in the code, the door flings wide open and two thin arms wrap around my neck.

"Are you okay?" Riley asks. She steps back, hands gripping onto my biceps as she looks me over, making sure I'm not hiding any feelings. Her eyebrows raise before dropping in satisfaction. "Yeah, you're fine. So, was it awful seeing him like that?" A shiver ripples over her, causing a shudder.

"Uh, I really don't want to talk about it right now. I want to hear about you. How are you doing?" Riley's face falls, her eyes shift away from me and land on Brandt for a moment before she spins on her heels and turns away, sauntering over to the couch.

"Fine," she clips. My eyes roll, and I follow her to the couch and sit down beside her.

"He knows, I told him." Riley's head spins to face mine, red coursing under her skin as tears well in her eyes. Her jaw ticks.

"You. Told. Him? Elissa, it wasn't your news to share!" Seeing the hurt in her eyes makes me feel small. I sigh, my shoulders dropping as I cradle her hands in mine.

"I know, but I had to tell him. We're trying to do this thing right and no more lies," I say as my eyes dart to Brandt. Riley relents, her body relaxing into the couch, tugging her knees to her chest. "So, what did Rhys say?"

Riley bites into her lip and rubs it between her teeth before answering. "Well, he didn't say much, but he said so much in so little. At first, he was huffy and smug because he thought I wanted him back," she scoffed. "As if. But when I told him about my *situation*, he didn't even ask if it was his. He demanded a paternity test! Like, why else would I be here if I thought it wasn't yours? You know? Why would I tell him about a random hook-up's baby? Sometimes I swear he's not the brightest— sorry, Brandt."

He shrugs in a nonchalant way as he's barely paying attention, rummaging through the cupboards, clinking glasses together as he looks for something. A moment later, his hands are holding glasses and a bottle of white wine. His large, thick hands uncork the bottle and pour two glasses. He goes to the fridge, gets a bottle of sparkling water, and pours it into the third glass. He brings the drinks over, passes one to each of us, and sits on the chair over in the corner closest to the television.

"I just… I understand why he wants a paternity test. I do. But for that to be the first thing, and only thing, out of his mouth just hurts. I lov—" her voice breaks as she tries to grab hold of her emotions bubbling up inside. I rest my palm against her thigh and give a gentle squeeze.

"It'll be fine. Like I said, I'm here for you and the little nugget, whatever happens." Riley's soft hand slips over top of mine and squeezes back, her eyes staring into mine, full of love and hope.

CHAPTER TWO

RILEY

When Elissa and Brandt excuse themselves for the night and slip behind Elissa's bedroom door, I'm left alone, sitting in silence. I sigh. I look around the room, taking in the quiet and loneliness I feel in this moment, preparing myself for the pending life I'm sure I need to get used to—being on my own.

I stare into the colourful red, green, yellow, and blue lights that glow on the bare Christmas tree in the corner of the room, opposite the chair Brandt was sitting in. A few opened presents sit under the tree, waiting to be put away. I sink deeper into the couch, staring into the warm glow of the tree's lights until my surroundings melt away, and I'm back at Rhys' apartment.

Bundled up in my black pea coat and white woolly infinity scarf, I fluff my straight black hair and toss it over my shoulders as I roll them back, straightening myself into a confident pose. My shiny red nail glimmers in the sunlight streaming into the lobby of Rhys' building as I reach for the button to buzz up.

"Hello?" His familiar voice echoes in the tiny room, wrapping around me in a warm embrace. My insides melt at the warmth that seeps through the intercom.

"It's me," I say. "We need to talk. Can I please come up?" I wait for Rhys to say something, but nothing comes. It's got to be a full three minutes and I'm about to give up when the buzzer sounds, and the door clicks unlocked. My hand wraps around the handle, the cool metal stinging the palm of my hand, and I pull on the door with force as if it's going to lock in an instant because Rhys changed his mind.

I take careful steps to the elevator mumbling under my breath. Mumbling about what I want to say, what I should say, what I need to say. I mumble imaginary counterarguments he might give me, but also the happy, hopeful answers a tiny piece of me wants but knows are unlikely. Realizing I probably sound and look like a crazy person stalking the stretch of hallway to the elevator, I pick up my pace and hit the elevator button before anyone has a chance to see me.

When the elevator comes to a stop, my heart hammers in my stomach. The pulse is so strong, it's making me nauseous, and this time I can't blame pregnancy. Bumps prickle on my skin as I near his door, raising the hairs on my arms and back of my neck. The hallway suddenly feels a thousand degrees warmer as beads of sweat form and roll down the centre of my chest. I take a steadying breath, running through all the words I need to say to Rhys, and raise my fist to knock on the door.

It opens before my hand connects to the heavy metal door. Rhys steps back, opening the door wide so I can slip inside. I peek out of the corner of my eye and damn, does he look good. His black hair is darker and slick as he's fresh from the shower, and as I pass him the warm, comfortable smell of Old Spice tickles my nose. He's wearing basketball shorts, no shirt. His broad shoulders are exposed and so are the delicious bumps that ridge his core down to his...

Focus, Riley. I clear my throat as I kick off my boots and bend over to tug my socks up that slipped off partway. I shrug off my jacket and turn to hang it up and see Rhys' face staring at me in amazement, but not in a good way. Like he can't believe I'm getting comfortable.

When I'm finished, he brushes past me, and another cloud of his body wash fills my lungs, and my heart aches to capture that scent for later. He pads towards the couch and sinks into it, sprawling his arms across the back, his shoulders pinching together and showing off his mouth-watering muscles. I have to tear my eyes away in order to focus and make my way to the living room and sit at the opposite end of the couch.

We both sit in silence, only the clock ticking makes noise. Finally, he sighs. He leans forward, braces himself on his knees, folds his hands together, and turns his head to face me.

"What is it, Riley?"

My tongue freezes. My whole body ices over, and my heart races. I hear my loud breathing in my ears, and I'm momentarily paralyzed. My mouth drops open, but clamps shut again. I'm losing all the words I had prepared. I'm sitting here like a mute fool, mouth gaping open. Rhys sighs.

"Riley, I don't know if I want to get back together, okay. There's just—" *Excuse me?* My hand flies into the air to stop him.

"I'm sorry. You think *I* want to get back together? Me? The one who was dumped ruthlessly and then used a few weeks later because you thought I was an easy fling? Fuck that." And suddenly, part of me changes my mind, I don't want him to know anything that's going on. My mind is telling me to move my feet and just leave. Forget him and his ignorant bullshit. But my feet and body keep me rooted in place. *No, Riles. He deserves to know. Scratch that. He needs to know; he doesn't deserve shit.*

I shake my head and clear my thoughts.

"I'm pregnant." I wait for a response, there's nothing. He's just staring at me with hard eyes. I tilt my head, furrowing my brows. "It's yours," I confirm. More silence. He finally moves, leaning back into the couch with a rigid posture. His muscles are tight, and his neck is straining. I can tell he's uncomfortable.

"I want a paternity test." His words sink my heart like the Titanic. A paternity test. I mean, yeah, sure. But how can he not believe me?

"But you never used a condom when you hooked up with me last; it's yours." He says nothing, gets up from the couch, and walks over to the door, holding it open.

"I'll call you when I set up an appointment to get this done. You can leave now." My mouth drops open. Doesn't he want to know anything else? I'm floored and can't think straight as I float off the couch towards the door. I slip on my boots and shove my arms into my jacket. I stop in front of Rhys, looking at him but not really looking. My stare is vacant, and I can't believe the conversation, or lack thereof, I just had with him.

My mind is reeling and blank all at once as I step outside onto the sidewalk. I bunch my coat up around my neck to keep warm, and I realize that I left my scarf at his place. Well, I'm not going back now. The icy wind bites at my cheeks as I walk down the road, staring up at the skyscrapers as I walk, the late afternoon sun glittering off the snow. People bustle around me as I take my time walking back home.

My eyes flutter closed as my head falls to the back of the couch, and I'm back in my apartment when I open my eyes. It feels like a lifetime ago that this happened, but it's only hours since I told Rhys. My shoulders collapse as I exhale a heavy breath and push myself off the couch. My feet shuffle me off to my room, and I slip behind the door, closing it with a soft click. My hand slides down the wooden grain of the door as my other hand releases the handle. I press my forehead into the doorframe and exhale. I flip the switch to my room, and the light bursts on.

I grab my phone off my bed, plug it into the charger, and sift through the clothes on the floor to find my PJs from this morning. Once they're on, I switch off the light and climb into bed. As I slide in between the cool sheets and duvet, sadness envelopes me, as well, and I realize that I'm in this on my own. I'm all alone. Elissa will be too busy with the company and Brandt, and who knows about Rhys.

I roll over and pick up my phone, squinting into the glow. I scroll through my messages and find the one person in the world that I need—my mother.

Me: *I miss you. Love you.*

A few moments later, the swoop comes in.

Mom: *I love you too, baby. Xx*

I click my phone off, place it back on my nightstand, and stuff my arm underneath my pillow. My other one hovers down and wraps around my bloated belly.

I'll love you just like my mother loves me. I'm all you'll ever need.

www.ingramcontent.com/pod-product-compliance
Lightning Source LLC
Chambersburg PA
CBHW011131190726
48289CB00012B/3001